FEARFUL SYMMETRY

DCI Will Blake Book 2

J.E. Mayhew

OBOLUS BOOKS

ISBN: 978-1-9998407-5-4

Cover design by Meg Cowley

This book is for:
Clare Hulme, Jan Jones,
Amy Rebecca Thomas, Laura Colwell,
Suzanne Thomas, Frauke Hoffman
and John Moorhouse.

Although the story is set on the Wirral, the names of some establishments and roads have been fictionalised to protect the unloved and godless... but you can have fun guessing...

JON MAYHEW

Tyger Tyger burning bright,
In the forests of the night:
What immortal hand or eye,
Dare frame thy fearful symmetry?

WILLIAM BLAKE

Everything is ready. My checklist is full of ticks; all the props and players are in place. All the deeds have been done. Nothing has been left to chance.

Once I met a writer and he told me that every story, film, or book has what he called an inciting incident; the moment when something happens that throws the hero into the centre of the story. When they find the remains of the girl on the beach in Jaws and Chief Brody realises he has a shark problem is a good example, apparently.

I wouldn't really know, I'm not a writer. I always thought stories start at the end of something. I mean, what events made Chief Brody afraid of water? Don't characters have a life that forms them before that one event? Isn't being born an inciting incident? Or is the first action someone takes against you the inciting incident? The first slight, insult or blow? Aren't they the things that form you and make you react the way you do? Or is that back story?

Anyway, the writer did warn me that inciting incidents are hard to see sometimes; a lot happens at the beginning of a story. My kind of story always starts with a grisly discovery...

SATURDAY 8TH FEBRUARY

CHAPTER 1

The curtains were the first thing Dot Taylor noticed. They were drawn closed. She'd had a conversation about this with her husband, Dave, three weeks ago, as they locked up the house. "Keep 'em shut, Dot," He'd said. "It'll fool the burglars!"

"Curtains drawn all day tell any would-be burglar that we're on holiday just as much as undrawn ones all night," she'd said, and he couldn't argue with that. He never really argued with her. Never had in all their forty-five years of marriage. Sometimes, she wished he had. The curtains were shut now, though, and unless Dave had popped back from their hotel in Cape Verde one night just to make a point, someone else had been in their house. She gripped his arm, as they pulled up to their bungalow in Hilbre Grove.

"There's something wrong, Dave."

Dave frowned and patted the back of her hand. "Calm down, missus," he said. "Probably just a faulty alarm and Jean from next door has been in. We did leave her a spare key, didn't we?"

"No, she's away too, remember?" Dot said, pulling her hand away. "Won't be back for another week. Honestly, I'm sure you're going doolally in your old age."

"Well, maybe it's Don Pleavin, then. You know what a busybody he is with his Neighbourhood Watch. Bloody weirdo, that man, if you ask me..."

Dot smacked Dave on the arm. "Mind your language. Don Pleavin doesn't have a key, thank goodness. Now go and look!"

Dave heaved himself out of the car with a grunt. The bungalow crouched in the cul-de-sac; a dark silhouette against the bright, afternoon sky. He shivered, hesitating at the metal gate that led into his front garden. Everything looked just the same but somehow it seemed quietly threatening. The front door was shut and there was no sign of any broken glass which suggested to Dave that if anyone had broken in, they'd got in through the back. He fumbled with his key in the lock and, finally, the door creaked open.

The heat hit him first; a wave of fetid, hot air that rushed from the house to dissipate in the cold February night. A fusty gloom filled the hall; whoever had drawn the front curtains had also closed all the others. The air was thick with an earthy, sewer smell that crawled into Dave's mouth and up his nose. He swallowed and then wished he hadn't. "The heating must be on full," Dave muttered to himself, trying to keep his mouth shut against the reek.

"What's that stink?" Dot said, appearing behind him and making him jump. "Smells like the drains have backed up."

"Smells worse than that," Dave muttered, a feeling of dread creeping through him. He knew that smell; he could never forget it and the horrors that accompanied it. "Dot. You'd better stay back, love," he whispered. Covering his nose and mouth with the crook of his arm. He crept into the hall and pushed on the living room door. With a strangled oath, he staggered from the room, cracking the back of his head against the wall and crumpling to the ground.

Dot ran forward. "Dave!" She crouched next to him, trying to pull him up. Dave moaned and Dot choked on the foul stench from the living room. She made the mistake of glancing in through the door.

At first, Dot thought someone had dumped a huge rag doll on the armchair by the fire; it was bloated and shapeless. And then she realised it was a body. One baggy arm hung down the side of the lounger. It lay, head to one side, face swollen and distorted. A mop of lank, blood-soaked hair draped over the stretched, blackened skin. The body looked like a balloon and had burst out of the blue blouse that tried to contain it. A cloud of irritated flies buzzed around the corpse, battering into each other. The armchair was normally a cream colour but now it was rust brown and Dot could only think that it was soaked in blood. But one detail seared itself into Dot's memory; the scissors, with their rounded finger guards, poking out of the poor creature's devastated eye. Whether it was the suffocating air or the sight in her living room that stopped Dot from screaming, she never knew. Instead, abandoning her prone husband, she crawled out of the house on her hands and knees and sat shivering on the roadside by the car. That's where the neighbours found her.

CHAPTER 2

The insect drone of the clippers filled DCI Will Blake's ears and he felt drowsy as they carved a path up the back of his neck. He'd managed to keep his interaction with the hairdresser functional and cursory without being rude, indicating he wanted it short at the back and sides but with a bit of spikiness on the top. Then he'd studiously avoided eye-contact while she ran the clippers around his head. It wasn't that he didn't like a bit of human company, nor did he blame hairdressers for being friendly or conversational. It was just that the conversation always went a little haywire the moment he said he was a policeman. Rather than kill any conversation, it generally seemed to encourage any hairdresser to give his or her considered opinion on prison sentencing or, even worse, result in a long and detailed account of their latest encounter with crime. Which was usually from TV.

But he knew what the hot topic would be if he gave the game away now: Ellen Kevney and he really didn't want to talk about her right now. A mobile hairdresser, she'd been missing for over two weeks. She'd dropped her two children at school in the morning before going on a call and hadn't been seen since.

Sometimes, Blake would say something non-committal like 'I work in an office.' This often worked better than the truth and wasn't really a lie. Most of the time, Blake did work in an office. He just happened to be poring over the gory details of a recent murder, assault or robbery rather than a spreadsheet or a quarterly report. Not that he didn't have his fair share of those either.

"So what do you do in the office?" The woman said, clicking off the clippers and giving him a tight smile.

"Oh. You know. Paperwork and stuff," he said, rolling his eyes. "All that paper. And answering the phone. Never stops ringing."

Once he had lied and made up a story about going on holiday to South Africa to visit his parents who owned a farm and bred antelope. He felt bad about that, though and realised he couldn't go back to that particular hairdresser without perpetuating the lie. Right now, it was all he could do to stop from looking skyward and praying for the woman not to rumble him.

"You're a copper, aren't you?" The hairdresser

said.

Startled, Blake looked up at her reflection in the mirror. For all his tough-guy act at work, when he was confronted so baldly, he found it hard to keep the lie going. There was something about being stuck in the chair that made him feel vulnerable as well. She was a short, round-faced woman with a golden ponytail that pulled her face tight. Her almond eyes and small mouth made her look mischievous. "Sorry," he said. "Is it that obvious?"

"It's all right," she said, with that tight smile again. "You get a kind of sixth sense when you do this job for long enough. People who don't want to talk. The one's that are telling porkies. Some people are downright creepy. But you probably know that already."

Blake nodded slightly. "How long have you done this, then?" Maybe if he controlled the conversation, he'd get out before the subject of Ellen Kevney came up.

"I've been cutting hair for about eight years now. Working here on and off for about two. I run a mobile service too."

Inwardly, Blake groaned. "You like it?"

She nodded. "Yeah," she said. "I like being my own boss. It's hard work, mind. On your feet all day."

Blake's phone buzzed on the counter beneath the mirror. He nodded at it. "D'you mind if I check that?" he said, reaching from under the gown that smothered him before the hairdresser could reply. It was a text from Laura: *Where are you? Thought I'd pop round if you're not too busy.* Blake frowned and clunked the phone on the side. It'd been four months since Laura Vexley had rescued Blake from his mother's cat, Serafina. The cat was a behavioural nightmare, with a seemingly psychotic hatred of Blake but somehow Laura, a self-styled animal psychologist had a magic touch with the fiend. Since then, Laura had slipped into his life almost seamlessly. At first anyway.

"Not work then?"

"No," Blake said, easing himself back into the chair. "Not work."

The hairdresser raised one eyebrow. "You sound almost disappointed."

"Just someone... a friend," he found himself saying. "It doesn't matter."

"Someone being a bit pushy?"

"Have you nearly finished?" Blake said, barely concealing the irritation in his voice.

The hairdresser's eyes hardened but she kept the professional smile. "I have if you want to walk out of here looking like you've brushed your hair with a toffee apple. I need to comb it down and layer it a bit."

"Okay. Sorry. Just a bit tense." A gulf of silence began to open up and, for some stupid reason, Blake felt obliged to fill it. "You said something about a mobile service. You go to people's homes, then?"

"That's generally what the 'mobile' bit means," she said, scraping the comb through his hair and snipping. "But I'm picky about my clients. I usually meet them in a salon first or know them from somewhere else. Too many nutters around. Wouldn't want to end up disappearing... like that Ellen, girl…"

"Yes. Quite," Blake said, trying not to groan with frustration. He'd walked into that one. "I was just thinking. Often I'm too busy to get a cut or I forget and then my boss tells me to get tidied up." The gown felt tight around his neck. "Would you be able to include me in your rounds? It might be more convenient…"

The woman paused and looked Blake in the eye. "Yeah. I could," she said at last. "I usually have old dears who can't get out the house or kids who have autism and don't like the salon but I can do you, too. My name's Keeley. I'll give you my card."

The phone rang almost as Blake left the salon, pocketing Keeley's card. Kinnear sounded as if he was being strangled. "Sir, you better come quick… we've found a body."

"Is it Ellen Kevney?"

Kinnear blew a long breath into the phone. "It'd be hard to say, sir…"

CHAPTER 3

Police cars, vans and ambulances filled the tiny cul-de-sac of Hilbre Grove. The small estate in Upton had never seen such activity and curtains around the Grove were twitching furiously. Some residents stood at their front doors watching the coming and going of uniformed police and scene-of-crime officers. A few kids leaned against their bikes at the end of the Grove, shepherded away from the house by an eagle-eyed community support officer.

Seeing the congestion, Blake had abandoned his car in the next road and walked, pulling his collar up against the cold February drizzle. He nodded to a few familiar faces and signed himself in on the crime scene register. DC Kinnear waited in the front garden of the bungalow, dressed in the obligatory white body suit. His face mask was pulled down around his neck and he gulped the air. Normally, Kinnear looked like he had a permanent smirk on his round face. Sometimes, people mistakenly interpreted that as flippancy. Today, he just looked sick to his stomach.

"That bad, Kinnear?" Blake said, catching a note of decay on the air as he neared the house.

Kinnear nodded. "Yeah, sir. The body's been there a while, and the heating was turned up full," he said, swallowing. "It's a mess."

"The house owners?"

"Dorothy and David Taylor, a couple in their late sixties. Just came back from their holidays and found this. They've been away three weeks."

Blake looked around at the bustling scene. "Where are they now?"

"Arrowe Park Hospital, sir," Kinnear said. "Mr Taylor fell and cracked his head, Mrs Taylor is in shock." He gulped more air down. "Nobody should have to see that."

Blake nodded as he pulled on his coveralls. His stomach squirmed. He'd been at this game for almost twenty years, but he never became immune to that feeling of dread when approaching a murder scene. The coveralls felt tight and restrictive over his big frame. Pulling up the hood, he trudged towards the front door of the bungalow.

The front door had hung open since the discovery of the body but the stench in the air still hadn't taken the hint and buggered off. Even with a face mask on, it pushed its way into his senses. "Oh God," Blake muttered as he entered the living room, swatting at a lazy, bloated fly that droned around him.

Mallachy O'Hare, the Crime Scene Investigator gave Blake a feeble wave, his long face greyer than usual. Another figure stooped over the decomposed body that filled the armchair. As Blake moved around the room, the figure turned and Blake's heart sank.

"Ah, Will," Jack Kenning, the pathologist said. "Just attending to our unwanted guest here." Blake gave a curt nod. Kenning had seen one too many television crime dramas and thought of himself as something of a comedian. Normally, he tried to cultivate the nonchalant attitude of an eccentric scientist, more interested in the body and clues than the person whose life had been so brutally taken. Even Kenning was struggling today.

"Unwanted?"

"I'm guessing from the reaction of the householders that they didn't *invite* our friend here into their living room," Kenning said.

Blake looked away. "I try not to guess, Jack. It's murder then?"

"I can't imagine anyone sticking a pair of scissors into their own eye like that," Jack said, his chirpy tone faltering. "There's blood everywhere, which would suggest she died here. But if you're wary of guessing, I'd say that it's suspicious at the very least."

"Yeah, I get the suspicious bit," Blake muttered, losing his patience. "Any ID?"

Mallachy shrugged. "Not so far. We're waiting for Jack to finish, so we can start checking pockets."

Blake glanced at the bloated misshapen body, trying to keep some level of professional distance. The victim had been a living human being, with loves and hatreds, dramas in their life; people who might be missing them. But right now, he had to be dispassionate; to think clearly. "Might it be Ellen Kevney?"

Jack shrugged. "Hard to tell. Certainly female. I'd say the victim has been here at least two weeks. The Taylors were away for three, so it's possible she's lain here longer. Whoever did this put the heating up and it's advanced the decomposition..."

"Jeez," Blake muttered. "They did it deliberately?"

"Now who's making guesses?" Jack Kenning said with a tight smile. "The Taylors could have left it on but, first responders remarked on the house being stifling, so I suspect it was turned up after the victim died. This level of decay is going to make any post-mortem testing tricky."

Blake scanned the room; a picture of bland normality apart from the scene of horror in one corner. A bookshelf full of Readers Digest condensed books lined one wall, a garish oil painting of a mountain stream hung on another, and the TV sat in one corner. Another picture hung crookedly over a chest of drawers. It showed a child sitting under a tree with his mother and a poem was printed beneath it. "What do you think of that?" he said to Mallachy, nodding at the picture.

Mallachy tilted his head and read the title. "The Little Black Boy," he said and shrugged. Blake always winced at Mallachy's frustrating, non-committal shrugs. "Dunno," the dour looking Irishman said. "Don't ask me. I'm a Philistine."

"So are the Taylors, if that oil painting is anything to go by," Kenning muttered. "That's a crime that should be reported immediately." Blake almost managed a smile. "You should recognise that Will," Kenning added. "It was written by your namesake."

Blake frowned. "What?"

"That's a William Blake poem," Kenning said. "You must have heard of him: Jerusalem? Tyger, Tyger burning bright..."

"Yeah, right," Blake said, holding up a hand. "I used to get a lot of that at school. Mainly from English teachers." He read the title again. "Not one of his better-known poems. Funny thing to have on your wall, don't you think?"

Jack put a hand on Blake's shoulder. "We're here

to investigate a suspicious death, Will, not criticise the décor."

The room closed in on Blake and he shook himself. He'd be more use outside interviewing neighbours or reading through witness statements, not staring at a picture. "You're right," he said. "Let me know when you're finished."

Back in the street, Blake welcomed the fresh air in his lungs. Some colour had returned to DC Kinnear's cheeks and he headed for Blake as soon as he emerged from the house.

"Sir, there's..."

Blake held up a hand to silence him. "Give me a moment, Kinnear. You know what it's like in there. Just let me catch my breath." He scrubbed at his face with his palms as if washing away the images from inside the house, but he knew he never could. "Now, what were you saying?"

"Sorry, sir, there's a Donald Pleavin who's eager to see you. He's the Neighbourhood Watch co-ordinator. Lives opposite the Taylors..."

"Couldn't you speak to him? Uniform? They're doing door-to-door anyway," Blake snapped. "I can't be doing with some self-important busybody, right now."

"He's quite insistent, sir. Asked for you by name."

Blake let out a huge sigh. "Sorry, Andrew," he

said. "It's just... I mean, who does that to another human being?"

Kinnear knew better than to shrug. "I don't know, sir. Let's catch the bastard and ask him, eh?"

"That's the most sensible thing I've heard all morning," Blake said, rubbing his cold hands and surveying the Grove with its low walls and neatly clipped hedges and lawns. "Why here, Andrew?"

"Sir?"

"Why did that poor soul end up here?"

"I don't quite follow, sir."

"Whoever killed her could have dumped her in a ditch on the side of a road or a copse somewhere. There's plenty of woodland on the Wirral. Why kill someone in someone else's home?"

"Privacy, perhaps, sir? Less chance of detection?"

"Possibly, but you'd have to know that the house was empty for some time and you were going to be undisturbed."

"Yes, sir," Kinnear said.

"If I was a gambling man, I'd say this was a local crime committed by someone with very local knowledge. Come on, lead the way. Let's see what Mr Pleavin has to offer us."

CHAPTER 4

Donald Pleavin stood in front of his bungalow, hands in his beige, M&S slacks; a walking stereotype of a Homewatch Coordinator. He was a tall man, as tall as Blake. Short, cropped hair silvered the sides of a shining bald patch. A neatly-clipped moustache sat in the middle of his craggy face. He looked like he kept active despite his advancing years and Blake found it hard to pin an age on him; early seventies, maybe?

"Mr Pleavin, I'm DCI Blake and this is DC Kinnear, I believe you wanted to talk to me?"

Pleavin shook Will's hand vigorously. "Yes, I know who you are, Detective," he said. "I remember you from that TV Crime programme, Searchlight. I never missed it..."

Blake felt a flash of annoyance and his cheeks reddened. "Well, that was a while back, now, sir. Do you have any information pertinent to this incident?" Blake glanced at Kinnear but the young DC kept his eyes fixed on Pleavin. His team loved it when the topic of Searchlight came up, Blake knew that; a great opportunity to watch their boss squirm.

It had been a fixture on early evening TV between 2004 and 2007; various crimes were reported, and a mixture of celebrities and real police officers had presented it. Blake, a young police constable back in 2004 had been encouraged to apply for it as he was 'easy on the eye' and a good communicator. The role, although part time, had made him a prime target for ribbing and banter from his colleagues. Some senior officers didn't approve. It shouldn't have surprised him how often Searchlight cropped up or that it was still used as a stick to beat him with. Even now, so many years later, those three brief years and their aftermath, haunted him.

Pleavin frowned. "As soon as I saw you striding across the Grove, I knew we were in good hands. I never know why they axed Searchlight. It was providing a very useful service. You were great on it. You did all the CCTV footage; shop holdups and street violence, that was it wasn't it?"

"I did, sir, but right now, I'm trying to investigate what happened over the road and you said you had information," Blake said, through gritted teeth.

Pleavin's face fell. "Forgive me, Detective Blake," he said. "I was quite a fan. Come this way." He led them up the path to the front door and into a bland, oatmeal hallway, so spotless it reminded Blake of a show home he'd visited recently; the kind of place that is so tidy, it has lost any sense of character. He half expected Pleavin to ask them to take their shoes off. The lounge was almost identical in layout to the one across the road, but without the body, bloated by weeks of decay. Pleavin sat on an armchair and flicked through a pile of notebooks on a small table beside him. “Here we are.” He pulled one of the books out of the pile with a flourish.

Blake could feel his nerves snapping; he was up to his eyeballs with the Kevney case and the need to know if the body in the house was Ellen or not gnawed away at him. He really didn’t have time for this. “And what’s this, sir?”

“Comings and goings,” Pleavin said, waggling his bushy, grey eyebrows. “For the last three weeks. I keep a careful note of anyone who calls at the Grove, Detective Blake, or the wife does if I’m not in.” He handed the notebook over. “If our killer arrived in a van or a car, then either I or Helen will have jotted it down. I know it’s all big data with you policemen nowadays; perhaps this can add to the picture.”

Blake took the notebook, his mood lifting a little. “This could be very useful, Mr Pleavin, thank you,” he said, scanning through the last three weeks and a seemingly endless column of the words ‘white’ and ‘van.’ People must have stuff delivered all the time. But it could be handy; there were dates, times, and registration numbers. “This will give a good picture of the movements around the Grove.”

Pleavin gave a conspiratorial wink. "Always glad to help, sir," he said. "I keep in close touch with our Police Community Support Officer, too. If you want the low down on any of the Grove's residents, just ask. You'd be surprised. We've got all sorts living here."

"All sorts?"

Pleavin leaned in close and Blake caught a whiff of soap and mouthwash. "Well, the Whites at number four for a start. Young couple. Never seem to go anywhere. Curtains drawn all day," he murmured, twisting his mouth in disgust. "I mean, haven't they got jobs to go to? The Jones at number five are always arguing."

"Thank you, Mr Pleavin," Blake said, straightening up. "I'll be sure to bear all that in mind."

Blake shivered in the cold February breeze and surveyed the organised chaos that filled Hilbre Grove. He handed Pleavin's dossier to Kinnear. "Get someone to go through these registration numbers, track down the drivers. It's worth checking."

"Yes, sir. Do you want to check any of the other people Mr Pleavin mentioned?"

Blake sighed. "We'll need to interview everyone in the Grove eventually ..." he stopped. A slight, hunched young man hurried past the Taylor house, pulling a hood over his face as he ran. "Where did he come from, Kinnear?" Blake started towards the young man. "Excuse me, sir!"

Blake saw the youth's eyes widen and his pale face framed in the hood, then the youngster broke into a sprint. "Stop!" Blake bellowed.

The community support officer at the end of the Grove saw the young man running towards him and opened his arms like a goalie awaiting the shot. The group of kids he was containing jeered and one of them must have given him a shove just as the young man ducked under his elbow. The PCSO crumpled to the floor and the kids took to their bikes, scattering in all directions.

"Don't just lie there, man, get after them!" Blake yelled as he ran to the end of the cul-de-sac but it was clear that the youth in the hoodie had vanished. Blake hissed through his teeth in frustration. "Did you get a good look at him, Andrew?"

"Red hair, young, maybe late teens. Freckles," Kinnear said. "He certainly legged it in a hurry."

"Might be something or nothing," Blake said. "He looked shifty as he passed the Taylors' house. Where did he come from?"

"I think there's an alley that leads between the houses at the end of Hilbre Grove, sir. There was meant to be a constable covering it."

Blake shook his head. "Get that plant-pot who was having a lie down to find those kids. They obviously knew the runner, so he must be local. Then meet me at the car. We'll go and see the Taylors."

CHAPTER 5

Tina White fidgeted with the curtain as she watched the police officers and people in white suits bustling in and out of the house, loading bags and boxes into cars and vans. It was like being on the set of a crime thriller. And she'd seen enough of those to know what came next; the knock on the door, the questions.

"Come away from the window, for God's sake," Paul White snapped. "You'll attract attention."

Tina let go of the curtain and slumped onto the sofa. The TV was on, showing some politicians shaking hands, but Paul had turned the sound down ages ago. "But it's horrible, Paul. To think someone's been lying there all this time and we..."

"We had nothing to do with it, okay?" Paul's voice rose as he cut her off. She could see red spots on his cheeks under his neatly trimmed beard. That was all that was neat about him at the moment. He still had his striped dressing gown on.

"Don't shout at me. Maybe we should tell them. Fess up. It wasn't our fault, was it?"

Paul squatted down in front of her. She could

smell garlic from the kebab he'd had last night. "Listen to me. We can't say a word."

"But what if it's Ellen? What if it's her?"

"What if it is?" Paul snapped, then threw his hands up in the air. "No, that'd be horrible, of course but it's not our fault."

Tina's head throbbed and her face ached from sniffing and crying. "I don't know. We should say something..."

"We should say nothing."

The doorbell rang and Tina flinched. Paul jumped up and peered out of the front window. "It's a policeman. Probably just doing door-to-door enquiries. You stay here, I'll deal with it."

Tina nodded and sat, tangling her fingers nervously, and listening to Paul at the front door. "Yeah, we're all in a state of shock really. No, no, haven't seen anything unusual. It's a pretty quiet place. Mainly old people. Don Pleavin at number six, he runs the show around here. At least he thinks he does. He's our neighbourhood watch fella. Keeps a log of all vehicles that come and go."

Paul continued batting away any questions with a baffled kind of regret that he couldn't be more help. No, they hadn't seen anything unusual. No, they were working most days. No, nobody had come to their door recently. All quiet, all boring, nothing to see here. Move along please.

She straightened up on the sofa. How could he stay so calm in front of a policeman? That took some balls. It was a side of Paul that Tina had seen before; a cold and calculating steadiness. He was great at haggling with car dealers and once he'd actually talked a traffic warden out of giving him a ticket. She'd been with him for seven years, married for four of those. He'd always been adventurous and a bit of a risk-taker, yes. But this was different. How could he talk so calmly to the officer knowing what he knew? She wondered if he'd had dealings with the police before.

The door closed and Paul came back into the living room. He looked down at Tina. "There you go. Gone."

"For now," Tina said. "They'll be back, though. I don't think I can face them, Paul. I'm not as hard-faced as you."

Paul sat next to her and put his arm round her shoulder. "Hey. Don't worry, love. Look we've done nothing wrong..." Tina looked up at him and sniffed. He coughed. "Well, nothing to be ashamed of. Just keep your head down and leave it all to me." Tina nodded and buried her head in his shoulder. Paul gave her a squeeze. "There," he said. "What say we give work a miss today and go over to Liverpool. Do some shopping, grab a bite to eat? By the time we come back, this whole circus will have moved on and things will have calmed down again. Remember, it's nothing to do with us."

Tina nodded and dabbed mascara from her cheeks with a crumpled, soggy tissue. For now, she'd go shopping and bury her head in the sand; pretend nothing had happened. The truth would come out eventually, though.

*****

Dave Taylor filled his hospital bed so completely, that Blake found himself wondering if they'd used a crane to transport the man here and get him in bed. A pile of pillows propped him up and he looked stranded under the mound of covers that only just reached the sides. He had a cannula fitted on the back of his hand and a monitor clipped to his finger. A machine flashed numbers at Blake. He had introduced himself and Kinnear, and Taylor had nodded but it was clear the man was still processing what he had seen in his living room.

"I knew what it was," Dave Taylor whispered, staring at the foot of the bed. "I knew from the smell. It took me back to my army days. Aden, 1967. You never forget that stink. Death. It's horrible." He looked up at Blake like a hurt child. "Who'd do something like that, though? In my house?"

Blake shook his head. "I don't know, sir. I intend to find out, though."

"It was meant to be the holiday of a lifetime," Taylor continued. "We don't have a lot of cash. I mean, I've got my army pension but after I injured my back, I couldn't find any steady work. When we won the holiday competition, we were over the moon. Wish we hadn't gone now."

"You don't normally have a cleaner, then? Or anyone who comes into the house for any reason?"

Dave Taylor shook his head. "Couldn't afford a cleaner and Dot wouldn't have it anyway. Too house-proud. She'd be tidying up before the cleaner came. How is she? Is she okay? I should have stopped her following me. She shouldn't have seen that..."

"No, sir, none of us should. She's in shock, Mr Taylor but she's being well looked after. Do you know of anybody who might have known about you going away?"

"Most of the Grove, would've known. But Pleavin keeps that place under close watch," Taylor said. "Nobody would've got past him. He keeps notes..."

"Yes, we've been given access to Mr Pleavin's observations, sir. We'll check those out urgently."

"There was the young man, sir," Kinnear cut in.

Blake glared at him. "Thank you," he said. "We noticed a young man hurrying away from the Grove just before we came here, Mr Taylor. Late teens, maybe early twenties. Red hair, freckles. He wore a dark hoodie, but he ran away when we tried to ask him some questions. Does that ring any bells?"

Taylor blinked and licked his lips. "Could've been one of the local lads, I suppose," he muttered. "They're always causing trouble around the estate. Used to be a nice place. Still is when they're all at school."

"He seemed a bit old for school, sir," Kinnear said, earning another cold look from Blake.

"I'm sorry, I can't help you," Taylor said, his eyes fluttering. "I'm very tired. It's been a terrible day..."

Blake nodded. "You've had quite an ordeal, Mr Taylor. We'll leave you in peace for now. We will need to ask you some more questions soon, though."

The hospital corridors thronged with visitors carrying magazines, newspapers and bags of fruit. Kinnear hurried after Blake as he strode away from Taylor's ward. "D'you think he's hiding something, sir?"

Blake stopped and turned on Kinnear. "Judging by his reaction to that last question, yes. And I think if you had kept quiet, I might have got a little more out of him."

"Sorry, sir, I just..."

"You just need to hold off a bit, Kinnear. He clearly knows who we were talking about but he's not saying anything. If we'd approached things in a less direct way, it's possible we may have got an ID for our mysterious young man. Let me do the talking in future. Okay?"

Kinnear's cheeks coloured and he bit his lip. Blake's mobile broke the tension. "Yes? On our way." He looked over at Kinnear. "That was Alex Manikas. Ellen Kevney's car has turned up."

CHAPTER 6

Darkness pressed in on Ellen Kevney, intensifying the cold of the steel floor. She'd lost track of how long she'd been in this place. Forever, or so it seemed. She couldn't see a hand in front of her. Her wrists were handcuffed, and, with a little brave groping, she had found they were chained to a steel ring in the floor. Everything was metal; the floor, the walls, the chain. That wasn't strictly true; there was a commode in the corner made of plastic. She suspected that she was being kept in a shipping container.

For the thousandth time, she tried to remember how she had ended up here but it was all very hazy. She'd dropped the kids off as usual and then gone home. What then? She knew what she normally did that day of the week. But had she been this time? Is that where she had been taken from? The huge black hole in her memory frightened her almost as much as the chains and the black, echoing crate she lay in.

The whole room clanged as the door at the far end of the container swung open, groaning on its hinges. A familiar silhouette appeared in the square of daylight that dazzled Ellen.

"Who are you? What do you want?" Ellen

sobbed, lurching forward but being yanked down by the chains. She gasped as she hit the hard floor just like she did each time he came in. The figure squatted close and slid a tray towards her but said nothing.

Ellen could smell the baked beans and feel their heat. Her mouth watered and she fought the urge to plunge her fingers into the steaming bowl. "Let me go," she whimpered. "Please. My children will be worried..."

The figure rose, looming over her and backed away towards the rectangle of light.

Hot tears scalded Ellen's cheeks and she looked up at him. "Please, I'm begging you. Let me go. You must have a mum. How would you feel if she was...?" The figure froze and she stopped, somehow sensing that she was heading down the wrong track. Then the door clanged shut, plunging her into darkness once more.

Ellen sat in silence, trying to resist the smell of the food. Her stomach growled and she went through the same process that she had every day since she'd been taken. She pushed the bowl away with her foot and turned her back on it. It could be poisoned or drugged. She was pretty certain that however she'd got here, it involved a spiked drink or food. But she felt so faint and hungry. If she was to keep going, she needed fuel. She need energy to think of a way out, as unlikely as that may seem. There was no reason to think her captor would drug her again, was there? She shivered, pushing away the question of why he had taken her and what his plans were for her. Finally, she snatched up the bowl and began spooning the contents into her mouth.

Ellen chewed and swallowed automatically, not tasting the mush. Blinking back the tears, she thought of her children, Casey and Donovan. The memories of chaotic mealtimes when she had to cram their busy lives between school and bedtime; swimming, football, dance, playing with friends. What would the kids be thinking, now? Her mum must be beside herself with worry, too. She imagined reading to them and stroking their hair before bedtime but that just made the harshness of her conditions worse. She longed for her small two-bedroom house and its ordinariness. The chains chafed her wrists and made it hard to pull the thin blankets over herself to keep warm. She shivered, trying to keep at bay visions of what might await her. Despite the painfully hard floor and the cold, Ellen Kevney finally slept, but her dreams were far from sweet.

*****

DCI Blake slouched on the desk and searched the crowded Operations Room for familiar faces amongst the assembled officers. DC Alex Manikas sat next to DS Vikki Chinn and, inwardly,

Blake smiled; those two were bomb proof. His brow creased as he saw DI Kath Cryer and DC Andrew Kinnear sat next to each other. They had a complicated relationship; Kath still had a splint on her wrist from when she'd taken a shotgun blast for Kinnear. Blake would never describe them as bosom buddies, though. In the past, some of Cryer's comments had been borderline homophobic. He was certain, Kinnear was going to make a complaint against her before she saved his life. Nothing more was said, but Blake worried about them both. He worried about Ellen Kevney more. Kath fiddled with the Velcro straps that secured the splint; fastening and unfastening them as if she couldn't get the splint comfortable.

"Are you alright, ma'am?" Kinnear said.

Startled, Kath sat bolt upright. "Yeah," she said. "Just getting it sorted."

"Hey! Blakey!" A voice cried across the office. Blake groaned as DCI Matty Cavanagh strutted towards the assembled group. Cavanagh was a swaggering, young scouser who spent as much time checking his hair in the washroom mirror as at his desk. It was said that if you snapped Cavanagh in half, he'd have LFC written all the way through him, like a stick of rock. He was always backed up by DS Bobby Dirkin, a shrewd and pugnacious foot soldier who covered Cavanagh's tracks and did much of the spadework for him. If you wanted to cut through the crap in a case, Cavanagh and Dirkin were your men. But Cavanagh had an easy manner and an ability to get on with just about anybody. He was often seen perching on the edge of desks, chatting football or the latest episode of whatever was trending on Netflix. Cavanagh was a consummate networker; everything Blake wasn't and it nettled him.

"If you don't mind, Matty, we're just about to start a briefing."

"You're tanned, sir," Cryer said, giving Cavanagh an approving nod. "Been anywhere nice?"

"Mexico," Cavanagh said. "Cancun. Roastin' it was."

"God. I'd love to go there," Kinnear said, wistfully. "Chris says it's too expensive."

"If I can get us back on track," Blake said, instantly feeling ridiculous at the level of his irritation.

Cavanagh pulled a face. "Oops, sorry," he said. "I brought back some mingin' sweets for you all to break your teeth on. My brother-in-law's a dentist, you see. Anyway, they're on my desk. Help yourself. If you want any input on this case, Will, just shout, mate."

"Thanks," Will said, curtly.

Blake watched Cavanagh saunter back to his

desk and the chatter died. He cleared his throat. "Right. Ellen Kevney, 28, mother of two, mobile hairdresser. Missing for over two weeks. Yesterday her car, a Fiat 500, turned up in the carpark at Leasowe Station on the Wirral. Alex, any more details?"

Manikas nodded and rose to his feet. "Yes, sir. CSI are going over it now but, as you know, cars are often a mess of prints and DNA, depending on who's driven, or been in the car for weeks before. They *did* find a bag in the back containing some hairdressing equipment: tongs, clippers, some dyes, curlers and also a passport."

"She hasn't left the country then," Kinnear said.

"It wasn't Ellen Kevney's passport," Manikas replied. "It belongs to a Katerina Dragavei. A Romanian national. We're making enquiries with the Romanian Embassy, Immigration, Interpol but that will all take time."

"Time," Blake muttered.

"There was something else, sir," Manikas said, his voice breaking a little. "Something a little unusual."

"What?"

"A copy of the Radio Times."

"So?"

"From 2007. It had an interview. Erm... with you in it... your picture was on the cover. From when you were in that Searchlight programme on TV."

There was a ripple of murmuring across the assembled group and glances were exchanged. A few people folded their arms or shifted in their seats, knowing this was a weak spot of Blake's.

Blake pursed his lips. "Really? That's strange. Could just be coincidence of course... where did they find it?"

"In the boot."

"D'you think whoever has Ellen Kevney is trying to goad you, sir?" Kath Cryer said, her voice sounding like fingernails on a chalkboard.

Blake shook his head. "No, there are a hundred and one reasons that magazine could be in there, Kath. We've all put old newspaper down if we're transporting a pet or..."

"It's quite an old magazine, sir," Manikas said. "To even be around now is odd..."

"Not really. It could have been at the bottom of a pile. Plus, there will have been interviews with other people in that magazine. I don't know... Bruce Forsythe, maybe? Is the killer trying to goad him?"

"He's dead, sir," Cryer said, her voice flat.

Blake pursed his lips. "The passport. Let's focus on the passport."

"The passport holder might have been working with Ellen, perhaps?" Kath Cryer suggested. "Is there any news on the body from Hilbre Grove, sir?"

Blake shook his head. "No. We don't know the identity of the victim at Hilbre Grove, yet. Or if it has any connection with Ellen Kevney's disappearance. The body was badly decomposed; the heating in the house was on full. It'll slow things down."

"Sounds like that's what they wanted, sir," DS Chinn said. "Cover their tracks."

"Maybe, Viki, but we can't assume it has any connection to the Kevney case," Blake replied. He turned to Manikas. "Had Ellen's car been in the station carpark long?"

Manikas shrugged. "We checked CCTV, sir and it seems the car was left there three days ago. The images aren't very good. All we have is someone in a dark hoodie. Possibly male."

"Amazing, isn't it?" Kinnear said. "Satellites can see a sparrow fart from space but we can't make CCTV clear enough to pick out a face from twenty feet."

"Do sparrows fart, Kinnear?" Blake said, narrowing his eyes at the young DC. "And could you see it? Or would you hear it?"

Kinnear reddened again. "I dunno, sir, I was

just... you know..."

"So," Blake continued, leaving Kinnear to flounder, "who dropped that car off?"

"Whoever took Ellen Kevney?" DS Chinn said.

"Or Ellen herself?" Cryer added.

Blake nodded. "Both possibilities, I suppose. Though I'm not sure what Ellen Kevney stands to gain from disappearing. She lived for her kids and seems to have led a blameless life."

Kath Cryer pouted and shrugged. "People get depressed and wander off..."

"True," Blake replied, "but they don't then deposit their car a week after they've wandered off, do they?"

"No, sir."

Blake frowned. "Sorry, Kath. We seem to be going round in circles. If we knew just something about where she was before she disappeared..."

"She vanished on a Monday, sir, her day off," Alex Manikas said. "After dropping her kids off from school, nobody saw her. She'd told her mother she was going to do a spot of shopping but our requests for any sightings in town, Cheshire Oaks or any of the local shopping centres, have brought up nothing. ANPR hasn't picked up her car registration for that day."

"Her neighbour says she saw Ellen come home

in the morning. But she wasn't home in the afternoon because the neighbour had to sign for a delivery of hair dye on Ellen's behalf," Vikki Chin added.

Blake sighed. "Vikki, could you have a chat with the neighbours again? See if there's anything they missed. Any little detail. I'm getting desperate here. Kath can you use your abrasive charm to see if we can speed up forensics people on the bag found in the car?"

Kath Cryer grinned. "They'll be snowed under with the murder, too. I'll do my best, though, sir."

"What about the Radio Times, sir?" Manikas said.

"Forget that, for now, Alex," Blake said. "You and Kinnear concentrate on Leasowe station and see if you can have a word with the staff..."

The team dispersed and Blake spent another hour or so scanning files and papers, trying to find something, anything that may give him a lead. His phone buzzed and he read the text: *Come home. Bring some chips.* He smiled; that didn't seem like a bad idea.

*****

It was almost eleven by the time Blake climbed out of his old Opel Manta outside Rock Lodge, the place he called home. It was a small building in comparison to the old Victorian mansions that stood nearby along the banks of the Mersey. Once, more than a century ago, this whole area had been the playground of the rich. Villas and gardens that led onto an esplanade where women in silks walked with top-hatted gentlemen. That was all long ago and since then, the park had been bisected by a dual carriageway. Some of the mansions had fallen into disrepair and even collapsed. A few still stood in their own grounds, sealed off from the estates of New Ferry and Rock Ferry by iron gates and the A41. Blake's house had been a DIY project started by his parents when his father retired. He'd passed away and his mother, who developed dementia, had wandered out of the front door a couple of years ago, never to be seen again.

He squashed down the memory of the door hanging ajar. Tried not to let the feelings of panic and guilt well-up in his tightening chest. At the time, he'd been so busy with his work, chasing villains and playing the efficient law man, that he hadn't noticed the danger. The times he'd come home at night and found her in the garden calling for her husband or thinking he was someone else. He should have sorted things out sooner and got the support she needed, but he didn't.

Blake shook himself and held the chips under his arm like a rugby ball, as he fumbled with the keys in the lock. Pushing the door open, he called out, "Chips!" Serafina, his demon Persian cat came up to him, meowing and rubbing at his ankles so persistently, that it nearly tripped him over. "Okay, okay! Calm down, cat."

Laura Vexley leaned against the doorframe of the living room. "What time do you call this, Mr Policeman?" she said, a smile playing about her lips.

"Sorry," Blake said, accepting her hug but holding the chips at arm's length to avoid them getting crushed. "Rotten day."

"I texted you," she said. Her green eyes flashing. *Cat's eyes*, Blake always thought. *That's why she gets along with Serafina. They're kindred spirits.*

"You did," Blake replied, scraping the chips onto two plates. "Several times, I noticed. Couldn't reply. Too busy."

"You found time to get a haircut, though," she said, raising one eyebrow.

"Jeez, what is this? I could grow it long, if you want, and tie it back in a ponytail for you!"

Laura sniffed and folded her arms. "Just saying, you weren't too busy to pay attention to your rugged good looks. Was she pretty?"

"What? Who?"

"The hairdresser, running her fingers through your luscious locks. Was she pretty?"

Blake shrugged. "I don't know. Maybe. I didn't really think about that...It was meant to be my day off. I just thought I'd get a cut while I could..."

"She did a good job," Laura said, scooping up a plate of chips and striding back to the living room. "Come on. Your chips'll get cold."

He watched her tall, angular body disappear into the other room and shook his head. He'd only known her a matter of months and yet he'd cheerfully given her a spare key to the house and let her into his life. Or some of it. Sometimes, though, Blake felt manipulated, played even. He knew it was his own suspicious nature, something that made him a good policeman but a quality that worked against him in his private life. Or maybe he just couldn't understand why this lively, beautiful woman would be even remotely interested in damaged goods like him. He looked down at his plate. She was right about his chips getting cold, though. And he needed to eat; tomorrow was another day and hopefully, it would bring fresh leads.

I didn't really enjoy the killing. It didn't feel like I'd thought it would. Not how it was in books or on the TV. It didn't excite me or make me feel powerful. It was just something that needed to be done. It was a bit like when I worked in the slaughterhouse. Most of the people there were kind of removed from the actual job of killing the cattle.

Thinking about it now, that'll be something they'll pick up on. I can see it now: 'Our killer spent some time working in an abattoir, taking pleasure in tormenting the poor animals as they went to their deaths.'

It won't be true, of course, but it'll help with the whole mythos. That's an important word; there has to be a whole load of speculation and story spun around my past. It has to be a folk tale. You think of all the infamous murderers, the really big ones. They all had troubled pasts that experts and enthusiasts pore over for years after, keeping the flame burning. So, I did feel sorry for the poor woman, but, just like a cow or a chicken or a lamb, she had to go. For the greater good.

One thing that really shocked me was the amount of blood. I really didn't expect that, in spite of my past work experience. It went everywhere. I like to think she died quickly and relatively painlessly. I'm quite proud of that.

I wasn't too worried about the blood. I mean it's not as if I have to clean it up. But I have to be careful. I mean, if I made it too easy, I may as well just go and hand myself over and where's the fun in that? And anyway, greatness must be earned. Soon, the plot thickens, as they say.

SUNDAY 9TH FEBRUARY

CHAPTER 7

Ellen Kevney's house sat in the middle of a neat row of terraced houses on Rowson street. Vikki Chinn pulled up outside. The house was built of old red engineering brick, probably built in the early nineteen hundreds. It looked like so many houses across this side of the Wirral, and over in Liverpool too; white UPVC doors and windows, blinds and a small, well-kept postage-stamp front garden. She thought, proudly, of her own flat in the middle of the city and wondered if Ellen Kevney had been pleased with her little house, too. Probably.

Vikki's parents were always asking her when she was going to get married and move out of her flat. That struck her as rich, given that they spent most of their years living in three rooms above a restaurant. Vikki had grown up there. But they wanted more for her, which is partly why they were so disappointed when she joined the police instead of going to university. She shrugged and got out of the car. The net curtains twitched in Ellen's house and Vikki frowned. Somebody was in there.

She rapped on the front door and waited. No response. She knocked again and, finally, the door creaked open. A young woman with dyed purple hair peered out. "Yeah?" she said.

Flashing her warrant card, Vikki introduced herself. "Can I ask your name, please? And can you explain what you're doing in this house?"

"I'm Blaise," The woman said. "Blaise Kevney. I'm Ellen's cousin... I didn't mean any harm. I had a key and I was just..." her face crumpled and she burst into tears. She turned and strode back into the house, leaving the door wide open. Vikki went in and found her sitting on the sofa in Ellen's living room.

"You were just what?" Vikki asked, perching next to her.

"Hoping she'd come back. I thought if I came here, I'd find her having a cup of coffee, watching telly or something," Blaise shrugged. "Stupid, I guess."

"You must have been close to her," Vikki said. "To have a key..."

Blaise nodded. "We grew up together. We were more like sisters. Went to school together and everything." She wiped her nose with a tissue.

"We're trying to trace her movements before she disappeared on the Monday, would you have any idea where she might have gone that afternoon, Blaise?"

"I told the policeman everything I knew,"

Blaise said, glancing at the carpet. "Mondays were her 'me time' because she worked all Saturday..."

Vikki frowned at Blaise. "Yes, we know that, Blaise. I feel like there's something you aren't telling me, though."

Blaise glanced at Vikki and then looked down again. "There's nothing to tell."

"Try me," Vikki said. "Look, Blaise. This is serious. Ellen's life could depend on any information we can get. Even if it seems trivial."

"Okay," Blaise said and drew a breath. "I guess you need to know."

*****

Leasowe station struck DC Kinnear as a confusing jumble. The main road, Reeds Lane crossed the railway line, which meant that a level crossing was needed to allow trains through. There was also a footbridge which masked the station from the road. Any old-world charm the station might once have possessed was smothered by brutal metal platform shelters, litter bins and signage. "I'm not even sure where to park," DC Andrew Kinnear muttered, peering into the drop-off point.

"Use the main carpark on the other side of the road," DC Alex Manikas suggested. "We can have a look at that while we're here."

Kinnear pulled into the carpark. It was large and surrounded by mature trees. It being Sunday, there weren't many cars parked. "I bet it's chocka on a Monday," Kinnear said. "Full of commuters. It's a wonder whoever it was dropped off Ellen Kevney's car found a parking spot."

"Can you imagine if they hadn't?" Manikas grinned. "Driving around and around. Maybe that's why they left it in a disabled space."

They climbed out and scanned the carpark. "Yep. Looks like a carpark," Kinnear said, with a shrug. "So glad Blakey sent us out to do this."

"He's got a real chip on his shoulder about that Searchlight programme, hasn't he?" Manikas said. "I swear I thought he was going to go off pop when I mentioned the magazine."

"Yeah," Kinnear muttered. "I kind of get it, though. You do one thing and it haunts you for the rest of your life."

Manikas gave him a sidelong glance. "You aren't going soft on me, are you?"

"Is that what she said last night?" Kinnear said, giving Alex a dig in the arm. He caught Alex's eye and grinned.

"Ha," Manikas laughed, looking away, quickly and striding across the carpark towards the station. Kinnear caught up with him. "If I said that to you, you'd have a right gob on you," Manikas said.

Kinnear opened his arms and looked surprised. "What?"

"You know," Manikas said. "I heard you gave Kath Cryer a right earful for making some snidey homophobic comments."

"Yeah, well, that was ages ago," Kinnear said. "We're okay, now. Anyway. If you'd said it, you wouldn't have meant it in the same way. Sometimes, it ain't what you say, it's the way that you say it."

Manikas shrugged. "Fair enough. Don't want to get on the wrong side of you though..."

"Why not?" Kinnear said, frowning.

Manikas smirked and gave Kinnear a sidelong glance. "It'd be a PC gone mad..."

"I should arrest you for that. I'm sure there are laws against crap jokes, you know."

They crossed Reeds Lane and entered the station. "There won't be anyone around today," Manikas muttered.

"Are you here about the car?" A gruff voice said from behind them. Kinnear turned to see a man in a Merseyrail uniform. His long, grey sideburns intensified his scowl, somehow. "I can spot coppers from a mile off."

"I'm DC Kinnear, this is DC Manikas. And, yes,

we're here to find out more about the car, if that's possible."

The man grimaced and looked around the empty station. "Fraid I'm rushed off me feet at the moment," he said and then gave a brief smile. "My name's Ian Saxby. It ends with a 'y' if you're writing that down. Course I can help, come in." Saxby ushered them into a side office which contained a table and a couple of chairs. A sink and a water geyser occupied one corner and a confusing array of mugs, cups and magazines cluttered the table. "So the car was reported blocking a disabled bay yesterday but it had been there a couple of days by all accounts. Is it true that it belongs to that Kevney girl? I hope they find her. She was a lovely kid..."

Kinnear frowned at the old man. "You knew her?"

Ian Saxby seemed to redden under his grey bristles. "Yeah, I knew her. It's a bit delicate, though..."

*****

Laura sat in the kitchen, swirling some orange juice in the bottom of a glass and staring into it. Serafina rubbed up against her legs. "It's Sunday, Will, why do you have to go to work?"

Blake raised his eyebrows. "Really? You're asking me that? You knew what I did when we first met. There's a murderer and a missing woman out there."

"I know but you aren't the only policeman on the force, surely..."

"I'm in charge of this case Laura. How would it look if my team are all up first thing on a Sunday morning while I'm having brunch with my..." he paused. What was she? Partner? Girlfriend? Lover? "Anyway. I've got to go. I'm sorry."

"It's fine. I understand," she said, hugging him. "See if you can get back early tonight, yeah?"

Blake nodded. "I'll see."

He hurried out of the house and climbed into the Manta, crossing his fingers that it would start first time. It had been his father's pride and joy and Blake had developed a similar affection for it. But the years hadn't been kind to it and it didn't always repay his loyalty. This time, however, the engine roared into life. As he drove, he mused over what he'd learned from Chinn and Kinnear. The houses of Rock Ferry flashed by and he passed the shining industrial buildings that occupied the old Camell-Laird shipyard. A few cranes still loomed above him but there wasn't as much activity there as when he was a boy. The tunnel was quiet, even for a Sunday and he soon found himself parked at Canning Place and heading up to the Operations Room.

Cryer, Chinn, Manikas and Kinnear were all waiting for Blake as if it was a surprise birthday party. "Okay, so run this all by me one more time," he said.

Vikki Chinn piped up first. "So, I found Blaise Kevney, Ellen's cousin in Ellen's house. She told me that Ellen goes to the Aphrodite's..."

"Where?"

"It's a swingers' club in Birkenhead," Kath Cryer said, reddening. "It's a converted pub down by Birkenhead Docks."

"That was a quick answer, Ma'am," Manikas said, smirking.

Kath pulled tongues at him. "Maybe I'm a regular, Alex."

"So was Ellen there recently?" Blake said, steering the conversation back from the brink of banter.

"Apparently, they have these 'No Strings Mondays' where single mums can go and meet up with men and... you know... Ellen Kevney was a regular."

Blake rubbed his temples. "Let me just get this straight. Ellen Kevney was last seen two weeks ago at one of these swingers' parties?"

"Possibly, sir," Manikas said. "Ian Saxby at the station went along frequently and often saw Ellen there. Of course, people weren't keen on coming forward because they were scared of being judged..."

"Jeez, I'd judge them more for not giving us vital information when we needed it," Blake snapped. "Right. We need to get round there, right away. Any volunteers?"

CHAPTER 8

At first glance, Aphrodites looked like any other closed-down street-corner pub. Metal sheets covered the downstairs windows and thick curtains covered the upper ones. But there were no weeds growing from the gutters and the huge red door looked newly painted. Blake wasn't a stickler for grammar and correct punctuation; he wasn't a man of letters at all, really, but even the lack of an apostrophe grated on him. He knocked hard and waited for a response.

A muffled voice called to them from behind the thick wood. "Yeah? Who is it?"

"Police, we'd like a word with you please," Blake shouted. He glanced over at Kath Cryer who had seemed really keen to accompany him. She raised her eyebrows.

"What's it about?"

"Do you really want me to shout it all down the street? I'd rather talk face-to face," Blake said.

There was a second's pause then bolts and locks rattled from behind the door and slowly it opened. A bald, round face peered at Blake. "What can I help you with officer?" the man said. "I was up quite late last night. So you'll have to forgive me. I haven't started tidying up yet." He pulled back the door and Blake saw he was short and round, wearing a thick, white dressing gown. Blake had expected someone younger; this man was in his late forties at least.

Blake and Cryer stepped into the main reception area of the club and Blake was quite surprised. He wasn't sure what he'd expected but the place looked quite classy; a bar stood in one corner of the room and leather chairs dotted the stripped floorboards. A few strategically placed mirrors made the place look bigger than it actually was. There was an 'after party' smell to the place, sweat, perfume and alcohol. "DCI Blake, this is DI Cryer," Blake said. "Are you the owner of this establishment?"

"I am. Bob Courtney," he said and extended his hand. Blake shook it briefly. "What seems to be the problem? It isn't the house on the corner? I've told them before; I make sure guests arrive and leave quietly. We're fully licenced by the authority to do this and we keep within the law..."

"No," Blake said. "No complaints, sir, we want to ask you a few questions about Ellen Kevney."

Bob Courtney's eyes widened for a fraction of a second and then he regained his composure. "The girl who's gone missing..."

"The mother of two who's gone missing, sir," Kath Cryer said, sternly. "She was a regular here, I believe."

"Yeah. I know her, but she was fine when she left here," Bob Courtney said, with a shrug.

"Didn't you think it was worth letting us know that she came here, sir?" Blake said. "Given the circumstances and the seriousness of the situation."

"I dunno," Bob said. "I have to be careful with people's privacy. Like I say, she was fine when she left with Ralph. It's not like she was on her own. I just assumed he would get in touch, maybe."

"Ralph?" Blake glanced over at Cryer.

"Yeah. Nice guy. Bit of a regular. Younger fella. Dark hair, slim. Quite a looker. She hooked up with him a few times. They seemed very keen on each other. She left with him. It all looked fine."

Blake shook his head. "And you can tell us where this 'Ralph guy' lives, I suppose?"

"Yeah, I could as a matter of fact. All our guests have to register and bring along some ID," Bob said. "Trouble is, I've also got a duty to protect my customers' privacy. Aphrodites is all about privacy as you can imagine. People won't want to come here if they think it'll become public..."

"I appreciate that, Mr Courtney," Blake said. "But Ellen Kevney has been missing for two weeks and your pal, Ralph, is the first lead we've had in all that time. Now, I can go and get a warrant which *will* be granted but will take time and Ellen just doesn't have that time. Do you want her blood on your hands?"

"Oh, come on..." Bob began to say.

"Think of her poor kids," Kath Cryer said, folding her arms. "Anyway, sir, there's nothing to stop us parking a police car outside and asking punters for information as they arrive at the club, is there?"

"No, Kath, I don't think so. I imagine Mr Courtney's Licence to sell alcohol will be coming up sometime this year. We may be asked to comment on whether we think it's wise to grant one."

Bob drew a deep breath. "Okay, okay but you're not looking through the guestlists. I'll give you this Ralph's full name and address and you leave me alone. Right?"

"For now," Blake said. Courtney disappeared behind the bar and rummaged around in a cupboard at the back. Finally, he pulled out a rather ragged-looking A4 notebook with red covers and flicked his way through it, muttering and pulling loose sheets of paper out. "Here we are. Ralph Vaughan, 28, Mere Lane, Hoylake." He scribbled it down on a scrap of notepaper and handed it to Blake.

As they drove away, Blake looked in the rear-view mirror at the club. Bob Courtney was just a blob of white on the doorstep, but Blake knew he was watching them vanish. "What d'you reckon Kath? More to find out about Mr Courtney and Aphrodites?"

"Dunno, sir. He might just be protecting his customers. They aren't really doing anyone any harm and what people get up to behind closed doors isn't anyone else's business. Least of all ours."

"As long as nobody comes to any harm and it's all legal," Blake added.

"Yes, sir," Kath Cryer said. She gave him a sidelong glance. "Perhaps we should send Alex and Vikki along on a party night. Undercover like. See what happens."

"You're a terrible person, Kath Cryer," Blake said, a smile spreading across his face. "I don't think there'd be much cover to be under."

"Do you think we should ask for backup, sir? I mean, we don't know anything about this Ralph Vaughan, do we?"

Blake shook his head. "Let's assess the situation when we get there."

They drove in silence for a while. The industrial estates and social housing of Birkenhead were replaced by more leafy suburbs and then, briefly, into countryside. The land became flatter and the sky bigger as they drew nearer to the sea. "You're never far from the sea on the Wirral," Cryer said. "It seems like it, when you're down in some of the big housing estates but water's never far away."

"Technically, The Wirral is an island, did you know that? If you count the streams and rivers at the Southern end."

"Interesting, sir," Kath said, with a smirk. "It's an education working with you."

Mere Lane was a small line of cottages not far off the North Parade that skirted the sea. It linked two bigger roads of large semi-detached houses with impressive, mock Tudor frontages. The cottages in Mere Lane were clearly old fishermen's homes, with thick sandstone walls. Blake could imagine them huddled together against the storms before all the development around them.

It was early afternoon and Blake's mouth watered as the smell of Sunday roast drifted through the air to taunt him. For a moment, his mind drifted to Laura's complaint this morning and he wished he was tucking into a roast somewhere with her. "Come on," he said. "Let's get moving. I'm starving."

Ralph Vaughan didn't look like the sort of person who would frequent swingers' clubs; nor did he look particularly young. He may have been a little younger than Blake; mid-thirties perhaps, with a thin, stubbly, beard that was clearly never going to thicken. He wasn't dark either but a blazing redhead. Blake noticed a cream shirt and what looked like a tank top beneath a flowery apron splashed with gravy. He stood frowning in confusion at Blake.

"Can I help you?" he said and then noticed the wooden spoon he was brandishing at them and lowered it. Blake introduced himself and Cryer and asked to come in.

The house smelt of cooking and rang with the squeals of toddlers thundering around upstairs. Toys littered the floor as they picked their way across the living room to a flowery sofa that had seen better days.

"You'll have to forgive the mess," Vaughan said. "Kids don't really show much mercy when it comes to tidying up, especially twins." He scanned the room, as if seeing it for the first time. "They're quite efficient mess-makers..."

Blake glanced over at Cryer who reflected his own doubts about the credibility of Vaughan as a prime suspect. He cleared his throat. "Yes, I'm sorry to bother you, Mr Vaughan but we're investigating the disappearance of Ellen Kevney. You might have heard about it in the news?"

Ralph Vaughan blinked at them through his bottle-end glasses. "I'm sorry Detective Blake, unless it's on CBBC, I haven't kept up with anything for months."

"Right. Can I ask you, Mr Vaughan, are you familiar with Aphrodites?"

The man frowned. "No. Is it a Greek restaurant?"

"It's a swingers' club, sir," Cryer said. Her voice was abrasive, but she had perfect timing and could wrong-foot the most hardened liar. "Are you a member?"

Vaughan blinked again and gave a short, disbelieving laugh. "Me? What? No. God you're serious, aren't you?" he spluttered and glanced at the door. "Look, what's all this about? I've never been near a swingers' club. I wouldn't know the first thing about..."

"Ralph? What is it?" A woman appeared at the living room door with two identical toddlers clinging to her dress. Her brown hair was cut in a pageboy style which seemed to have come straight from the seventies. The rings around her eyes betrayed her tiredness. One of the toddlers broke from the cover of her mother's dress and rushed onto her father's knee. "Who are these people?"

Ralph reddened and frowned as if trying to solve a difficult puzzle. "They're police officers, love. They're investigating someone going missing." He looked distantly at her. "They want to know if I've ever been to a swingers' club..."

Blake stood up. "Forgive me..." he fished for a name.

"Andrea," she said. "Andrea Vaughan. I'm Ralph's wife..."

"I'm sorry, Mrs Vaughan but during our investigations, your husband's name has come up in connection with Aphrodites Club in Birkenhead. I don't know if you are familiar with it but..."

"No. I'm not. And he's not, either," Andrea Vaughan said. "Whatever you're accusing him of, I can tell you now that when he's not at work, Ralph has been here looking after the twins with me. Honestly, just look at us. Do we look like we have the time, the energy or the inclination to go to a... a... *swingers' club?*"

"Swengers cleyub!" One of the toddlers said.

"Shwinger Club!" The other one giggled, picking up on her brother.

"Oh god! They'll be shouting that all over Sainsbury's now!" Andrea Vaughan said.

Trying to wrestle the conversation back, Blake turned to Ralph Vaughan. "So, what is it that you do for a living?

Vaughan settled the child on his knee. "I work for the council. I'm a clerical assistant. Housing..."

"And you work Monday to Friday?"

"Yes," Vaughan said, his cheeks reddening. "Nine to five. Then I get in my car and drive here and give Andrea a couple of hours respite."

"Can you think of any reason why your name would appear on the register of Aphrodites, then, sir?" Kath said. "The club is quite strict. They require photo ID and an address."

Ralph Vaughan went pale. "Oh no," he said. "My driving licence. I lost it a few months ago."

"Yes," Andrea said. "At the Sizzling Platter pub in Greasby, we think. We went there for my birthday."

"I had my coat on the back of my chair while we were eating and when I looked down, my wallet was on the floor. The licence was missing. I thought it had fallen out but..."

"I presume you reported this and replaced the licence," Blake said. "So that'll be a matter of public record."

"Yes," Vaughan said. "Maybe someone used it to become a member of this swingers' club."

"I'm afraid we may have wasted your time, Mr and Mrs Vaughan," Blake said, rising to his feet. "My apologies. We will have to check your hours at work, but we can do that discreetly with your manager."

Mrs Vaughan showed them out and, once in the car, Blake rubbed his face with both hands. "If ever there was someone who had never committed a crime in their lives, it's that man. Damn!"

"One thing is for sure, sir. Ellen Kevney's disappearance seems certain to be an abduction now, and a premeditated one at that."

Blake sighed. "Could be. Looks like it's back to Aphrodites."

We're all slaves to something, aren't we? I mean, some of us submit to tyranny quite willingly. We sell our souls for drink or drugs, the latest phone or even a bit of recognition from our friends. How many people are addicted to social media now? Craving 'likes,' tweets or 'mentions.' We give away our privacy just to get that momentary dopamine hit and then we're back to square one, seeking more. Yes, we're all slaves to something. I'm as bad as anyone else, in that regard. But some of us are taken deeper into slavery by others; those who are trafficked, kidnapped, held against their will. Some are duped into slavery; they marry the perfect charmer only to find a whip and drumbeat replaces the wedding march. The worst thing is to be a slave and never even realise. The people of Hilbre Grove taught me that.

In a way, I feel like I have liberated them all. Their petty little lives will be smashed to pieces after this. Broken. But sometimes, you have to break things to make them stronger.

MONDAY 10TH FEBRUARY

CHAPTER 9

The clang of the huge bolt that locked the door to the container made Ellen Kevney flinch. Her backside and legs felt numb from the hard surface. In the darkness, she'd lost all track of time but her growling stomach told her that she hadn't eaten for a good while. Once more the blinding light filled the room and she heard footsteps as her captor came in. The door clanged shut, plunging them into darkness and she heard someone settle in the corner.

"Why are you doing this?" Ellen said. She could hear the strain in her own voice, the fear, too. "Just let me go. I promise I won't tell. I don't know where I am anyway. Please. I'll do anything. Just let me go home and see my kids..."

"Did you ever watch Searchlight, Ellen?" A voice whispered in the darkness. It sounded male but smooth and soft. Not a gruff voice. "You'd have been old enough I think when it was on."

"Searchlight?" Ellen struggled to follow.

"It was a crime programme. With Ross Armitage and Emerald Fisher. They used to pick crimes that had happened all over the country and show re-enactment videos. The aim was to get the public to help them."

"No," Ellen said, hoping it was the right answer. "No. I don't remember that one."

"I used to love it. Shame it finished. If it was on now, there'd probably be a reconstruction of you on it. Imagine that. An actress playing you leaving Aphrodites with a tall, dark stranger called Ralph..."

Ellen bit her lip as fragments of memory came back to her. The club. Ralph's bare chest. Then in the car but not driving. Had her drink been spiked at the club? "Where's Ralph?"

"Ralph's not here anymore, Ellen," the voice said again. "You won't see him again."

Ellen's heart thumped. "What have you done?"

"I was telling you about Searchlight," the voice said, firmly. Ellen swallowed down her fear. She found it hard to focus on the words; more images of Ralph swirled around each other in her mind. More questions. She didn't really know him that well as a person. The sex was great and whenever he was at the club, she would seek him out. She thought maybe it could go further. It seemed to be heading that way. They'd met for coffee a couple of times but there had always been this barrier between them. When did she last see him? Was he there when she was taken? Oh my God! Had he tried to defend her and ended up hurt? Or worse? She snapped her attention back to her captor. "There was always a feature on the programme where a real policeman would show CCTV footage of shop robberies or street muggings," the whisperer said, "and it was always introduced by a PC Will Blake."

Ellen frowned. The name seemed familiar. She half-remembered her mum saying something a bit saucy about wanting to be arrested by PC Will Blake. Ellen had been a teenager. They'd been watching telly and Ellen had been mortified, as any teen would when their parent makes even a remotely suggestive reference. Maybe that's why it had stuck in her head.

"The same Will Blake's looking for you now, Ellen. He's still on the force. Got promotion, too," The voice said. Ellen frowned, did her captor sound *excited* by the idea? "He'll find you. Mark my words."

"But you could just let me go," Ellen said. "He doesn't have to find me. And you could get away."

There was a moment's silence as though her captor was considering the options. "No. That wouldn't work. Wheels are in motion. Don't worry. You won't be lost forever. I'll make sure of it."

She heard him rise to his feet, the door squeaked on its hinges and she crushed her eyes shut at the glare. And the full impact of what he said hit her. *He'll find you. You won't be lost for ever*. Ellen Kevney wept at the finality of those words.

*****

To say that Bob Courtney didn't look pleased to see Blake and Cryer would be an understatement. The man looked like Blake's presence caused him physical pain. "Really?" he groaned. "Back so soon?"

Blake stepped past him into the club. "I'm sorry Mr Courtney but it turns out that your Ralph Vaughan wasn't the real Ralph Vaughan. Did he verify his ID with a driving licence by any chance?"

Courtney's shoulders slumped. "Probably. Look, how am I to know it's fake or been tampered with? We do a lot to keep our members happy and safe here. It's a responsible community."

"If it was that responsible someone would have come forward days ago," Blake said, stony-faced.

Bob Courtney drew a breath. "Look, Inspector Blake, we got off on the wrong foot earlier today. I've got nothing to hide. People come to this club for all kinds of reasons and on different days of the week. They're lovely, ordinary folk. A lot of them won't even know that Ellen came to the club too. Others might but didn't think it was relevant or haven't seen her for a while anyway."

Blake grunted. The man had a point. "Fair enough. But I'll need to see a full membership list."

"Let me put the word out about Ralph, first. Someone will come forward, mark my words," Bob Courtney said, looking pained again.

"You do that, and in the meantime, I'll apply for a warrant," Blake said. "But I really don't have the luxury of time, Mr Courtney."

"Look," Courtney said, wincing. "I'll send an email out today and make a few calls. You can look at the register just let me warn people first, okay?

*****

It was late again, by the time Blake finally arrived home. The house lay in darkness; Laura must have gone home. It troubled Blake that she had never really offered to return the spare key for the Lodge after he had been in hospital. He'd nearly been burned alive whilst trying to rescue a suspect from a blazing charity shop. Laura had volunteered to feed Serafina while he recovered and so needed a key. It was true that Blake had never asked for it back. But she'd hung onto it and turned up when he least expected her. Blake never objected; somehow Laura was an expert at moving things in the direction she wanted. She wasn't an animal behaviourist for nothing and often, Blake felt she was working her magic on him. But the house seemed cold and dark without her there.

Serafina's plaintive meow greeted him. "Are you starving to death?" he said to the cat. As he closed the front door, he noticed a white van roll past at the end of the drive. He frowned. It was late for any kind of commercial vehicle to be around here. In this neck of the woods, the properties were quite far apart, set in large gardens and secluded. Few people came down here. Occasionally, a strange car would cruise through the unmade roads, the driver peering at each property and Blake just knew they were criminals searching for their next target. These were big houses, and the people who lived in them were well-off.

The van had rumbled past the gateway in an instant. There had been a logo on the side but Blake didn't have time to register it; his eyes had been focused on the dark figure in the driver's seat. Despite the fleeting glimpse, he could tell the driver was looking at him.

Opening the door again, he looked out onto the garden. He could picture his mother standing there in her nightdress like a ghost, calling out his dad's name or Jeff's, his little brother. And when he'd brought her into the warm house, she'd insist that someone was there. So much so that, spooked, Blake would search the garden, even the house sometimes.

Shaking his head, Blake slammed the door shut and bolted it. Ghosts were one thing he didn't need.

CHAPTER 10

Superintendent Martin sat back in his chair and listened to DCI Blake as he laid out the main lines of investigation for him. He was an older man with a whipcord frame and hawk-like features. Blake imagined him to be a formidable copper in his youth. The man had risen through the ranks and Blake respected that. What Blake always found frustrating was the strategic view that senior officers had to take. How things might affect the force's relationships with the community, how the force might look in the media; things that Blake didn't like to concern himself with, too much. He knew they were important; he just didn't want to hear about them.

"So we're no nearer to finding Ellen Kevney... Unless of course the body we've just found turns out to be her?" Martin said, a glimmer of hope in his pale blue eye.

"Possibly, sir. But we can't be certain and the level of decomposition was such that..."

Martin silenced Blake with a wave of his hand. "That's fine, Will, no need for the gory details. We need to get somewhere with this case and fast. Reporters are beginning to get impatient and that's never good for the force."

"No sir... not good for Ellen Kevney either..."

Martin gave Will a tight smile. "Yes, I know, Will. Don't think I've lost sight of that. But we need the public on our side here. We've got nothing otherwise."

"To be fair, sir, we have Aphrodites. We know where Ellen was before she went missing."

"And that is just what the press will pounce on. It's a juicy story, Will. A good-looking woman goes missing from a swingers' club? Someone being left with scissors in their eyes. We'll have the nationals down here like a shot. Let's keep that under wraps, for now, shall we? The last thing we need is a media circus down here, with you at the head of the parade..."

"With respect, sir, I don't go courting publicity..."

"No. It just seems to find you, doesn't it, Will? Rescuing people from burning buildings, psychopaths running around with shotguns; it's all in a day's work for you. Just keep this all calm and discreet, can you?"

Stinging from the comments, Blake walked out of his meeting with the Super and straight into a phone call from Jack Kenning, the Pathologist. Much as he disliked the man, the call had never been so welcome.

"I've been working overtime on the body,"

Kenning said. "On first examination, it looks like the victim was killed by a straight stab wound to the neck. Probably with the scissors. It cut the artery. She'd have bled out quite rapidly. We're still *combing* through the crime scene but it's a mess and it'll take a while. I'll keep drip-feeding you details as they become available."

"Right," Blake replied, trying to hide the impatience in his voice and ignoring the feeble hairdressing pun.

"We've managed to extract a couple of objects which had been hard to remove from the corpse because of its advanced state of decomposition."

"Go on."

"One was a St Christopher medal with an inscription on the back in a language we've identified as Romanian. There was also a card from Happy Homes Cleaning Services. It's an identity card for staff members and it has a name on it..."

Blake's heart sank. "Don't tell me. Katerina Dragavei."

"That's impressive, Blake. I take it you've already been searching for this young lady?"

"No. Her passport turned up in Ellen Kevney's car," Blake said, already wishing the two cases hadn't just become one and the same.

"Well, we need a formal identification somehow. Medical or dental records maybe. God knows how otherwise. I don't think her own mother would recognise her..."

Blake winced "What about the scissors that were used to kill her?"

"Professional grade. Salontech brand. Very sharp. Left-handed, too. Your friend Ellen's DNA was all over the handles along with some that's as yet unidentified. She's a left-hander, too, right?"

"Yes, so they're her scissors," Blake sighed. "Is there anything else?"

"I've sent all I have so far in an email, Blake. Do you not turn your computer on first thing?"

"You know I don't, Jack," Blake said. "That's why you rang me. That's why you always ring me. Anyway, I've been walking the Super through the finer points of the case and haven't had chance to."

Blake leafed through the notes he had made and read Kenning's email which gave a more technical and detailed account of what they had found so far. One woman missing, one dead. It didn't look good for Ellen Kevney; she could be dead, or kidnapped. A pair of her scissors were in the dead woman's eye and Katerina's passport was in Kevney's car but Blake didn't think she was the killer. Blake called the team together and briefed them on the latest development.

"So anything we can dig up at Hilbre Grove might lead us to Ellen Kevney, sir," Kinnear said.

"Possibly," Blake said. "Have a look through the door-to-door notes that uniform have made and I think we'll need to go and talk to the neighbours again. One of them might have some link to Kevney. Vikki, could you arrange a visit to Happy Homes Cleaning? See if we can find more about the victim. Manikas, you come with me. We're going to have a look at the crime scene again."

"Sir?"

"Looking at it with the knowledge we have now might give us a different view. Come on."

*****

Although the heating had been turned off and the body removed, a stench lingered it coated everything and rose up to greet Blake as he stepped through the front door. A few Scene of Crime Investigators, dressed in white protective suits, still buzzed around the other rooms, taking photographs and searching cupboards. Blake led Manikas into the room where the armchair sat, soaked in blood.

"So the killer brought the victim here? Met her here? What?" Blake muttered.

"I'd say met her here, there, sir. Otherwise our killer would have to persuade her to come to the house. Not impossible but trickier. It's easier if it's a business transaction."

Blake nodded. "Yes. The Taylors have a landline still. A home cleaning service would be easy to call from here. And then just wait."

"Like a sort of dial-a-victim service?" Manikas said. "That's a bit grim, sir,"

"I hate to say it, but I wonder if Ellen Kevney is lying somewhere in an empty house," Blake said. "She was a mobile worker, too. Our killer could have done the same to her. Another part of me wonders if Kevney might be responsible for the death..."

"Really, sir?"

"Her scissors ended up in the woman's eye and the passport was in Kevney's car."

"But why would Ellen Kevney kill Katerina?"

"Why would anyone kill her? Like that too. It's horrible. We need to check the phone records for... Are you with me, Alex?"

But Manikas had his head tilted and a curious frown on his face. "Sorry, sir," he said. "It's just that picture..."

Blake turned and saw 'The Little Black Boy' still hanging, slightly tilted on the wall. "Oh, that. Yes, it caught my eye, too."

"It looks out of place, sir..."

"Yes," Blake said, a sinking feeling growing in his stomach. "It's a William Blake print apparently..."

Manikas looked at him but said nothing.

"You think that was placed there? By the killer?" Blake said, at last.

"I don't know, sir," he said, looking sheepish. "I'm just saying, there was that Radio Times in perfect condition in the car and now this. I'm not being funny but look at that oil painting on the other wall; it fits in with the rest of the house. But the print looks wrong and it's by William Blake..."

"It could be pure coincidence, Alex," Blake said, trying to convince himself more than Alex; he'd thought the painting to be curious when he first came to the scene. "I'm not so big-headed as to think somebody is trying to attract my attention with all this..."

Alex Manikas shrugged. "But we should consider all possibilities. All we have to do is ask the Taylors if they own a William Blake print, sir. Then we'll know."

"Fair enough. Ring in and get someone to ask the question."

Manikas went out into the hall and Blake stood shaking his head at the scene. "How did the killer know?" he said as Manikas returned.

"Know what, sir?"

"That the Taylors would be on holiday? The killer must have watched them, but how do you know how long somebody will be away for?"

"The number of bags they stick in the car, sir?"

"Maybe, but it would be hard to assess..."

"Well, it doesn't really matter, sir, once the deed is done, does it? I mean, if they're away for a week, the poor victim is still dead. If they're away for a fortnight, then there'll be more decomposition. More distance between the crime and the killer. Three weeks is a bonus."

"True but he must have been keeping a close eye on them to know that they'd be gone for more than a day. It would all need to be planned. How could he book a cleaner without knowing when the house would be empty?" Blake edged around the blood stain on the hearth rug and looked out of the front window. The Grove was quiet, nobody in their front gardens or cleaning their cars. "Any of these other houses would give you a great vantage point and the neighbours would be the most likely people to know each other's movements."

Manikas joined him at the window. "You think the killer might be that local, sir?"

"It's a strong theory, Alex," Blake sighed and wandered into the kitchen. "Or at least there's a strong local connection. Why is there tape around the sink?"

"Apparently, there were two coffee cups in there. One had lipstick on the rim."

Blake shook his head. "The killer had coffee with his victim first? Jeez."

Manikas's phone rang. "Yep? Right." He gave a long breath. "Thanks."

Blake raised his eyebrows. "And?"

"Better get that picture bagged and tagged, sir," Manikas said. "Mr Taylor has never heard of William Blake and has never had a painting of a Little Black Boy in his living room. That's been put there deliberately."

But Blake wasn't listening. He strode up the hall and out into the front garden, staring at the bungalow next door. It lay silent and still; curtains drawn tight. "Who lives there, at number three?"

Manikas flicked through his notes. "That's a woman called Jean Quin. Single, lives on her own. Currently on holiday... sir, you don't think..."

"I'm hoping not but we both agreed, Ellen Kevney must be somewhere. We need to check."

CHAPTER 11

Happy Homes Cleaning was clearly the kind of place you phoned to book a cleaner; anyone who had come direct to the office would have run a mile. Google maps had led DS Vikki Chinn off the Dock Road, down a narrow street that led into a crumbling alley. This had all been warehouses once but since the shrinking of the docklands, garages, wholesalers and woodyards occupied the area. The new businesses stood between decaying warehouses with empty, staring windows, overgrown with opportunistic weeds and bushes. Vikki had been told that more goods went through the port of Liverpool than ever before, but the decay here seemed to contradict that.

A little door, its tired blue paint peeling in huge flakes, stood lost in a wall of blackened brick. The sign above was functional but hardly sang Happy Homes Cleaning. One tiny window at the side of the door was so grimed with dirt and dust from the street that it was impossible to see inside. Vikki tried the door and it shuddered open, the bottom snagging on old linoleum.

A woman stood behind an old counter in a tiny room. The whole place looked faded and in need of a good wiping down and a lick of paint. A few faded posters of cartoon cleaners holding thumbs up clung to the wall, slowly losing their grip by the corners. Three chairs sat along one wall but a large, bald man dressed in black sat on the middle one, effectively making the other two unusable. He scrolled through his phone without looking up.

"Can I help you love?" The woman said. Vikki weighed her up. Mid-fifties, perhaps, dyed blonde hair, her heavily-made-up face had a mean, pinched look about it.

"DS Vikki Chinn. I'm here enquiring about an employee of yours. A Katerina Dragavei?" From the corner of her eye, Vikki noticed the big man stop scrolling and look up at her.

The woman behind the counter blinked and then gave a curt nod. "Ex-employee," she corrected. "Cleared off a few weeks ago. Haven't heard from her since. Took her uniform with her, too. Is she in trouble?"

Vikki scribbled in her notebook. "I'm sorry. I didn't get your name..."

"Joynson," The woman said. "Heather Joynson. Manager of Happy Homes Cleaning."

"Thanks, Heather. So when did you last see Katerina?"

The man to Vikki's left shifted in his seat, his

leather jacket creaking.

Heather Joynson exhaled deeply. "I dunno about three weeks ago. She went on a call and didn't come back. I tried ringing her but there was no answer. Bloomin' annoying if you ask me."

Vikki consulted her notebook. "Would that call be to number two Hilbre Grove, Upton on the Wirral?"

Heather Joynson gave a grumpy sigh and pulled out a huge appointments book. She flipped it open and flicked through the pages. "Yeah... Hilbre Grove, Wirral... Mrs Taylor..."

"And you took the call?"

"Course I did."

"Can you remember anything about the caller?"

"No. We get hundreds of calls in here every day," she glanced down at the silent phone. "Well lots anyway. How am I meant to recall every punter?"

"Please. If there's anything. It might be important. Was it male or female?"

"Well, it says 'Mrs Taylor' in the book but... hang on, now you mention it. It was a male voice. A young man. He said he was ringing for his grandma."

"Local accent?"

"Think so, yeah."

Vikki frowned "When she didn't come back; weren't you worried about her?"

Joynson shrugged. "These casual workers come and go. She hadn't been with us all that long. I just figured she'd gone home. I wish she hadn't taken the uniform with her. I go through loads of them."

"Do you have an address for her?"

"I'm afraid I don't, sorry," Joynson said, pouting. "I did ask her a few times, so I could put her on the books properly but she kept putting me off. Said she was just in the process of moving."

"You'll have to forgive me, Heather," Vikki said, lowering her notebook. "But that sounds awfully odd. You didn't know where she lived and yet you employed her. Don't you need references? Don't you vet your employees? How on earth did you pay her?"

"Cash," Heather Joynson said, staring coldly at Vikki. "I suppose you're right. I should've done more background checks but, to be honest, it's so hard finding staff who'll stick the job. I'd take you on if you wanted to fill in the time between your shifts."

The bald man grunted and Vikki flashed him a look. His grin faded.

"What about friends. Did she know any of your other employees?"

"No. Not really. Ours is more of an agency model. The girls don't work together much and Katerina came in alone. What is this anyway? I feel like I'm being interrogated, here..."

"Katerina's card and uniform were found at a crime scene," Vikki said. "It's essential we trace her last movements and any next of kin."

If Vikki Chinn had expected to shock Joynson, it didn't work. Instead, her face hardened. "Well, I don't think I can help you other than that. Now, unless you have any other questions, I'd like you to leave."

The big man stood up and took a step forward but Vikki didn't move. "I don't think there's any need to be like that, Ms Joynson. I'm investigating a serious crime. If I have to come back here with a warrant, I think there may be a number of other interested parties who might like to tag along. HMRC might be a start. Possibly a couple of immigration officers too. What d'you think?"

Heather Joynson didn't blink. "I think you'd have to have a bloody good reason for getting a judge to agree to a warrant, Detective Sergeant Chinn. Now I asked you to leave."

Vikki clenched her teeth but turned and left. As she climbed in her car, she glanced up at the windows high above the door. Someone had wiped the grime from the inside and a pale face stared out at her. A piece of paper was pressed against the glass and it had one word written on it: HELP. Then a hand wrapped around the girl's mouth and dragged her away from the window.

CHAPTER 12

Even as he approached the door, Blake could smell it. That familiar stink of death. He pushed at the front door but it was locked. "We'll check round the back," he said and led Manikas down the side of the house. "Why didn't anyone pick up on that smell when they did the door-to-door?"

"Dunno, sir," Manikas replied, a handkerchief to his mouth and nose. "Maybe they just thought it was from the Taylors' house..."

A side gate led them into a garden and to the back door. There was no sign of any forced entry. "Gloves," Blake said to Manikas, producing a pair from his jacket pocket. Blake tried the handle and it opened. A gust of warm, fetid air caressed Blake's face and he grimaced. The brightness of the kitchen only made the hall darker. It lay waiting for them, shrouded in shadow. Blake inched forward, pressing the back of his hand to his mouth. The smell grew stronger and thicker, until he felt that if he opened his mouth, he would taste the air itself.

The body lay on the living room floor. Its legs were straight but the arms were extended, as if the poor soul had been crucified. The face was grey and swollen, but Blake could see a dark beard, matted with blood. The whole body was puffed up, straining at what looked like dark overalls. A pair of scissors protruded from one eye.

As Blake backed out, something caught his eye. A picture hung, crookedly on the wall above the fireplace. Half the frame was occupied by a poem, the image below showed a boy with a sack on his back. "It's the same style as the one at the Taylors'," Blake said, trying hard to hold his breath and speak at the same time.

"The Chimney Sweeper," Manikas read aloud from the painting. "Is it a William Blake, poem, sir?"

Blake gagged on the smell. "Jeez! I dunno, Alex. let's get outside."

They staggered into the fresh air, the smell clinging to them. Manikas retched and doubled up over the hedges in the front garden. Gesturing to one of the Scene of Crime Investigators who was leaving the other house, Blake leaned against the gatepost, bending over and sucking in air.

"You okay, sir?" The CSI said.

Blake nodded. "I'll be fine. There's another one in there..."

"Another what, sir?"

“Another body,” Blake snapped. “Call in. Get another team down here quickly.”

The man’s eyes widened and he sprinted to the van parked outside number two.

Blake watched the man go and then groaned at the sight of Don Pleavin marching across the Grove. “Are you all right Mr Blake?”

“Yes, Mr Pleavin, I’m fine. Just made a... discovery...”

Pleavin’s eyes widened. “Another murder? In Jean’s house?”

Blake straightened up and Manikas had managed to recover himself, too. “I’d rather you kept this to yourself until we have a team to secure the area.”

“Absolutely,” Pleavin said, nodding. He seemed pleased to be involved in some kind of official secret. “Was it him?”

“Who?”

Pleavin winked and made a stabbing gesture to his eye. “You know, the Scissor Man. Was it him?”

“The Scissor Man?” Blake said.

Pleavin looked taken aback. “I thought that’s what you called the killer. The Scissor Man. He stabbed the woman in the eye with a pair of scissors, didn’t he?”

“Where did you get that from?”

"The PCSO who called round told me. Tom Dacre. Nice fella."

"With respect, Mr Pleavin, he shouldn't be divulging details of the crime scene to members of the public. I'll be having words with him as soon as I can. mark my words."

"I see," Pleavin said. He looked as if he was trying to think of a way to make amends. "Is there anything I can do to help? I could stand guard over Jean Quinn's house..."

"No. No," Blake said. "We need to keep the place secure until an official team arrives. I'm sure you understand."

"Right," Pleavin said, still standing there.

"Maybe a mug of hot tea?" Manikas said, his eyebrows raised, expectantly. "Or coffee. We've had a shock, Mr Pleavin..."

"Ah! Right!" Pleavin said, giving them a thumbs up. "Yes. I can do that." He hurried off, glad to have a role.

Blake gave a bleak smile. "Good thinking, Alex. The last thing we need is Mr Pleavin gumming up the works. If I catch up with that PCSO, I'll tear him a new one. Gossiping with the bloomin' public. Is that what they're calling the killer? The Scissor Man? Jeez."

"Beggar's belief, sir." Manikas scanned the houses. "For what it's worth, I think you're right.

Whoever did this is likely to have a close connection with Hilbre Grove…"

"And whoever did this, has Ellen Kevney. If she isn't dead already."

*****

Tina White looked out of the front window of number four Hilbre Grove and caught her breath. She dropped the curtain and slid out of view.

"Paul!" She cried. "Paul!"

Paul rushed into the room. "What is it? What's up?"

"There are two policemen in the road. They just came staggering out of Jean Quinn's house. Oh my God. D'you think they've found another body?"

"Don't be daft!" Paul snapped, grabbing Tina by her arms. "You've been watching too much Columbo!"

Tina didn't smile at his feeble joke. "Well why else would they come running out of that house? The tall dark one threw up in the front hedge. He wouldn't do that unless he'd seen something horrible, would he?"

"No," Paul said, quietly. "No. I don't suppose he would…"

"Oh. Paul. What are we going to do? They're

just hanging around out there. They're bound to come asking more questions. We have to tell them!"

"Stop it!" Paul snapped. "We don't! All we have to do is sit tight. So what if they ask us questions? We don't know anything. Do we?"

"But what if it's her? What if it's her in Dot and Dave's house? Or what if it's her in Jean's?"

Paul looked out of the window. Don Pleavin had come out with two mugs of tea for the policemen. "Trust him, Mr Neighbourhood Watch. If they knew what a creep he really was. Wouldn't surprise me if he did it..."

*****

Once more, Hilbre Grove was full of vehicles as Crime Scene Investigators buzzed around both houses. Blake had brought the team down and now they stood in a huddle outside Number two. A line of uniformed officers stopped the large crowd of gawkers that had grown at the entrance to the road. Blake cast an eye to the alleyway that led between number four and number five. The PCSO blocking that route raised a hand to him and Blake nodded. "Is that the fella who was pushed over by those kids the other day?"

"I think so, sir," Kinnear said.

"Bloomin' hopeless," Blake muttered. "Go and tell him to keep the far end of the alleyway shut.

He'll have half the neighbourhood blocking it as they peer over into the garden of number three."

"Will do," Kinnear said and jogged across the Grove.

"Oh and Kinnear! If his name is Tom Dacre, tell him I'm putting in a complaint about him blathering on to the residents about the crime scene."

Blake watched Kinnear gesticulate to the man who went pale, nodded and vanished down the alleyway with appropriate haste.

"Right. No need for anyone to go into the house. I've seen all I need to see and more besides," Blake said once Kinnear had returned. "We'll let CSI do their job. I want to focus on the residents here. Talk to them. Find out all you can: how well they know the Taylors or Jean Quinn, what they think of each other, attitudes, any relatives with criminal records, anyone who visits regularly, anything that might give us a clue as to who selected this Grove to be their dumping ground for bodies and why."

"Okay, sir," Cryer said. "D'you have any preference for who we talk to?"

"Yes. Could you talk to the people at number four and five? Kinnear, can you have a chat with the ever-helpful Mr Pleavin. Manikas take number one. I'll check out number seven..."

"D'you want us to ask about the pictures?"

Blake cleared his throat. "Only if you can do it carefully, Manikas. If someone is fixated on me, for whatever reason, I need to take advice on that. If you get a chance to look at their bookshelves or notice anything relevant, fine. Right. Let's go."

Blake turned and headed for number seven Hilbre Grove.

CHAPTER 13

Tightening the straps on her wrist splint for the fifth time, Kath Cryer walked up the cracked concrete drive to the front door of number five. She looked down at the splint; the straps weren't straight. The Velcro top piece on the first fastening was at an angle and a loose bit stuck out. It wouldn't do. She pulled it open and smoothed it straight back down. Her heart thumped as she approached the door. It looked ordinary enough; the kind you would see on any suburban bungalow. But then the house she'd been shot in had been ordinary, too. And had a similarly unremarkable door. She squeezed the fabric of the splint, hearing it creak. Taking a breath, she knocked on the door.

"Will someone get that?" A male voice bellowed from inside the bungalow.

"Someone? You mean me, you lazy bastard?" A woman yelled back. "You get it, I'm busy!"

"Honestly! It's not like I've got a day off..."

Cryer rapped again, cutting the argument dead. The door swung open and she held her warrant card high before anything was said. The man in front of her had three day's stubble, long, straggly hair and a faded Red T-shirt. His face, which seemed to be losing the fight against forty years of gravity, dropped even further. "DI Cryer, sir, we're investigating the murder at number two, can I come in?"

The man stepped aside and allowed Kath Cryer into the hall. The bungalow looked as tired as its occupants. Wallpaper peeled at the corners and dust and dog hairs coated the laminate flooring. An old grey-muzzled sheepdog staggered up to Kath giving her a feeble wag of its tail before turning and heading back down the hall. A woman in a baggy hoody and jeans stepped from the kitchen, wiping her hands on her front.

"DI Cryer," the man said sullenly. "Asking about the murder."

The woman brushed a strand of greying blonde hair from her worried face. "Come in, Detective... erm... officer..."

"Kath's fine, ma'am," Cryer said, with a warm smile. She'd decided that this woman had enough on her plate without an arsey police officer giving her a hard time. Kath could change tack if she needed.

The woman ushered her into a large living room which, again, would have benefited from a redecorate and a quick hoovering round. Framed album covers hung on the walls. They sat down. "So, it's Mr and Mrs Jones?"

"I'm Gretchen," Mrs Jones said. She couldn't

help curling her lip. “He’s Graham.”

“Great,” Cryer said, pulling out her notebook. “You’ll be aware that a body was discovered at the Taylors’ a couple of days ago…”

“Yes, horrible,” Gretchen said, pulling the sleeves of her hoody over her fingers. “We spoke to the police officer who called round then.”

“Has there been another discovery?” Graham Jones asked. “Only, there’s a lot of activity around Jean Quinn’s place.”

Kath Cryer nodded. “I’m afraid we’ve found another body, sir.”

Gretchen gave a squeak and hugged her knees to her chest. “That’s horrible. How… how long had the body been there?”

“We don’t know yet, Gretchen,” Kath said. “We’re working on establishing as much detail as possible. I need to ask a few questions. I’m afraid some of them might seem impertinent or intrusive but I hope you understand.”

Gretchen nodded. “If it helps find the bastard who did this, then ask away.” Graham nodded.

“So, Dot and Dave Taylor what are they like?”

Graham shrugged. “Quiet. Dave’s a bit of a blowhard. Always going on about his army days. Dot’s house proud. They spend most of their time polishing and cleaning the house.”

"Dot always told me they didn't have much money. So when they finally bought their own place, they were made up. It's all they wanted," Gretchen said, giving Graham a sidelong glance. "Content with their lot, is how I'd describe them."

"Anyone who doesn't like them?"

Gretchen and Graham shook their heads in unison. "We're not a close bunch," Graham said. "Not in and out of each other's houses..."

"Not physically, anyway," Gretchen muttered.

"This is more of a wave to each other as we put the bins out sort of place," Graham finished off, ignoring Gretchen.

"When did you ever take the bins out?" Gretchen said.

"How about relatives?" Cryer asked, heading off any argument between them. "Has anyone visited the Taylors' house recently who seems suspicious?"

Gretchen shook her head. "Nah. Like I say, they're a lovely couple. Their son visits every now and then and their grandson pops round more often. Nice people."

Kath nodded. "Great. Thanks."

"I dunno what you're worrying about the Taylors for," Graham said, staring out of the front room window at the busy scene playing out in the Grove. "It's that Pleavin, fella, I'd be looking at if I were you."

"Graham!" Gretchen snapped.

"Yeah, well, it's true. The man's a flippin' weirdo."

"He's not a murderer though, is he?"

"I'm sorry," Kath Cryer said. "If there's information, however trivial or irrelevant it seems to you, you really must share it with me."

"Pleavin," Graham said, darkly. "He makes himself out to be a pillar of the community but he's a pervert..." Gretchen snorted and looked pointedly at Graham, who blushed. "I don't go round groping other people's wives, Gretchen!"

Kath raised her eyebrows. "Are you saying that Mr Pleavin has assaulted someone in the Grove?"

Gretchen shook her head and sighed, her face and neck reddening. "It was years ago. Honestly. When we first moved in, we thought it would be a great idea to throw a barbecue for everyone in the Grove. We all had a lot to drink."

"He was a bloody animal. Slipping his hand up your skirt every time you went past him. You had to slap his face."

"Well, it wasn't a great party. Paul and Tina got drunk and a bit loud. Dave had an argument about BREXIT with Graham..."

"Bloody idiot," Graham muttered, then held up his hand. "Sorry..."

Kath leaned forward in her chair. "Assault is a serious allegation, Mrs Jones. If you wanted to take that further..."

Gretchen shook her head again and scowled at Graham. "Nah! I put him in his place. Men, eh?"

"Apart from the party, has Don Pleavin caused any other kind of trouble in the Grove?"

"We had some washing go missing from the line," Graham said. "Gretchen's smalls, tights, that kind of thing. Paul White at number four reckoned he'd seen Pleavin in our back garden while we were out one day. It really wouldn't surprise me. He's always sniffing around Jean Quinn, too. Acting the he-man protector."

"Okay," Kath said, scribbling down notes. "Do you think Mr Pleavin might have a key to Ms Quinn's house?"

"Possibly," Graham said. "I wouldn't give him our key, I'm telling you. He'd be through Gretchen's smalls drawer like a ferret up a drain-pipe..."

Gretchen looked pained. "Don Pleavin is a bit of a nuisance," she admitted. "But I can't imagine him killing anyone." She looked over at Graham. "Mind you, he's not the only one on the Grove with certain... proclivities..."

"Gretchen don't," Graham said.

Kath sat up. "What do you mean?"

Gretchen drew a breath. "The Whites at number four. Tina and Paul are quite the exhibitionists." She gave Graham a sidelong glance. "You'd be amazed what they get up to in their back garden and who I caught watching them..."

"I didn't... it wasn't like that," Graham muttered and stared at the carpet. "They were just having fun..."

"Yeah, right. So were you, by the look of it..."

Graham clamped his mouth shut and glared at Gretchen.

Kath raised one eyebrow and made a note. "Unless you make an actual complaint about that," she said. "There isn't much we can do. Getting back to the Grove. What about, deliveries, vans, cars? This is a pretty quiet cul-de-sac, you obviously notice unusual activity."

"He does," Gretchen muttered. "I'm too busy."

Graham winced and scratched the stubble on his chin. "Vans come and go all the time. What is it they say? If you want to stay invisible, wear a hi-vis jacket and sit in the passenger seat of a white van. Nobody notices you."

"Mind you we're out working most of the day," she said. "So who comes and goes then, I couldn't say."

"And what is it you do?"

"I work in a nursing home," Gretchen said.

"I'm a musician," Graham said. "Local gigs and YouTube mainly but…"

"Graham's an IT technician at the local high school," Gretchen said, firmly. "So, we're both out all day."

"Thanks," Kath muttered, making a note.

"Come to think of it, there was a chimney sweeps van parked outside Jean's last week," Gretchen said. "The trouble is, the Grove is a cul-de-sac so people don't always park directly outside the house they're visiting. I didn't think much of it."

"When was this?"

"Monday or Tuesday, I think," Gretchen said. "Jean's on holiday for two weeks. Not back until Saturday." Gretchen put a hand to her mouth. "Oh my God. Has anyone told her?"

"We're getting in touch as soon as we can. Do you know of any family she might have? Anyone who might break the news gently to her?"

Gretchen shook her head. "I don't think there's anyone. She lived there, looking after her mother. When she passed away, Jean was left on her own. She never mentioned any brothers or sisters."

"Used to see her wheeling her mother around the Grove," Graham said. "Other than that, she always seems to be alone."

"You don't really know people, do you?" Gretchen said. "I mean, you think you do but it's not true is it? I suppose we don't know half of what goes on round here."

"Clearly," Graham said, sitting back.

"This van," Kath said. "The chimney sweep. Can you remember anything about it? The registration number or maybe a name on the side? Anything that might help us track it down?"

"Chimeree," Gretchen said. "Yeah, Chimeree. That was the name on the side. I thought it odd, you know. A bit Mary Poppins."

Kath Cryer closed her notebook and stood up. "Well, thank you for your time. That's been very useful," she said. "If you do think of anything that might help, just let me know." She passed them a card. As she left the house she looked next door at number four and thought about what Gretchen Jones had told her about the Whites. This was going to be a curious interview.

CHAPTER 14

Against her better judgement, DS Chinn climbed out of the car and strode back over to the Happy Homes Cleaning office. The woman she'd seen at the window was in immediate danger and needed help. Calling in for back-up, she gripped the expandable baton handle, hoping she didn't have to use it.

Heather Joynson's eyes widened as Vikki Chinn came back into the office. Vikki noticed that the big man was no longer in his chair. "I thought I made it clear..."

"Mrs Joynson, I have reason to believe there is someone being held against their will in the upper storeys of this building..."

The huge man burst through the door at the back of the office and gripped Vikki's wrist tightly. Vikki felt her grip on the baton weaken. Fumbling in her jacket pocket with her free hand, she found what she needed.

The man bellowed in surprise as the pepper spray took effect. He clawed at his eyes, rubbing and cursing in a foreign language. Vikki pushed him towards the chair he had sat on, and swung his arm behind his back, quickly cuffing him. "Stay down!" She barked.

Joynson cowered behind the desk. "Keys," Vikki snapped. "Now."

Flinching at the sound of distant sirens, Joynson snatched up a bunch of keys and slid them across the counter. "It wasn't me," she said. "I didn't want to do this. I was in debt so much. They threatened me..."

Vikki snapped open the baton, more for effect than anything else and pointed to the back door behind Joynson. "Lead the way," she said.

The door opened into a large, empty warehouse. A metal staircase led up two flights. Joynson fumbled at the lock and looked pleadingly at Vikki one last time. "It wasn't my idea, honest." She pushed the door open. "They made me do it."

The smell of stale sweat and long-confined bodies struck Vikki. In the dim light she saw five women sitting on mattresses on the floor. They looked terrified and confused. "It's okay," Vikki said, holding up her warrant card. "Police."

One woman's eyes widened and she sprang up trying to barge past Vikki, almost knocking her over. Another one shouted something in a language Vikki didn't know but sounded eastern European and the struggling woman shouted back, angrily. Vikki pushed the girl back. "It's okay, I'm here to help!"

The sirens were loud now and another of the

women looked out of the grimy window. Vikki could see the 'HELP' sign discarded on the floor. The woman at the window said something else and the one struggling with Vikki, slumped and fell back down onto the mattress, weeping.

Vikki Chinn turned to Heather Joynson as the sound of police officers barking orders drifted up from downstairs. "Heather Joynson, I'm arresting you for False Imprisonment, you do not have to say anything. But, it may harm your defence if you do not mention when questioned something which you later rely on in court. Anything you do say may be given in evidence. Do you understand the caution?"

Heather Joynson nodded wearily.

*****

Don Pleavin handed DC Andrew Kinnear the plate of biscuits. "Help yourself, son," he said. "You'll need the energy."

Kinnear smiled and nodded. *Never a truer word was spoken*, he thought. Pleavin had regaled Kinnear with numerous stories about previous occupants of Hilbre Grove and how they'd been a cut above the current riffraff. The man had an endless supply of pointless tales. Kinnear balanced the plate on the arm of the sofa. "Thanks," he said, thinking ruefully about the gym membership he wasted every month and the tightness of his belt. He'd been trying to keep off the biscuits for the last five days, but they were a weakness of his. His partner, Chris, would start nagging him about the pounds he was putting on if he didn't do something soon. "If I can get back to the investigation, Mr Pleavin..."

"What? Ah, right. You'll have to forgive me. I lost track, there. So how is the investigation going? Have you tracked down all those van numbers I gave you?"

Kinnear shifted in his seat. "We have a team working through them as we speak, Mr Pleavin, thanks. Can you tell me who might know that Dot and Dave, and Jean Quinn are on holiday?"

Pleavin frowned. "You mean locally? Most people on the Grove. I make a point of alerting other neighbours when houses are unoccupied, so they can keep an extra-special eye out. Possibly not Albert at number one. He keeps himself to himself."

"What about family, friends?"

"Well, Dot and Dave have quite the social life; Bingo on a Thursday evening, bowling on a Tuesday afternoon, they're always down at the British legion Club. They could have told anyone there. They were chuffed to bits about winning the holiday..."

"You seem to have quite a comprehensive knowledge of their weekly schedule, Mr Pleavin," Kinnear said.

Pleavin almost preened himself. "It's part of the job, isn't it officer? No point being a Neighbourhood Watch Coordinator if you don't know the comings and goings of the *neighbourhood*, right?"

"Quite, sir. What about Jean Quinn? Who might she tell?"

"Nobody, I should imagine. She lives alone. No family," he sat back in his chair. "She's particularly vulnerable. At risk, I think you might say?"

"I'm sorry?"

Pleavin levelled his gaze on Kinnear. "Well, an older single lady. Living alone. Prime target for any scumbags looking for a quick burglary or theft, wouldn't you say?"

"So, Miss Quinn doesn't go out much?"

"Not that I'm aware of and very little gets past me..."

Kinnear couldn't help himself. "Apart from the two murders in the houses opposite..."

Pleavin's cheeks coloured and his toothbrush moustache twitched under his nose. "I try my best, DC Kinnear. I can't be here all the time and my wife is somewhat lacking in observation skills."

"Where is Mrs Pleavin, by the way?"

"She's in the garden, putting some washing out.

Why?"

"Well, I just thought it would be useful if I spoke to you both at once, to save time and resources."

"Do you have to speak to her? She doesn't really notice things. Better in the kitchen than anywhere else, if you see what I mean?" Pleavin gave a ratty grin which Kinnear didn't return.

"I think I'd like to have Mrs Pleavin here, too, please."

"Suit yourself," Pleavin muttered. He stood up and headed for the door, swiping the plate of biscuits from Kinnear's side and taking them out with him. Kinnear pursed his lips, having just decided he would take one.

Mrs Pleavin was a small, mousey woman in every sense of the word. Her hair was a greying light brown and her eyes glittered with a nervousness that set Kinnear on edge. She sat on the edge of her armchair like she had no right to be there.

"Here she is," Pleavin said, pointing at her. "She won't be any use though. Not detective material, this one." Mrs Pleavin gave a fleeting, injured smile and looked down at the mat that lay spread out in front of the fireplace.

"Hello, Mrs Pleavin, I'm DC Kinn..."

"I've told her who you are. Just get on with the

questions," Pleavin snapped. Kinnear raised an eyebrow. The man's demeanour had completely changed. He was rubbing his hands together and one foot tapped rapidly on the carpet.

"So, Mrs Pleavin, I'm DC Kinnear from Merseyside Police. I wondered if you'd noticed anything unusual or suspicious in the last couple of weeks?"

Mrs Pleavin glanced over at her husband who gave a brief nod. "No," she said. "Just the usual delivery vans coming and going." Her face crumpled in disgust. "Especially to number four. They have a lot of stuff dropped off."

"But nothing out of the ordinary?"

Mrs Pleavin shook her head. "It's a quiet little spot, really. All this that's happened, I've never known..." She sounded bewildered, which Kinnear could quite understand.

"And you don't remember seeing any kind of cleaning company van or car? Anyone calling at the Taylors' or to Jean Quinn's?"

Again Mrs Pleavin shook her head. "We do keep a close eye on the place. Donald would have noticed anything untoward on his rounds, wouldn't you, dear? I try to keep an eye out when he's away but there's so much to be done, keeping the house just so."

Kinnear nodded. "And what days were you

away over the last three weeks, Mr Pleavin?"

"I'm not sure," Pleavin said, reddening a little. "There'd be the weekly Tuesday afternoon shopping trip. Then I'm out Wednesday morning for The Greasby Ramblers, it's a walking group..."

"It's good for you both to keep fit," Kinnear said, smiling.

"I don't go," Mrs Pleavin said, and Kinnear realised that he didn't even know her first name.

"She prefers to stay in the house, don't you, dear?"

Mrs Pleavin gave a tight smile and seemed to shrink into the seat further.

"Just for the records, Mrs Pleavin, could I have your full name, please?"

"Helen," she said.

Kinnear gave her a warm smile. "My favourite aunty is called Helen," he said. "She used to spoil me rotten when I was a kid."

Helen Pleavin's face uncreased into a genuine grin, for a moment. She glanced over to her husband and Kinnear noticed a glint of mischief in her eye. "You haven't told Mr Kinnear about Monday afternoons. Sometimes you go out on Monday afternoons, don't you, Donald?"

The muscles in Pleavin's jaw clenched. "Sometimes, yes," he said. "I just go for a walk in the hills. North wales usually. Moel Famau. There are some great little rambles round there."

"Even in the winter, Mr Kinnear," Helen Pleavin said, her eyes fixed on her husband. "Comes back in the dark sometimes."

"I'm sure the detective doesn't want to hear about my adventures in the countryside, dear. That's enough now." There was an edge in Pleavin's voice that Kinnear didn't like.

"So, can I ask, Mr Pleavin. Helen mentioned your 'rounds.' What do these entail?"

Pleavin swallowed and stared at his slippers. "Well, I check everyone's houses are secure..."

"So you check them front and back?"

"Usually. I make sure the houses are locked if people are out. Check if their windows are closed, keep an eye on garden sheds."

Kinnear frowned. "And everyone is okay with this?"

Pleavin shrugged. "Mostly..." He looked up and saw Kinnear's quizzical expression. "The Whites don't like me going in their back garden, so I don't..."

"Unless they're out," Helen Pleavin murmured. "Then you do..."

"They'd thank me if I stopped a burglary, wouldn't they?" Pleavin said, his voice a petulant whine. "I don't overstep the mark."

"And how often do you do your 'rounds,' Mr Pleavin?"

"I haven't recently, have I? Not since you lot warned me off..."

"Somebody made a complaint?"

Pleavin nodded. "One of those fake policemen... you know...Community Support fella. He knocked on the door a few weeks ago and said I shouldn't be going into people's back gardens. Put me in my place, didn't it? But now look what's happened."

"And you don't know who complained?"

"No idea," Pleavin said. Kinnear noticed a tiny smile had crept onto Helen's face and made a mental note to come back and talk to her when her husband wasn't in. There was more to Helen Pleavin than met the eye.

CHAPTER 15

Albert Green, who lived at number one, Hilbre Grove was an oddball. That was the only word Alex Manikas could come up with to describe him. Green had answered the door wearing a long kaftan decorated with red and blue swirling dragons. He wore a little pillbox hat and smoked a cocktail cigarette in a holder.

"Are you the policeman whose coming was foretold?" he asked when Alex started to introduce himself. "Do come in but please try and keep to the plastic mats. I'm trying to preserve the carpets."

Alex wrinkled his nose. The atmosphere in the other two houses had tested his sense of smell to destruction but the stink in here was running them a close second. "Do you have pets, Mr Green?" he said, glancing around at the desiccated excrement that lined the edges of the stained hall carpet.

"Several cats, as you shall soon witness, young man! They're old and wise and my best friends!"

Albert Green's living room heaved with feline bodies. Alex counted at least twelve lying in various places around the room. Piles of magazines and newspapers cluttered the floor and made movement difficult. "You have a lot of cats," Alex said.

"I do, I do. Take a seat, why don't you?"

Alex scanned the chairs, each one occupied by a cat and covered in a thick layer of hairs. "I'm fine thanks."

"Suit yourself," Albert said, smiling. "Can I get you a cup of tea or anything?"

"No! Really!" Manikas almost shouted. "I had a drink just before, thank you. You're very kind."

Albert nodded. "Very well," he said, sitting down heavily. Alex thought for a second that he had actually sat on top of the cat that lay there but right at the last moment, it slid up onto the arm of the chair and settled itself onto his lap. "So, tell me officer, with what particulars can I furnish you?"

Alex stared for a second and then remembered what he was doing and pulled out his notebook "Ah, yes, if I can ask you. Have you noticed any unusual activity around Hilbre Grove in the last three weeks?"

Albert Green stroked his chin and then the cat. He frowned and looked up at the ceiling. "Yes," he said, at last.

An awkward silence fell across the room as Alex waited but it seemed that was the sum total of Mr Green's answer. "And... what have you noticed?"

"There are a lot of policemen around," Mr Green said. "The cats think it's because of that horrible man who came to the house two weeks ago."

"You had a visitor?"

"Yes."

"Why was he horrible?"

Mr Green shrugged. "I don't really know. Maybe he'd had a bad upbringing. A good role model is so important for a child, don't you think?"

Alex began to wonder if this was some kind of wind-up. "Sorry, Mr Green. In what way was the man horrible?"

"He tried to sell me cleaning equipment. It all looked a bit cheap and shoddy but then he told me the price. Ten pounds for a duster. Well, I mean, that's daylight robbery, isn't it? I told him so!"

"And this man didn't like that?"

"No! He began to verbally abuse me. He even tried to kick one of the cats as she ran out. Disgusting way to treat such a wise and venerable creature. You know, the Egyptians used to worship cats as gods..."

"This man. What did he look like?"

"Like a demon," Mr Green said, his eyes widening. "Stubbly short hair, and a stubbly beard. And a tattoo of an inverted cross on his neck. Can you imagine that? Hideous!"

"Did he threaten you?"

"He said he'd been in prison before and he was sick of 'stuck-up gets with too much money' telling him his stuff was too expensive!"

Alex raised his eyebrows. "Shocking."

"Exactly. I told PC Esso about it and he said they were looking into it."

"PC Esso?"

"Yes, the young police chap. He had one of those new-fangled hats on... a baseball cap, that's right!"

"Did he say he was a PCSO by any chance?"

"Yes, that's what I said. He's the fella."

"Right," Manikas said, making a note. If the PCSO had followed the complaint up, then it would save him a lot of time. "Well, thank you for your time Mr Green. You've been very helpful. Apart from the unpleasant salesman, have there been any other strangers around?"

Green stroked his chin and made a huge pantomime of thinking. "No," he said, at last. Then he leaned forward in his chair. "But I tell you this: there are few people stranger than Donald Pleavin."

"In what way is Mr Pleavin strange?" Alex Manikas asked, wondering what you'd have to do before Green decided you were strange.

"In and out of people's gardens. Nosing on people all the time. He watches everyone. He watches everything. Making notes. Scribbling things down. Mark my words. That one's a strange fish and no mistake."

Alex closed his notebook. "Well, thank you, Mr Green," he said. "No need to get up. I'll show myself out."

*****

The curtains rippled as Kath Cryer walked up to the door of number four Hilbre Grove. Clearly, Paul and Tina White had been watching what was going on at their neighbours and anticipated a call.

Kath tugged at the wrist splint. After throwing herself in the path of the shotgun, back in October, she'd come away with nothing worse than a painful wrist. Apparently, she'd sprained it when the blast of the shotgun knocked her off her feet. There was some damage to the muscles and tendons that would take a while to heal. In some ways, it was an indignity; a gammy leg and a cane would have held more gravitas. Theo, Kath's boyfriend, always pulled a face when she slipped the splint on. He called it her 'old lady glove' and made no bones about what a turn-off it was. He was constantly telling her that she shouldn't need it anymore and to try and go without it. But she needed it.

The door to the Whites' house swung open and a stocky, well-groomed man smiled out at Kath, taking her by surprise. "Paul White?" she said, fumbling for her warrant card. "DI Kath Cryer. Can I have a chat?"

"Yeah, sure," White said, leaning against the door frame. "Is it about the Scissor Man?"

"Scissor Man?"

White snorted. "Yeah, that's what Don Pleavin said you'd called the killer. Is that all part of the gallows humour you police are meant to have?"

"If we could discuss things inside, please..."

White frowned. He was a good-looking man in his early thirties. A little on the plump side but then who was Kath to hold that against him? He looked like a man who was careful about his appearance, with his trimmed beard and open shirt. Paul White hesitated for a moment. Kath could sense his hesitation. "Sure," he said, at last and stood aside. "Welcome to Chez White."

Kath gave the briefest of smiles and stepped into the hall. The décor matched Paul White completely; pastel blue walls, a few tastefully arranged ornaments and a mirror to glance in as you left the house. A murmuring came from one of the rooms at the end of the hall. It rose and fell, sounding faintly seductive but Kath couldn't make out the words. "Is your wife around at all? I'd like to talk to you both."

White glanced down the hall and then back at Kath. "She's working at the moment. In a conference call. Can't be disturbed."

Kath shrugged. "You'll have to do then," she said, giving another grimace. White led her into the front room and she sat down on the leather sofa without waiting to be invited.

"So what's going on?" Paul said, his arms open. Everything about him put Kath on edge. He was overfriendly, trying too hard. Smarmy, that's what Kath's mum would have called him. When she was a teenager, dancing around her handbag with her friends, he's the kind who'd come slithering up to them; twice their age and three times as handsy.

"We've found another body," Kath said. "At number three, this time. Jean Quinn's house. She's on holiday, too, apparently."

Paul's face fell. "Another body?" he sat down. "That's awful. Was it a woman or a man?"

"That's an unusual question, Mr White," Kath said. "Why do you ask?"

Paul White shrugged. "I don't know. It might have a bearing on who I saw. If a woman was hanging around number three, I might notice more."

Kath frowned. "I'm sorry, I don't follow."

"Dunno," Paul said. "I don't pay much attention to workmen and delivery fellas but women tend not to do those sorts of jobs."

"I see," Kath said, not really agreeing with White's logic and thinking it said more about his attitude to women than his observational skills. "Well I can't really divulge that information. I'm sorry. Do you get on with Jean Quinn?"

"Yeah," he said. "She's a no-nonsense sort of woman. I like her. She just says, 'hello,' and then gets on with her day. Not a great one for chitchat. Doesn't poke her nose where it doesn't belong."

"Whereas some other people on the Grove do?"

Paul pulled a face. "I suppose so. It's not a bad place to live. Dot and Dave are pleasant enough."

"How about Gretchen and Graham Jones?"

"Oh them," he snorted. "Have they been bitching about us? What have they said?"

"They did mention that you'd been spotted having sex in the back garden, yes. They weren't making a complaint."

"I bet they weren't," Paul snorted. "Especially not Graham. He didn't quite have his binoculars out but..."

"You don't get on, then?"

"None of my business what they think is it? I don't bother them; they don't bother me. Graham's a bit of a dreamer. Thinks he's the next Ed Sheeran, missing the point that he's past it. Pretty average pub singer, in my opinion."

"So you haven't seen any suspicious activity in the Grove at all? Vehicles outside the Taylor house or Jean Quinn's? Anything at all?" A muffled, wordless groan drifted down the corridor into the room.

Paul White stood up and closed the door. "No," he said, raising his voice. "As I say, white van man comes and goes but I haven't seen anything..."

The groaning became louder and a thump accompanied it. "If you don't mind me asking, Mr White, what is that noise?"

Paul's face reddened. "That? Oh just Tina having a laugh with some of her work colleagues..."

An insistent screech, muffled by something other than the door filled the air, now. Kath's scalp prickled and she jumped to her feet. It sounded like someone who was gagged trying to attract attention. "I'm sorry, Mr White but I'm going to have to investigate that..."

"No!" Paul White stood up too but Kath was at the door already. He followed her down the hall. "Please. It's not what it looks like!"

“Let’s see shall we?” Kath threw open the door to the room at the end of the hall and her eyes widened.

Tina White sat, gagged and bound tightly to a wooden chair with rope. She wore a gingham dress and what looked like a blonde wig tied in plaits. Tears mixed with tracks of black mascara that coursed down her cheeks as she stared up, pleadingly at Kath.

CHAPTER 16

Kath Cryer prised the gag from Tina's mouth, and the woman snapped, "What d'you think you're doing?"

"I thought you were in trouble, I..." Kath looked across the room to an expensive-looking camera and microphone that was rigged up to a computer. "What's this? Lilly White?" A voice said from the computer. "I never said anything about a rescue. I tell you what though, how about you show the lady your appreciation? Eh?" The tone of voice made Kath shudder.

"I don't know who you are, sir but this is DI Kath Cryer of Merseyside Police and I'm in the middle of an investigation. Do you mind hanging up?" She looked at Paul White. "Do you mind explaining to me?"

"I told you it wasn't what you thought it was," he said.

But Tina had cut in. "I'm a cam girl," she said. "And you've just cost me fifty quid."

She was quite good-looking, but Tina didn't strike Kath as a typical model type; underneath all the make-up, Kath reckoned she probably looked like most women in their late twenties or early thirties. Maybe that was the appeal: the girl next door. Attainable.

Now, as Paul slowly untied her, Tina explained. "Some of the clients have specific requests. He's one of my regulars. Goldilocks bondage."

"Right," Kath said, biting her lip and not daring to ask if any bears became involved later on. "I'm sorry, I just heard the noise and assumed..."

"Assumed what? That I was holding someone captive?" Paul White said, seizing on Kath's apology. "What do you take me for? Some kind of weirdo?"

Kath gave Tina a brief glance, taking in her gingham dress and wig. "I don't know, Mr White. What exactly is your role in all of this?"

"I know what it looks like but none of this is illegal," Paul said, reddening. "I do all the technical stuff. And the marketing, advertising, monetising the Instagram feeds and all that."

"I see, sir," Kath replied, trying to process half of what had been said. "And you're right. It isn't illegal but at the same time, if you'd warned me then I wouldn't have jumped to conclusions."

"Anyway, it isn't us you should be questioning," Paul said, letting his indignation build again. "If you're looking for a shady customer, you should head over to number six."

"Donald Pleavin?"

"Paul, don't..."

"Why not? He's always lording it up and down the street like he's better than the rest of us with his Neighbourhood Watch," Paul snapped. "Well, let's just say that he's fond of a bit of Goldilocks, too."

*****

After looking at number seven Hilbre Grove and finding it locked and empty, Blake had taken himself back to HQ at Canning Place. He was relieved that the house held no surprises; having stood empty since its owner had died, it was a prime location for the killer to use. He was a little surprised that the killer had gone to all the bother of using a house that was occupied when a vacant one was available. On the flip side, at least he hadn't found Ellen Kevney's rotting corpse.

Having spent the afternoon working on the case from his desk, Blake called the team together to see what they had gleaned from the Grove. One name cropped up time and again.

"Donald Pleavin," Andrew Kinnear said. "Gave me the creeps. The way he spoke to his wife was horrible."

Blake shrugged. "We can't call him in because he gives us the creeps, Andrew. Anything more substantial?"

"He's got an intimate knowledge of people's comings and goings, sir," Kinnear said. "He knew the Taylors' weekly social calendar like it was his own. If anyone could plan this, it would be him."

"Albert Green didn't have a good word for him, either, boss," Manikas said, flicking through his notebook. "Said he was always in and out of people's gardens."

Blake nodded. "He's certainly a character," he said. "Come on, Kath, you're bursting to tell us something. Spit it out."

"So, first off, Gretchen Jones from number six said that Pleavin tried to touch her up at a party. He seems to have something of a predatory reputation. Plus, Tina and Paul White run a cam-girl service from their home. She calls herself Lilly White. All manner of people pay to direct her over the internet..."

"Direct her?" Blake said.

Kath went red around the neck. "Yeah, you know, tell her what to do. Talk dirty to her. But Mr Pleavin likes a bit of bondage; ropes and gags and the like, apparently."

"The dirty old man," Kinnear said, grinning at Kath. "What does her husband do? Is he a looker too?"

"Calm down, tiger," Kath said, grinning. "He

just sets up the cameras. And no, he's a flake."

"Shame," Kinnear said.

"Just for that, Andrew, you can take a closer look at this Lilly White. See if there might be any connection."

"Kath, you get Pleavin in, if you can. Getting him off his home turf might work to our advantage."

"Could I have a word with Mrs Pleavin while he's out, sir?" Kinnear said. "I'm sure she has some dirt on him but won't say anything in his presence. I think she's scared of him."

"Okay, Andrew," Blake said.

"What about the magazine in Ellen Kevney's car, boss? And the paintings? Is that something Pleavin would do?" Manikas looked doubtful. "Plus, he doesn't really fit the description of Ralph Vaughan, the man who left Aphrodites club. I mean, he was using a stolen identity. It couldn't have been Pleavin."

"That's true, Alex," Blake said. "But we can't just ignore Pleavin, either."

"Almost the first thing he mentioned to you was the Searchlight TV programme, sir, d'you remember? He said he was a big fan," Kinnear said.

Blake pulled a face. "True. Let's give him a call. Get him in tonight or first thing tomorrow."

*****

Vikki Chinn sat in St Anne Street Station interview room with DI Bev McCallon of the National Crime Agency. She was a tall, dark-haired woman in a grey trouser suit. Opposite her, Heather Joynson twisted a soggy tissue between her fingers.

She'd waived the right to a solicitor, even though one had arrived at the station almost before Vikki had. McCallon had introduced herself to Vikki.

"That was a bit rash, Vikki," McCallon had said. "Happy Homes Cleaners is a tiny cog in an international trafficking ring. The guy you arrested could easily have been armed."

Vikki nodded. "I know, Ma'am, I should have waited..."

"Ah well," McCallon had said. "Looks like you struck lucky." She turned to the solicitor, a tall, bespectacled man, in an expensive suit. He looked oily to Vikki, with his slicked back hair and smug grin. The grin faded when McCallon announced that his services would not be needed.

"Who did actually send you, by the way? Ms Joynson hadn't made a call."

The solicitor inclined his head. "That I can't divulge, I'm afraid. Let's say someone who is concerned for Ms Joynson's welfare."

Now, sitting in the interview room, Vikki could see how vulnerable Heather Joynson looked. Someone powerful had sent that brief and she had declined the help. It was bound to be seen as a slap in the face.

"You're sure you don't want a brief here, Heather?" Bev said.

Heather nodded. "Yeah. I want nothing more to do with that lot. They've made my life a misery for months and now that poor girl is dead."

"So, the women in the upper floor of the building that houses your cleaning company. How did they come to be there?"

"I didn't pay attention to that," Heather said. "I was approached by some men who wanted to hire the upper floors. They said they would pay good money if I didn't ask any questions. I was desperate because my business was going down the toilet. Couldn't get decent staff. I was losing money right, left and centre."

"These men. Who were they?" Bev asked.

Heather shrugged. "I don't know. The rent money just went into my account. The faces changed all the time and they all spoke another language. Romanian, I think."

Vikki caught Bev's eye and she nodded. "Heather. How did Katerina Dragavei come to be working for you?"

Heather's hatchet face softened. "Once I realised the girls were being kept up there, I tried to think of some way I could help them without getting into trouble myself. These men were like leeches; they hooked into my business, watched me all the time and I couldn't say anything."

"So you hatched a plan?"

"I thought if one girl could get out, maybe she could raise the alarm and save the others. And one day Katerina sneaked downstairs. She was a bright kid. We thought if I could persuade them to let her work for me as a cleaner, then it might give her a chance."

"Go on."

"Well it worked, didn't it? I got her passport to hold over her as a threat and she got to work for me. The deal was to do a few cleaning jobs and not run at first. Gain their confidence, see what I mean?"

Bev nodded. "Right. But then what happened?"

"She didn't come back from one of the jobs. They dropped her off but when they went back to pick her up, the house was closed up and there was no sign of her. I thought she'd done it. Got away and run for it." Heather Joynson dabbed the tissue to her face. "Instead, she was murdered."

"Do you think it's possible that the gang that rented your building killed her?" Vikki asked.

"I'm sure they're capable of it," Heather said. "They treat people like cattle. I'm not worried for myself. I don't care anymore. I couldn't bear what they were doing. Those poor girls getting shipped around the country for God knows what."

Later, when they'd finished, McCallon passed Vikki a coffee. "D'you think they killed the girl?" Vikki said.

"It doesn't seem likely," McCallon said. "They aren't stupid. If they were going to do it, they'd dump her somewhere that couldn't be traced back to Happy Homes Cleaning. "Besides, weren't there other features to this case? A picture connected to your celebrity DCI?"

Vikki grinned. "William Blake? Yes, ma'am."

"I can't imagine the traffickers spending time adding touches like that. Besides, the girls are a commodity. They're sold into slavery. No, I'm afraid poor Katerina was just in the wrong place at the wrong time."

"Slavery," Vikki muttered. "The Little Black Boy poem was meant to be about slavery, I think."

"A very subtle touch. Whatever sick bastard's doing the killing, Vikki, I don't think they're part of this outfit."

"Which leads us back to the residents of Hilbre Grove," Vikki muttered. "Literally a dead end."

It didn't surprise me that it took them so long to find my second victim. In my plan, it would have been a little later before the second one was discovered. It's a bit like timing fireworks to go off. Maybe they're smarter than I give them credit for. Maybe.

Again, it was nothing personal. I didn't get any kind of kick out of killing him. There had to be another victim. Everything was done for a reason. Even if you're particularly sadistic or you mutilate the body in some hideous way, you're instantly forgotten if you just kill one person. You're just a person who has killed someone. The public might think you're a sick fuck but, in their minds, there's little difference between you and someone who kills in a fight. I know there's the whole thing about intent; obviously a careless driver is careless and didn't set out to murder someone. I suppose what I'm saying is that if you kill one person, you might be a murderer but that's all you are. When only one person dies, the public care more about the victim than the killer.

Kill more than one person and the public starts to pay attention. They start to wonder: 'Why did he do that? What drove him to such extremes?' More than one victim and maybe a pattern emerges. Or at least you search for one. Herd instinct begins to kick in; forget the individual, watch out for the killer. Instantly, the prey is forgotten, and the hunter takes the stage. Front and centre.

I'm glad they found him. Things are hotting up now. We're in the crucible where base metals are turned to sparkling gold.

CHAPTER 17

Blake reached home late again, too tired to even think about food. He just wanted to sleep. It had been another frustrating day and he was no nearer solving the murders or finding Ellen Kevney. Laura met him at the door, holding Serafina. "God, you look shattered," she said.

"I am," Blake replied, slipping past her into the house. "Between mad old men and cam girls, I've had about enough for one day."

"I texted you."

"I know. I can't really reply when I'm at work."

"Well what about lunchtime?"

"Lunchtime? What's that?"

"Surely you can take thirty seconds just to…"

Blake held up his hand. "Look, I really don't want to talk about this, now. I want to go to bed and sleep."

"Your brother Jeff rang. He didn't know about me. I had to introduce myself."

"I'm sure you managed," Blake said, rubbing his face. Two bodies lay in cold storage and Ellen Kevney was somewhere, either dead or close to it. Anything else was irrelevant. "What did he want anyway? As if I didn't know. Money. Have we sold this house, yet?"

"He's worried about you, Will..."

"He's worried about me getting too comfortable in this house. That's what he's worried about. Talking to you will only have increased his paranoia. He'll think I've moved you in; that we're taking up residence."

"Well what are we doing, Will? I come round here and find the house empty. You turn up late in the night exhausted and irritable. What am I meant to do? Stay? Go home? I don't know. It's like I'm meant to just be there when you need me and I don't know when that is."

Serafina growled in agreement.

"I'm going to bed," Blake said, dragging himself upstairs.

*****

The figure crouched in the darkness. Ellen knew he was there. She had managed to doze for a while but had been jolted awake by pins and needles in her legs. And she'd quickly become aware of him as he shifted position, a darker outline in the gloom of the container.

"It's always hard to know what to do for the best, Ellen," he whispered. "I take no pleasure in the suffering this causes you or anyone else. You must understand that."

"Then let me go," Ellen said. "Blindfold me. Take me somewhere quiet and deserted and let me go. I won't ever know who you are or where you've been keeping me."

"What I was going to say was that I *do* take pleasure in how things are unfolding. Did you ever play with dominoes as a child, Ellen?"

"Dominoes?"

"Yes. You know, those wooden tiles. Did you ever set them up in a line and knock the first one over, taking pleasure in the knock-on effect as each domino in the line fell in turn?"

"Yeah," Ellen said, trying to keep up with the whisperer in the dark. Her head throbbed and she felt hollow with hunger. "I did."

"It's like that. The dominoes are falling just like I intended and it's fun! But there's no way to stop things once you've flicked that first domino and that happened a long time ago."

"Where's Ralph? What have you done with him?"

There was a moment's silence as if the man was thinking. "So, after almost three weeks, you still think about him. Do you miss him? Do you think he might turn up and rescue you?"

Ellen curled up into a ball, hugging her knees to her chest. "No."

"Forget him. He's dead and gone. The dominoes are falling, Ellen, one by one. and we're all dominoes in this little line that I've constructed. Except I've noticed a glitch..."

"What do you mean?"

The man shifted in the darkness and Ellen knew he had stood up. "It would take too long to explain, Ellen but, in a nutshell, I'm afraid someone is going to have to die."

*****

Andrew Kinnear pulled up outside his small, detached house. It was a new-build on an estate on the edge of Knowsley, just by the M57. It was far enough away from the centre of town to be quiet and trouble-free. The constant rumble of traffic filled the air as he climbed out of his car. He and Chris had fallen in love with the house the moment they saw it and decided to settle there. It was nothing special; three bedrooms, brick-built with a white cladding, but it was Kinnear's castle. Chris had nurtured the small garden after digging what seemed like another house-worth of bricks out of the clay soil. The upstairs light was on; that meant Chris was still up and working.

Letting himself in, Andrew shouted up the stairs. "I'm home!"

"Up here, finishing off assessments," Chris called down. "There's some lasagna in the oven if you're hungry."

Andrew grinned. He kicked off his shoes and shuffled into the kitchen, pulling a bag of crisps out of the food cupboard. "Not really that hungry. Going to watch some cam girls. You interested?" he grinned as he heard feet thumping down the stairs.

Chris poked his freckly face around the door. "You what?" His jutting jawbone and cheeks, gangly arms and knobbly knees gave him an angular kind of appearance. With his mop of unruly blond hair, Chris wasn't classically handsome, but he always managed to look good. He did to Andrew anyway. Andrew Kinnear often said it was Chris's kindness and selflessness that shone through and made Chris so attractive. To which Chris would put his hand on his heart and say, "Babe, that's the sweetest thing anyone's ever said to me. Have you got a bucket I can be sick in?"

Andrew waggled his eyebrows. "Just thought it'd be a change, that's all..."

"Tell me Blake hasn't given you the job of watching some dodgy porn," Chris said, looking pained. "I was thinking more something on Netflix?"

"Thought you had assessments to do. Those children will want to know if they've passed, you know, Mr Teacher."

"They'll keep. Not due in until next week," Chris said, giving Andrew a hug and a peck on the cheek. "Anyway, what're these?" Chris snatched the crisp packet from Andrew's fingers. "I made a vegetarian lasagna; all calorie controlled for you and this is how you repay me."

"I'm just not that hungry..."

"You never are until you pass a Gregg's and the call of the steak slice draws you in!"

Andrew laughed and went into the living room, picking up his tablet from the glass coffee table. "We're investigating this murder and it involves a cam girl called Lilly White..."

"God it sounds like a sanitary towel," Chris muttered. "So this woman makes money by showing off in front of a webcam?"

"Supports her husband, too..." Andrew said.

"If you keep wiggling your eyebrows like that, Andrew Kinnear, I'm going to shave one off when you're asleep."

"It's hardly an effective alter-ego either, really; it's so close to her real name."

It took a little searching but eventually, Andrew found a site that advertised Lilly White and he recognised Tina White's face. "Here we go… oh," he said, staring at the paywall sign.

"How are you going to claim that back on expenses?"

"I'll get it off Blakey. I'm sure he'll stump up," Kinnear lied. He put his card details into the site and began scrolling through Tina's page. There were links to pictures, videos and numerous calls to click and say, 'Hi!' Some of the images and videos had comment boxes beneath them filled with lewd remarks.

Every now and then, either he or Chris would utter a gasp or a, 'Oh my word' as they were presented with various bizarre images and scenarios.

"Some of this is seriously flaky," Chris said. "Why did Blake pick you to look at it?"

Andrew pulled a face. "I kind of accidentally volunteered. Ooh, hello."

"What?"

"Ralph 69 – Anytime you want your rug cleaning, my beauty…" Kinnear read out loud.

Chris rolled his eyes. "God, it's like a Carry-On film."

"No, listen, we're looking for a bloke called Ralph in the Ellen Kevney case. Or rather a guy *not* called Ralph. He stole some poor man's ID." Kinnear clicked on the link in Ralph 69's comment and revealed a tangle of naked bodies. He watched two woman and two men on the screen as they grunted and twisted into ridiculous, impossible positions. "Tina and Paul White at number four. She's the cam girl. I bet that's…"

Andrew's voice faded. In his career as a policeman, he'd seen plenty of porn, some of it hideous but what stunned him now was the backdrop; an ordinary living room, with a pale sofa and armchairs, a fluffy rug in front of a gas fire. And a garish oil painting of a mountain stream on the wall. Even though he'd only stood there once, Kinnear recognised it almost instantly.

"Oh my God. Chris, that's the Taylors' living room and *that's* Ellen Kevney."

TUESDAY 11TH FEBRUARY

CHAPTER 18

If he was feeling intimidated by the clinical coldness of the interview room at Birkenhead Custody Suite, Paul White wasn't showing it. He sat back in his chair, arms folded as if he was waiting for a meal to be served. DCI Blake sat opposite him with Kath Cryer alongside him. "So, Mr White, would you care to explain how there appears to be a video of you two having sex with another man and Ellen Kevney in the Taylors' living room?"

Paul shrugged. "We didn't mean anything by it," he said. "It was just a bit of fun..."

"Fun?" Blake snapped. "A dead woman was found in that room only a few days ago and Ellen is missing. I'm presuming you didn't have the Taylors' permission, so it must have been filmed whilst they were away."

As soon as Kinnear had made Blake aware of the video on the website, Paul and Tina had been brought in for questioning. It was first thing in the morning and Blake hadn't even had chance to grab a coffee. Fleeing from the frosty atmosphere at home, and Laura's silent treatment, he'd imagined himself grabbing a drink or a bite to eat on the way in. It never happened.

"So you have a cheeky foursome in someone else's house, film it, and a couple of days later, someone winds up dead there," Kath Cryer said. "Are there any more surprises in your video collection, Mr White?"

Paul White licked his lips. "What? What d'you mean?"

"I mean, will we find a video of that poor woman being mutilated? Did you film her death? What about Ellen Kevney? Is her body lying somewhere?"

"No!" Paul almost shouted. "That's sick..."

"We see a lot of sick things in this line of work, Mr White," Blake said. "You wouldn't believe the perversions some people have..."

"Or maybe he would, sir," Cryer said, still staring intently at Paul White. "Maybe he knows exactly what some people want to see. Right Paul?"

"No. We aren't like that..."

"So talk me through it, Paul," Blake said, leaning forward. "Help me understand how breaking into the Taylors', having sex in their lounge and then killing someone is entertainment..."

"We didn't kill anyone!" Paul said, putting his head in his hands. "It was Ralph's idea. He said he knew where the Taylors kept a key. He wanted to make a porn film." He looked pleadingly at them. "He thought it would be funny because, even if the Taylors did recognise their own house, they couldn't do anything about it without admitting to watching porn."

"This Ralph character," Blake said. "Where did you meet him?"

"Aphrodites," Paul sighed. "We played with him and Ellen a few times..."

Blake frowned. "Played?"

"Had sex," Paul said. "There's no law against it. All consensual..."

"We got on really well. There was a chemistry between us," Paul said. "We invited him to the house a few times and he'd get us involved in the role play."

"Doctors and nurses?" Kath Cryer snorted. She drummed her painted fingernails on the desktop.

Paul looked bashful. "It was a home invasion thing. Burglars...masks, a bit of bondage, that kind of thing..."

"Sounds classy," Kath said.

"Then Ralph suggested making a film for the web channel," Paul said. "Tina was grumbling one day about doing the Cam Girl stuff. She liked it to start with but it got wearisome after a while and some days we hardly earned anything."

Blake frowned. "So people pay to..."

"To watch Tina, yeah. Sometimes I join in. The punters call the shots really. But we only do what we're comfortable with."

"So Ralph suggested making the film," Kath cut in.

"Yeah," Paul sighed. "He said we could show it some nights when we wanted a break or we could use it to draw traffic to our site."

"But you could have made that film in your own home," Blake said. "At your own leisure. Why break into the Taylors'?"

Paul groaned. "Ralph suggested it because he thought it would make it seem more real. He had a point. Sometimes you get more of a buzz when something seems like it's really happening. If it looked authentic to the punters, then it's a bit more of a thrill... a bit more transgressive..."

"Transgressive," Kath repeated, curling her lip.

"I know what it looks like," Paul said. "But we really didn't have anything to do with what happened to that poor woman. We went in, made the film and came out again. We had no idea about anything..." Paul White stopped as something finally dawned on him. "Oh my God. Do you think Ralph was involved in the killings?"

"We're certainly interested in Ralph," Kath said. "He sounds like a charmer. Would you be able to describe him?"

Paul frowned. "I can, but haven't you got a film of him standing billy bollocks naked?"

"When did you make the film?" Blake said, ignoring the comment.

Paul thought for a moment. "About three weeks ago," he said. "Yeah. The Sunday after the Taylors left for their holiday."

"And shortly after that Ellen Kevney goes missing and you didn't even think to contact us?"

Paul went pale. "We didn't think it was relevant..."

Blake stood up and leaned on the desk. "It's relevant all right. A young mum is possibly dead by now. And you're looking at being arrested for burglary, conspiracy to murder, kidnapping. I don't know where the public decency laws stand on you having it away with your friends in someone else's house but I'd say that's the least of your worries."

"How well do you know this Ralph?" Kath said.

Paul had lost all of his cockiness now. He sat slumped in his seat, staring at the desk. "Like I said, we knew him from Aphrodites but he didn't say much about himself. He told us he worked in the media and lived over in Liverpool."

"Where in Liverpool?"

Paul shrugged. "He never really said. He just seemed like a fun guy, you know? Full of energy, witty. Tina fancied him something rotten. Ellen would do anything for him. But we never saw either of them after that day. Ralph took Ellen home and that was it. He posted some comments up on the website but other than that, nothing."

*****

Tina White sat on her own opposite DS Vikki Chinn and DC Manikas. She scrubbed the remains of a disintegrating tissue under her nose and squished it onto the desktop. Like her husband, she had told them everything she knew. She seemed relieved to unload her knowledge. Like a burden had been lifted from her.

"Ralph was a good-looking fella. He seemed nice and charming," she said, sniffing loudly. "Ellen really liked him. She'd said something about wanting to get to know him more. But we never saw either of them after the session at the Taylors'. I told Paul we should go to the police but he said not to."

Vikki Chinn turned a biro over in her fingers. "How did you avoid getting spotted by Donald Pleavin when you broke in?"

Tina blinked at them. "Ralph had convinced me to send him an invitation to a free show but it was prerecorded. Pleavin wouldn't know that, though."

Manikas pulled a face. "Why not? Surely the moment he spoke to you, he'd know."

"He wouldn't," Tina said. "He's into watching women gagged and bound. I couldn't have replied even if he had said something."

"What you just lie there?" Vikki said.

"Yeah. Bound up like a carpet roll. I wriggle around and groan a bit but that's about it. It's the easiest way to make a few quid I know."

"So while Pleavin was watching a video of you on the bed, you were sneaking round the back of the Taylors'," Manikas said, slowly, trying to process the information.

"We went through the back gardens. Jean Quinn was away too," Tina frowned. "We had to carry the cameras and lights, so it was a bit awkward. It all sounds a bit too good to be true, doesn't it? The two houses empty. I'm starting to think Ralph planned it all."

After the interviews, DS Chinn joined Blake and Cryer outside the interview room. Blake heaved a huge sigh and stuffed his hands in his pockets. "It looks like our friend Ralph or whoever he is, has targeted Hilbre Grove and planned this all quite carefully."

"But what does he get out of it, sir?" Kath said.

"What?"

"Well, why go to all the trouble of grooming the Whites, setting up Pleavin and recording the video, then coming back a few days later and murdering someone on the same spot? There must be some kind of payoff."

"Maybe it's just the thrill," Blake said. "being 'transgressive,'" He shook his head as he said the word.

"Let's not forget this Chimeree Van," Kath said. "A quick Google search should give us a name and address for whoever owns that."

"Yeah," Blake said. "Could be important."

"Wasn't the picture left at Jean Quinn's house something to do with a chimney sweep?" Vikki Chinn asked. "The van could belong to victim number two. There was the slavery connection with the last picture..."

Blake grimaced. "God, I sincerely hope not."

"Unless it's Ralph we found lying there dead in number three," Kath said, simply.

"What?" Blake said, horrified.

"It's just a thought, sir. Suppose Ralph had been carrying on at the Taylors' and went back to make sure he hadn't left anything behind. He meets the killer who does him in and dumps the body in Jean Quinn's."

"Jeez," Blake said. "Get Mr Pleavin in, Kath. Tell Kinnear to go and see Mrs Pleavin, too. Let's see how much he actually knows."

CHAPTER 19

When he was a small boy, Andrew Kinnear's parents had taken him on holiday to Greece. In a taverna there, he'd met a small dog, mistreated by its owner. The poor creature was torn between an eagerness for young Andrew's kind stroking hands and its master's harsh words and hard boots. Looking at Mrs Pleavin's face as she opened the door reminded Kinnear of that poor creature all those years ago.

"I'm sorry, Mr Kinnear, but my husband isn't in," she said and frowned. "He's been called to the police station. I thought you'd know that."

Kinnear smiled. "It's not your husband I've come to talk to Mrs Pleavin. Can I come in?"

Helen Pleavin stepped back from the door, glancing around the Grove as she shut it, and led Andrew into the living room. The pristine cleanliness gave it a lifeless air and Kinnear wondered how anyone could tolerate such a tidy house. Chris was quite house proud and did the lion's share of the hoovering and cleaning; left to Kinnear, he was pretty sure the place would be a pig sty in a matter of days. Even Chris allowed a little bit of clutter. "Clean enough to be healthy, dirty enough to be happy," Chris always said.

"Do sit down," Helen Pleavin said, gesturing to the armchair. "Can I make you a cup of tea or coffee?"

That would be lovely, Helen," Kinnear said. "I can call you Helen, can't I?"

Helen Pleavin reddened. "Of course," she said and gave a nervous giggle. "I'll make the tea."

Not wanting to waste any time, Kinnear followed her out to the kitchen and leaned on the door frame. "The house is lovely," he said. "You must work every hour to keep it clean and tidy."

Helen didn't look at him but nodded her head as she filled the kettle. "It's a body's work," she said. "Donald likes things just so."

"I imagine he's out in the garden all day," Kinnear said, casually.

"No," Helen muttered, clinking the mugs and spoons. "Was it tea or coffee you wanted, Mr Kinnear?"

"Please, call me Andrew," Kinnear said. "People get so confused about how to address a policeman. Is it constable or detective? Oh, coffee would be great, thanks."

"Donald doesn't do a lot around the house at all, really," Helen said, opening the fridge. "Milk?"

"Just a spot," Kinnear said, patting his stomach. "Trying to slim down a little."

She passed him the mug of coffee. "It's all going to come out, isn't it?"

"I'm sorry, Helen?" Kinnear said. She looked frightened.

"What's going to come out?"

"Donald's..." she started to say, floundering for the words. "Donald's behaviour!"

"I'm not sure what you mean, Helen. Can you explain?"

She looked down into her drink and clasped the mug with both hands. "He's not a nice man, Andrew. He's bullied me for decades. I know what he does. He goes on the internet and looks at that Tina White and I know he goes to that club in Birkenhead. The sex club. He comes back smelling of perfume. He even told me once. Just to upset me. Told me he goes and watches them all..." She pulled a disgusted face, "... doing it. And I'm stuck here making sure his books are straight on his bookshelf, his magazines are in the rack by his chair, the TV remote control is placed at the correct angle on the coffee table. I don't think I can bear it any longer."

Andrew wanted to put his mug down and hug the poor woman. "Do you think your husband could be involved in the murder over the road, Helen?" he said, gently.

Helen Pleavin shook her head fiercely. "No. He's

a too much of a coward to actually hurt anyone. He's a watcher, Andrew. He watches the people in Hilbre Grove and sneers at what they do, he watches sluts on the internet but he'd never *act* on any of that."

"What keeps you here, Helen?"

"Where would I go? I've never worked. I can't drive. I've got no friends. Donald made sure of that."

This time, Andrew Kinnear put his mug down and wrapped his arms around Helen Pleavin's shoulders. "Sometimes you have to be a little bit brave, Helen. A leap in the dark can be terrifying but sometimes the landing is softer than you think." He lifted her chin and looked into her eyes. "That's what Chris, my husband always says," he gave a soft smile. "Mind you he's full of crap half the time."

*****

Kinnear stood outside Pleavin's house and pulled out his mobile. He hadn't really got much out of Helen but the link to the club was interesting. Maybe he'd helped her in some way. A quick call to Kath might be useful in case they still had Donald in the interview room. There was a chance Pleavin knew Ellen or possibly Ralph. Kinnear didn't buy Kath's hunch. He didn't think Pleavin was a likely candidate for the Scissor Man, but it was the kind of detail that Blake would pounce on and beat him with if he hadn't mentioned it. He respected Blake but some days, he wished the DCI would cut him some slack.

Kath Cryer answered the phone and, as Kinnear spoke, he watched an old lady striding up the Grove towards him. A wheeled suitcase rumbled behind her and marched with a sense of purpose. "I've got to go, there's a member of the public coming."

The woman stopped in front of Kinnear "Are you the man in charge?" she said. Her voice sounded clipped and a little too loud. Her tanned complexion spoke of years of outdoor life, sport and bellowing across fields to friends or teammates. She was a sturdy-looking woman. Her white hair was tied back in a tight ponytail and she surveyed the world with a permanent frown.

"I'm DC Kinnear. Can I help you?"

"Jean Quinn. I live at number three. Now what's going on? I got a phone call at my hotel saying there had been an incident. Jumped on the first flight home. Has there been a burglary?"

"Worse than that, I'm afraid," Andrew Kinnear said. "A body was discovered at the Taylors'..."

"Golly. That's horrible!" Jean Quinn said.

"I'm afraid we discovered someone dead in

your house too. Crime Scene Investigators are busy working there now."

Jean Quinn's frown deepened. "In my house? Gracious me. That's not good. Do you know who the poor victims are, detective?"

"We're still working on that, I'm afraid. Would you be able to talk in more detail? I know you've only just arrived home and must be very tired but..."

"No!" Jean snapped. "Come on in. Let's find the buggers who did this."

Kinnear gave an apologetic smile. "I'm afraid your house is a crime scene, Ms Quinn and, putting it as delicately as possible, the air in there isn't as fresh as it might be..."

Jean Quinn pursed her lips and frowned even more. "Really? Why's that?" Then her eyes widened and her face creased into a disgusted grimace. "Ah, right. Decay and all that. Foul. Where can we go then?"

Kinnear scanned the Grove and looked back at her apologetically. "Would you mind sitting in the back of a car?"

"Ooh! Not at all! Let's go!" She linked arms with Kinnear and led him across the Grove to the nearest police car. Kinnear pulled a face as they processed across the Grove, miming a cry of 'help' at the smirking constables at the gates of number four.

"So, Ms Quinn..." Kinnear began once they were in the back of the car.

"Miss... Miss Quinn..." Jean Quinn's voice was bombastic. It filled the vehicle.

"I'm sorry..."

"Oh, don't be. I'm happy being a 'Miss.' I can change a tap washer or a fuse and I'm quite capable of wielding hedge clippers. What use would I have of a man? Besides have you seen what's on offer to women of my advanced years? A sorry bunch. Carry on."

"Right," Kinnear said, thinking he wanted to take this woman home to meet Chris already. "There was no sign of forced entry to your house, Miss Quinn. Did anyone else have a key?"

"No," she said. "I wouldn't have left one with Don Pleavin; not to put too fine a point on it, he's a nuisance. If I gave him my key, I'd never get him out of my house."

"Really?"

"I don't tittle-tattle about people, Inspector but that man is a menace," she leaned in close. "He's tried it on with me several times. His poor wife. I don't know why she puts up with him!"

Kinnear nodded in agreement. "So, you can't think of any time when you might have given someone else access to your keys or lent them out? Anything like that. Did you lose them perhaps?"

"No, detective. I may be in my seventies but I'm not senile yet. I'd remember if I'd let those keys out of my sight and I haven't."

"Then, is it possible you forgot to lock the back door when you went away on holiday?"

Jean Quinn gave Kinnear a look that made him gulp. "It was locked. Of that I am certain."

"Right," Kinnear said. He flicked through his notes. "Can you think of any reason why your house in particular was targeted?"

"Other than the fact I was away on holiday, no."

"It would have to be someone local who had been watching the house to know exactly when you left and when you might return."

"I can't imagine any of the inhabitants of Hilbre Grove being capable of murder, Inspector," she leaned towards him, again, "but that doesn't mean they aren't, does it? Can I ask, what happened in my house and at the Taylors'?"

Kinnear thought for a moment, considering how much information he needed to give. "In your house a man was killed and laid out on the mat. In the Taylors', a woman was left in an armchair. In both cases the heating was turned up, we assume to accelerate decomposition..."

Quinn grimaced. "How fascinating," she whispered. "And what do you think the killer hoped to accomplish by that?"

"I'm sorry?" Kinnear said, frowning.

"I mean, I presume most killers want to cover up what they've done. Maybe they're a little frightened by it or by the consequences. Don't they usually try to hide the bodies? Why did this one put those bodies out to be found?"

Kinnear nodded. "A good question. Tell me, Miss Quinn, where did you go for your holiday?"

"Tenerife. I was lucky enough to win a holiday in a competition..."

"Really? Can you tell me more about that?"

"Well, it was after my mother died. I was at a bit of a loss what to do. Dot from next door had just won this holiday through a new travel blog. They're online, internet things, a bit like magazines. Very interesting, detective, they have crime ones too..."

"Call me Andrew, Miss Quinn. Yeah, my husband used to write a weekly blog about teaching. So this travel blog, what was it called?"

"Tarbock's Travels, Andrew," Jean Quinn said. "Dot said that Dave had been told that, because it was a new blog, they didn't have many readers, so the chances of winning a holiday were really high. And they were. I won." She looked a bit crestfallen. "Too good to be true, really, wasn't it?"

Kinnear nodded, sympathetically. "Probably. So did you have any correspondence with Tarbock's Travels?"

"Only by email. They bought all the tickets and sent the boarding passes online. Goodness me, Andrew. I've been had, haven't I? Your killer wanted me out of the house at the same time as the Taylors so he could do these terrible things. How awful." She clicked her fingers and started rummaging in her handbag. "I do have the correspondence, however. I printed it all off. Always feel safe when there's a hard copy to wave around at a complaints desk. Here."

Kinnear took the papers. "Thank you."

"I'm sorry I can't be more help."

"I think you've been a great help. We have a lead through this and the Tarbock's website you mentioned."

Jean Quinn shook her head. "I doubt it, Andrew. I bet you a tenner the Tarbock's Travels Blog is no longer online, and the trail is cold. All we have is a PO Box number. That might reveal something. A name maybe. I hate to say it, young man, but you have a clever psychopath on your hands, and he's goading you."

CHAPTER 20

It was dawning on Donald Pleavin that he hadn't just been called down to the interview room to 'clarify a few details' as Kath Cryer had suggested. His cheeks were reddening by the second and he looked as if he was sucking a particularly large and angry wasp. Kath suppressed her smile of satisfaction and pulled the sleeve of her jacket over her splint.

"You spend a lot of time watching the Grove, Mr Pleavin," she said, giving DC Manikas a sidelong glance as if she shared a secret with him. "Why is that?"

Pleavin scowled. "Why d'you think? I'm Neighbourhood Watch Coordinator, aren't I? I wouldn't be doing a very good job if I didn't watch things would I?"

"True," Manikas said, nodding slightly. "But that generally means keeping an eye out if neighbours are away or if you see suspicious activity in the area. It doesn't mean logging down the comings and goings of every van and car in Hilbre Grove."

"And that's a crime is it?"

Kath shook her head. "No. It could be very useful for us, but I couldn't help noticing that you log the movements of your neighbours too. Very convenient if you want to know when they're likely to be out."

"That's not why I do it," Pleavin muttered. He stretched his mottled hands flat on the tabletop and stared at his fingernails. "I just need to keep track of people..."

"But why? So you could break into their houses?" Kath said. "Your neighbours have concerns about you, Mr Pleavin, d'you know that? They don't like the way you roam freely through their back gardens..."

"I'm just checking up," Pleavin said. "No harm in that."

"I've also heard tell that you can be a bit 'hands on' with some of the female residents of the Grove. Is that right?"

"This is disgraceful," Pleavin snapped. "I came here voluntarily. I've a mind to make a complaint." He made to stand up but Manikas raised a hand.

"Please, Mr Pleavin," he said. "You have to appreciate that we need to look into every aspect of life at Hilbre Grove. Whoever killed those people there knew a great deal about Hilbre Grove."

Kath's phone rang and she stepped out of the

room for a moment. It was Kinnear.

"Apparently, Pleavin went to Aphrodites, and he was one of Tina White's paying clients. His wife just told me. She's not a happy bunny at all, poor woman. I just wanted to take her home."

Kath grinned. "You're a soppy get, you are, Kinnear."

"I've got to go, there's a member of the public here." He hung up and Kath went back into the room.

"So, Mr Pleavin," she said, sitting back down. "What can you tell me about Ellen Kevney and Aphrodites?"

Pleavin pursed his lips. "Who?"

"Come on, Donald," Kath said. "You follow the news avidly. You know that Ellen Kevney is missing. We know you were a regular at Aphrodites. If you want to draw this out, we can go and look at the membership list. You'll be on it, I'm sure. Ellen Kevney was a member too."

"I never did anything," Pleavin said. "I just went to watch..."

Kath looked bored. "I'm not really interested in what you do in your spare time, Mr Pleavin, as long as it's legal. Nobody is judging you. But if you know anything that might help us find Ellen Kevney then you should say."

"I didn't know she was a member, honestly. I

just went along once in a while. I didn't really speak to many people there."

"How about a man called Ralph Vaughan? Speak to him at all?"

"Never heard of him."

"What about Tina White?"

Pleavin's eyes widened as he realised just how much of his private life had been exposed to the cruel glare of daylight. "What about her?"

"You are one of her paying customers I believe," Manikas said.

Pleavin blinked, breathing rapidly. "What's that got to do with anything?"

"Cast your mind back about three weeks, Donald. It was a Sunday evening. What were you doing?"

"I think you already know. Stop goading me," Pleavin muttered. "I was watching Tina..."

"Are you alright, Mr Pleavin?" DC Manikas said. The old man looked pale. He winced and rubbed his left arm.

Kath continued to verbally bludgeon him. "Hogtied on a bed, unable to move. Is that your thing, Donald?"

Pleavin tugged at his collar. "I don't know what you mean."

"Boss." She felt Manikas touching her arm, but

she was in full flow, now.

"I mean, it's not a huge leap of the imagination is it? Going from that whole tied and helpless scenario to hurting someone. D'you see what I mean, now?"

"Kath, he doesn't look right," Manikas said again.

She stopped. Sweat trickled down Pleavin's forehead and he pressed his hand against his left shoulder. "I want to go home," he gasped. "I don't feel well at all." He stood up, swayed, and then crashed to the floor.

*****

Blake wanted to bang his head against a wall when he heard the news, either that or just walk out, jump in his car, and go home. Mind you, knowing his luck his ageing Opel Manta would choose that moment to give up the ghost. Instead, he leaned back in his chair and dragged his fingers through his hair.

"What were you thinking of, Kath? He's an old man, for God's sake."

Kath Cryer rolled her eyes. "I didn't know he had a dodgy heart, did I, sir? Anyway, you said to question him."

"I did, Kath. I didn't say to interrogate him. He's clearly not a suspect. I just thought he might be hiding something."

"Sorry," she said, tugging at the splint on her wrist. Blake had noticed how she fidgeted constantly with it. "He's such a flake though. Putting himself up there as a pillar of the community when really he's perving around people's houses. He nicked Gretchen Jones' underwear off her washing line."

"Allegedly," Blake said. "And anyway, that's hardly a reason to give him the third degree. He's in hospital now. Look Kath, are you sure you're okay?"

Kath frowned at him. "Yeah, course I am. What d'you mean, sir?"

"You seem to be on edge. I know you try to shrug it off, but the shotgun incident was a big deal. If you decided that you wanted counselling..."

"That's rich," Kath muttered and then bit her lip.

"What do you mean by that?"

Kath took a breath. "Well, you don't look too great yourself, sir. No disrespect but we've been running around in circles for weeks now and it's taking its toll on all of us. You included."

Blake wasn't sure he liked the tables being turned on him like this. What irked him most was the truth of what she said. Blake wasn't sleeping well, Laura was getting on his nerves and the whole issue of the house and what to do with it weighed on his mind more than it should. "I appreciate your concern, Kath," Blake said, at last, "but it's you we're talking about."

"Honestly, sir," Kath said, "I'm fine. Pleavin just got to me, that's all. I'll apologise to him if that helps. I don't know what else I can do."

"Let's see what happens, shall we? You've got my full support if he makes a complaint of any kind. You know that."

Kath gave a brittle smile. "Thanks, sir."

"Come on," Blake said. "The others will be waiting." He led her out of his small office and into the Major Incident Room where Kinnear, Chinn, Manikas and other team members waited.

Blake looked at the pictures jumbled on the board and drew a long breath. "Two dead bodies. Only one identified. No arrests. And we're no nearer to finding Ellen Kevney."

"Thanks to Andrew's extra-curricular internet activities," DS Vikki Chinn said, "we have a number of clear images of the mysterious Ralph."

Manikas grinned over at Kinnear. "I bet you never thought your dodgy porn habit would be a boon to the force, mate."

Kinnear pulled a face at Alex Manikas. "I don't have a dodgy porn habit and if I did, I don't think

I'd be watching that lot." he shivered. "Needed a bit of warm lighting. Gave me goose bumps..."

"I take it we're having them clipped down to headshots so they can be used for public broadcasts, sir?" Kath said. "Call us if you see this sex face..."

"I can't imagine the Super' would be happy about showing the full video at the next press conference, Kath," Blake said, happy to see she'd bounced back; she still seemed fragile to him, though. "But yes, we have a couple of clear headshots..."

Kinnear sniggered and Blake gave him a withering look. "What about Tarbock's Travels, Andrew? Any luck with them?"

"As we suspected, sir. The website is down, and the PO Box just leads to an office in the Baltic Quarter of Liverpool. We've put in a request for the identity of whoever set it up but nothing back as yet."

"But we do know that our killer went to great lengths to entice Jean Quinn and Mr and Mrs Taylor away. It must have cost a few quid, too. This person knows the Grove and has access to money."

"There is the *other* link, sir," Manikas said.

Blake groaned. "Yes, I know, I know. The Searchlight programme."

"Could the Scissor Man be using the show in some way?" Vikki said. "Maybe to taunt you?"

"That would be the height of my luck at the moment, Vikki, yes. It's possible, I suppose. Can we call him Ralph? I hate all this 'Scissor Man' nonsense."

"Except, we aren't sure Ralph isn't victim number two, sir..."

"True," Blake said. "All the same..."

"Jean Quinn made a good point," Kinnear said. "Normally, killers try to hide their victim's bodies. They don't leave them out on display like this one did."

"Jean Quinn? Who's she, some kind of Miss Marple?" Blake snorted. "I can see her point but, on the other hand, most bodies get found eventually and the killer got themselves three weeks' head start this way."

"But they were left to be found, sir," Alex Manikas said. "Plus, they went to all the effort of planting the pictures. It does seem designed to grab your attention or get at you in some way."

"You could have a word with some of your old colleagues, boss," Vikki said. "They might remember someone who made a nuisance of themselves when the show was on TV. It's got to be worth a try."

Blake shrugged. "Nothing to lose, I suppose.

Although the nearest person I know probably won't be too glad to see me."

CHAPTER 21

Blake pulled up his Opel Manta outside the high wooden gates of Bramble Cottage in Caldy. This was the most affluent corner of Wirral. Here, detached mansions sat in their own grounds, surrounded by high, sandstone ramparts and mature gardens. Footballers and minor celebrities lived here, using it as a bolt hole close to the motorways but more or less unknown to the outside world.

A less cottage-like entrance to a home, he couldn't imagine; the gates were set in a high red brick wall with a metal intercom panel set into the pillars. There wasn't a bramble in sight, either. Beyond the wall, grew a thick layer of bushes; rhododendrons and yew trees battled with each other to obscure any view of the house. Blake remembered the house well and knew that it was more of a mansion than a cottage. He sighed and climbed out of the Manta. He didn't want to be here, he knew, but he couldn't ignore the fact that there was a connection between him and the things the killer had left at the crime scenes. And they all pointed back to Searchlight. He just hoped Superintendent Martin didn't find out or Blake would never hear the end of it. Anyway, what's wrong with looking up an old friend? Though Blake would hardly class Armitage as a friend.

As far as he could remember, the last words Blake had uttered to Armitage were 'fuck you.' So he wasn't sure what kind of reception he was likely to get. It had been at a party at this house, in fact. The wrapping up party for the Searchlight programme. Armitage had been the frontman for the show along with Emerald Fisher. At the time, Blake had been devastated at losing the show. Armitage had shrugged it off with typical laddish bravado. He thought he'd got a secure future in television; he was good-looking, articulate and educated. He had started in the nineties, reading the regional news but quickly made his way onto national TV; breakfast television, reporting on serious crimes around the country and occasionally hosting.

For Armitage, Searchlight had been a steppingstone, but his future footholds in the industry became smaller and more precarious. Nowadays, he did the voice-over on a 'live footage' police programme that followed coppers on their duties. He'd done them all, over the years. They morphed and changed from titles like 'On the Beat' one minute to 'Camera Crew 999' the next but the content remained the same; a parade of the same targets of middleclass outrage: drunken weekend brawlers, or feral teenagers on mopeds and in stolen cars or travellers without insurance. They were hate figures and bogeymen paraded before the public and brought down for their satisfaction late on a Friday night. Other than those, Blake had heard Armitage's voice on an advertisement for house alarms and he'd cropped up on a celebrity quiz show once.

Blake could remember Armitage at that last Searchlight party, bumping into miserable researchers and runners who had lost their jobs, sloshing red wine onto the thick carpet and telling Blake to lighten up. To the likes of Ross Armitage, this was a celebration, not a funeral. At the time, it felt like the end of the world to Blake. He hadn't realised that would come later with the death of his daughter.

Blake pressed the buzzer on the intercom and waited. There was no guarantee that Armitage was even in. He could be filming anywhere in the country. What was he doing here anyway? Just as he was about to turn and head back to the car, the intercom fizzed and clicked. "Yeah?" Blake recognised Armitage's faux-cockney voice at once. He stepped into view of the CCTV on the panel.

"Hi, Ross. It's DCI Will Blake. I wondered if I could have a brief chat?"

"What've I done, now, Blakey?" The crackly voice said and a throaty chuckle followed.

Blake ignored the joke. "Just wanted to pick

your brains about something if you've got the time." The gate buzzed and he pushed it open.

Bramble Cottage hadn't changed; a two-storey pile with a dizzying number of windows. Blake's feet scrunched on the gravel drive that cut through the shaggy, unkept lawn surrounding the red brick house. He felt faintly ridiculous walking up the long drive which was clearly meant for cars. Nobody walked up to the house; they either left letters in the post-box built into the wall or they drove up.

Armitage stood on the steps up to his front door, dressed in a sloppy, but very expensive, tracksuit. A phone was pressed against his ear as Blake approached.

"Yeah. Just hurry up, okay? Good," he said and shoved the phone into his pocket. He'd grown his old spiky hairstyle out and now had it greased back; cut short round the back and sides. Blake noticed he hadn't gone for the beard; Ross Armitage's cheeky chappie image wouldn't survive under any serious growth.

The celebrity jigged down the steps as if he was in the opening scenes of a quiz show and shook Blake's hand vigorously. "Will, good to see you, mate. How you doing? Weren't you just in the papers or something? That Scissor Man case?"

Blake suppressed a groan; that name seemed to be getting everywhere. "Probably, Ross. That's what I'm here about."

Ross Armitage raised his hands. "Weren't me sir! I was with a Lithuanian prostitute all night," he laughed.

Blake winced. This was Armitage's stock-in-trade when he was off-camera, laddish banter, smut, and wearisome innuendo. He may appear slick and professional on television, but the man was somehow still trapped in the late nineties in real life. The reference had also brought Katerina Dragavei to mind and with it a whole host of uninvited images.

"It's probably nothing and I'm probably wasting your time," Blake said, almost choking on the half-apology.

"No worries, Will. Always glad to be of assistance, you know me," Armitage said, his face creased with concern. Of course, the man was working out an angle already; Blake could tell. Armitage might appear shallow and superficial but, before he jumped into the celebrity swamp, he was a trained journalist who cut his teeth on major national and international crime reporting. The man wasn't stupid, and he followed the news avidly. Blake suddenly felt the urge to walk away. Anything he said would be leaked if it benefited Armitage's career. The man was as watertight as a colander.

Blake gave an awkward cough. "It may be that

the person we're interested in may have some connection to the Searchlight programme."

"Connection? What d'you mean connection?"

"I can't really say, Ross. Sorry."

Ross squinted at Blake and he could see the incisive journalist come to the fore. "So, the killer has left references to the programme or to someone in the team?"

"I honestly can't tell you, Ross. More than my job's worth."

"It's you isn't it? The killer's fixated on you!"

Blake frowned. "Fixated? No! What makes you say that?"

"Behave, Blakey. I can see a guilty look a mile off and you can't hide that from me. What's he been doing? Writing you love letters?"

"If I could just ask you a few questions?"

Armitage threw his arms wide. "Ask away!" Blake noticed there was no invitation to come inside and, for a moment, he wondered if the joke about the prostitute was, indeed, a joke.

"So, you must have had your fair share of fan mail and crank calls. But does anyone stand out? Can you remember any names of people who bothered you?"

Armitage thought for a moment or at least made all the right noises. "There was that flash bird who used to hang around the stage door. You know the one with the big..." Armitage lifted his hands to his chest but the look on Blake's face stopped him from making the full gesture. "Oh, come on, Blakey, it was years ago. I can't remember members of the public I met last week let alone thirteen years ago. Can you?"

"As a matter of fact, I can. It's my job. There's nobody you can think of who stood out. Gave you the shivers? Maybe more recently. Has anyone contacted you about the Searchlight programme? Or just mentioned it in passing? It's important, Ross. Lives might depend on it."

Ross Armitage frowned and pursed his lips. "Nope," he said at last. "Your best bet would be to track down some of the runners or security people from the time."

Blake nodded. "There was Amy Tyson. Remember her?"

Armitage pulled a face. "God, yeah, mate. Wasn't she a dyke or something?"

"I wouldn't know, Ross," Blake said, grimacing. He did know, he just didn't like Armitage's turn of phrase. "Have you got her number?"

"Yeah. I might have actually. Give me a second. I might have it in an old diary. Bear with me..."

The oak door closed on Blake's face and Armitage disappeared into the house. For a moment,

Blake wondered if he was ever going to return. There were raised voices behind the door as if Ross was telling someone off. Blake frowned. He was speaking urgently but there was nobody replying. He reappeared with an apologetic smile. "Sorry, buddy, can't find it. She lived in Manchester somewhere. Didsbury or somewhere like that. I tried it on with her once, but she wasn't having it. Told you, bats for the other side."

Blake shifted back a little from Armitage. He'd always seen something flaky in the man when he was younger but thirteen years later, it suited him even less. "Right. Thanks. I should be able to find her anyway."

Ross Armitage took a step closer to Blake, so that their shoulders almost touched. "Funny to be fixated on you, though, eh?"

"How do you mean?"

"Well, like, not being funny or nuffin, Blakey but you weren't the star of the show, were you? I mean, why not get hung up on Emerald... or me? We were front and centre."

"Like I say, I can't comment," Blake said. "Thanks anyway. I'll have a look for Amy."

The sound of cars pulling up and doors opening and closing drifted from out in the lane. Blake frowned but couldn't see anything beyond the trees and bushes that fringed the grounds. "Tell me you haven't, Armitage."

From inside the house the buzzer sounded. "Hello," a crackly voice said. "Mr Armitage, It's Phil Planter from the Sun. Is he still here?"

Ross Armitage gave him a maddening grin. "Called 'em as soon as I saw you through the intercom. This could be an opportunity, Blakey," he said, suddenly draping an arm over Blake's shoulder and whipping the phone out of his pocket. "Have you thought about that?" he said and gave a brilliant white smile. Blake pulled away but the damage was done.

"What're you playing at?"

"Just a selfie, mate. For old time's sake. You and me. The old team. If you track this fella down, well, what a story, eh?" Armitage had dropped the cheeky chappy act and looked as sharp as a razor.

Blake took another step back. "Delete it," he said. "Get rid of it now or I'm telling you..."

"What?" Armitage said. "You going to wrestle me to the ground? Assault me? That'll be one for the press pack at the gates."

"Come on, Ross. This character is deranged. I don't know what you've got in mind, but any publicity could endanger the life of Ellen Kevney."

"Don't worry, mate," Armitage said. "Just want to get myself in the picture, that's all. This kind of thing is great for my profile. Just one little tweet, that's all. You won't feel a thing."

"Fuck you, Armitage," Blake said and stalked across the gravel, wondering what kind of nightmare Armitage's ego would bring down on them all.

CHAPTER 22

The front door hung open again. Just like it had two years before. Sitting in his Opel Manta, Blake found himself back at that time once more. That moment when all his fears came to pass.

It had been a long day, what with Armitage and the press scrum outside the house. Blake had managed to escape without having to say anything, but several pictures had been taken and Ross Armitage had even managed to entice a TV camera down there, too. No doubt, he'd followed Blake out to give a full statement about the nature of his 'cooperation' with Merseyside Police. After all, he wouldn't want to leave anything up to speculating journalists; he knew his own tricks best.

Blake had returned to the office and kept his head down. The journey home had flashed by. He hadn't noticed the tunnel or the roundabout or much of the route home at all; he'd driven them in some kind of flow state as he mulled over the various ways in which the next day might pan out. None of them were good. Lost in thought, he'd turned the car into the drive and seen the door. And he'd been dragged back to that moment when the door stood ajar.

He'd been caring for his mother for some time and had watched her slowly slide into confusion. He should have known that this was a possibility. That his mother would just open the front door and walk out. Behind him, just at the end of the drive the River Mersey flowed black and cold.

Blake shivered, snapping himself back to the present. The front door shouldn't be open now. Climbing out of the Manta, he crept towards the front of the house, wincing at every scrunch of gravel underfoot. Somebody was moving around inside in the dark.

"Don't move!" Blake snapped and flipped the light on. He glimpsed Laura's startled face and then saw her fist fly up. Stars blossomed before his eyes and he fell to the ground.

*****

Paul White frowned at Tina and slumped his shoulders. He looked like a little boy who'd just been told he couldn't have an ice cream. As the hours ticked by, Tina wondered more and more what she'd actually seen in this man. "Come on, love. It's big money. You haven't really been online for a few days and we're skint."

"I can't Paul," she said. "All I keep thinking of is Ralph and that room and the idea of a dead body... the last thing I want to do is get glammed up and show myself off for a load of dirty old men."

"He's offering £500. Just wants me to tie you up tight. No sex. He just wants you to wriggle around on the bed. Not even costumes. Just office wear."

Tina sighed. "Bloody hell, Paul. We've been in police custody all day. Can't you see I'm upset?"

"That's the beauty of it, love. You can be upset. It'll turn him on. Just an hour, that's all. Think about it. Five hundred quid!"

"Are we really that skint?"

"We spent a fortune at the shops the other day, remember? We need some cash to go into the bank. How about it?"

Tina shrugged. "Okay fine but not sex. Just ropes and a ball gag and I'll roll around on the bed trying to get free. Okay?"

"Great!" Paul said, grinning. "I'll message him back now."

Tina rolled her eyes and dragged herself off the bed. Who found that sexy anyway? A woman hogtied and rolling around. I mean, she could understand voyeurism, the thrill of watching something forbidden or just plain flaunting it if you got it. They kind of went together in her mind, like they were complimentary. But a lone woman tied up? Just dressed in a pencil skirt and a blouse? It never made sense to her. It was easy money, though.

She opened her wardrobe and pushed aside the slips and costumes and dragging out a coil of rough, hemp rope. She threw it on the bed and took a ball gag out of the drawer. "Paul," she called out of the bedroom door. "I'm gonna need your help, you lazy git."

Paul reappeared looking a little flushed. He switched on the spotlights dotted around the room and booted up the laptop. He took the dust cap off the expensive camera that stood on a tripod at the foot of the bed. Tina sighed and held up the rope. "I meant these!"

"Oh! Right, yeah!" Paul said and took the gag from her. He tied one end of the rope around her wrist and pulled her arms tight behind her back.

"Ow! Careful!"

"Sorry. He wants them tight, love."

"Yeah, well there's no need to rip my arms out of their sockets is there?"

Paul nodded and slipped the ball gag between her teeth. "Should've done that first," he muttered.

"Gnff!" Tina grumbled. She fell flat on the bed, her face down, arms tight behind her back.

Paul switched the camera on and gave Tina a thumbs up. She watched him make a little mime of drinking a cup of tea and then he tip-toed out of the room. She lay alone, straining at the ropes, testing them a little. When they did bondage sessions for the camera, Paul usually left a little slack. This time the ropes felt tight and unforgiving. She gave a little squeak of protest and rolled over onto her back.

Time slowed down. She wriggled a little and then pulled violently at the bonds. Paul had tied them well.

A moment of panic swept over Tina and all the anxiety of the last few days burst through. Her heart thumped in her chest and she felt clammy. She twisted and turned, kicking her legs to get free but the ropes seemed to tighten, if anything.

The camera light winked red and suddenly, Tina felt cold. Why would anyone in their right mind pay £500 to look at a woman tied up on a bed? She didn't even get that much for the more intimate sessions she offered. This was all wrong. The ropes bit into her wrists and she struggled to get free. What was Paul playing at?

A dull thud from the hallway made her stop and flinch. She tried to say Paul's name, but the gag reduced it to a grunt.

Footsteps shuffled down the hall towards the door and Tina wriggled to get free.

Her wrists and ankles burned against the rope, but it held tight.

The half-open bedroom door creaked slightly, and a shadow filled the gap.

*****

Will Blake sat in his armchair, pressing a cold flannel to his eye. Laura leaned over him. “I’m really sorry, Will, I thought you were…” she broke off. “I didn’t know who you were.”

Serafina rubbed around his legs, trying to find an opportunity to jump onto his lap.

“It’s fine,” Blake said, wincing and taking the flannel away from his eye for a second to squint at her. “That’s quite a hook you’ve got on you. Where did you learn to punch like that?”

Laura shrugged. “I took some self-defence lessons a while back,” she said and grinned. “Plus a bit of boxercise.”

“Why were you sneaking around in the dark like that?”

“The door was open,” she said. “I didn’t want to disturb any would-be burglar.”

“The door was open when you arrived?” Blake said, frowning. He looked around. Nothing seemed out of place. He’d seen plenty of burglaries and normally, the thieves didn’t worry about searching carefully for valuables; things would be strewn all over the place, furniture turned over, even slashed. He had even known some burglaries where the thief defecated on beds and living room mats.

Stepping into the front room, he stopped. “Oh my God.”

“What is it?” Laura said hurrying into the room.

“He’s been here.”

CHAPTER 23

Ross Armitage held up his phone and grinned, bracing himself for the flash. Looking down at the result, he grimaced and flicked through the filters. Another notification from Twitter popped up and he smiled again. Flicking onto it.

"YISSS!" He hissed, punching the air. "At last. A bloody retweet from Emerald Fisher!"

Emerald had been his co-host on Searchlight and had gone on to greater things; she'd done a couple of stints on the One Show and reinvented herself as a healthy eating guru. She was never off Breakfast Television, or any number of variants of Bake-off.

Another ping told him that hardman TV presenter Troy Griffin had retweeted, too. Once one of them did it, they all would; fearful of missing out on the tiniest glimmer of reflected limelight. This was doing his profile no harm at all.

The impromptu press conference had been a masterstroke. Ross had been following the Hilbre Grove case in the locals and a few of his old contacts in the force had given him some juicy morsels of gossip. When Blake turned up at his front gate, Ross hadn't hesitated to phone the press and tell them to get down here right away.

Once Blake had wrestled his way through the crowd of eager journalists, Ross had sauntered out of the gate behind him and held up his hands for calm.

He told them there had been a few developments in the case, that he was working with Blake in an advisory capacity and couldn't divulge any details; then he went on to divulge all the details he'd picked up from his sources at Canning Place. He dropped in the killer's apparent fixation with Blake; maybe garnishing it with a few exaggerations.

Ross looked at the selfie he'd taken on the doorstep before Blake left; it was perfect. Blake looked suitably morose in the shot, almost downtrodden whereas Armitage positively shone. The actual tweet had said, 'The dream team together once more. Watch out criminals!' He'd posted a few different tweets, same picture but new text: 'The Fun-Loving Crime busters' was one of his favourites as Blake's hangdog face screamed anything but fun. It made them seem like characters from a buddy movie; Armitage was the wild cheery one. He stood up and looked in the mirror, imagining himself as Mel Gibson to Blake's Danny Glover in Lethal Weapon. Ross gave a white smile and nodded; he was good-looking enough and he certainly drank as much. It was time for a relaunch. He was sick of those voice-overs; playing to the crowd of boomers, sitting in their living rooms, drunk on the Friday night bottle of red and terrified of the chavs they watched and sneered at.

Armitage sat down again. He had dismissed social media at first. Once he saw how Emerald Fisher had nailed it with her healthy eating YouTube channel, he'd changed his mind. It was so frustrating trying to catch up with it all.

'Be genuine' his people had told him. 'Just be yourself' but Armitage knew that would never work. The whole 'laddish' vibe was toxic to these 'woke' youngsters. He didn't want to be seen as some kind of dinosaur but that's what he was. He stared into his whiskey glass, desperately trying to recapture that buzz from the retweets but it was gone; replaced with a starving desperation; a need to be seen and heard.

His phone rang, startling him back to reality. Armitage snatched up his phone. "Ross! You dark horse!" The voice of his agent, Jerry Goldren bellowed, making Armitage hold the phone away from his ear.

"Jerry!" Ross yelled back. "I know right? This Kevney case and the Scissor Man murders. It's gold dust, mate!" Armitage pulled a contrite face. "I mean, shocking an' all that but every cloud, right? If I can get involved in this somehow. Make a public appeal or something. Might reignite something? Yeah?"

"Some people are going to hate you for it, Ross, me old mucker," Jerry said, adopting a warning tone.

"I've got broad shoulders, Jerry, you know me. I'm just performing a public service. Like in the old days and let's be honest, I could do with the publicity."

"It'll push you front and centre for a while, that's for sure. Might be a stint on Big Brother in this for you or I'm a Celebrity. You can always do your penance in a bush tucker trial. Show 'em you're a nice guy really as you eat a cockroach or a wombat's arse or something."

Ross grimaced. "How about a few magazine spreads? At home with Ross Armitage, Crime Fighter Extraordinaire..."

"Love it! Then we need to find a way to boost it. Maybe pitch some documentary ideas. I was thinking Crime International, you know, Ross Armitage investigates cold cases from around the world. What d'you think?"

"Genius, Jerry, now I know why I pay you your fifteen percent!"

"Great stuff. Keep those tweets going. I'll see if I can get your face all over the papers in the next couple of days."

"I'll get over to the Police HQ tomorrow. Pretend I'm giving a statement or advising in some capacity. I'll get myself centre stage again if it kills me."

Ross Armitage sank back into his leather armchair and took a long swig from his glass. Yep things were looking up.

The lights went out, plunging him into darkness.

"What the...?" Ross Armitage frowned and stood up, banging his shins on the low coffee table in the middle of the room. The house lay so far back from the lane that only a weak filter of moonlight made it into the room, reflecting blue off the tabletop and TV screen. Muttering, Ross shuffled across the room, holding onto furniture, and groping his way through the darkness. Then he stopped.

Something filled the doorway. Or rather, someone. A shadowy silhouette stood feet away from Ross.

"I'm telling you now, there are security guards on the way. This place is wired direct to the police station..."

"No, it isn't," the man hissed, his voice muffled by a face mask.

"Look, I haven't got any money here. Take what you want. Just don't hurt me, please!"

The figure shifted a little and Ross thought he heard the creak of leather gloves. "I never really liked you on the show, Ross; too smarmy. You weren't a proper copper, but you hogged the limelight. Now you can make amends. We're gonna get you centre stage, again, Ross!"

*****

Newspaper and magazine clippings lay arranged on the front room table in Blake's house. There were pictures of him as a younger man from his Searchlight days. An interview from the Daily Mail Magazine, some black and white head shots, done for the programme. Laura gripped his arm.

"Could he still be here?"

Blake shook his head. "I doubt it."

"How did he get in? He hasn't broken a window or forced a door."

"The locks on these doors are old. I've never really improved the security since my mother... went... Jeez. I'd better phone CSI. Don't touch anything!" he snapped as Laura reached for a magazine clipping.

It was from another Sunday Supplement. Blake's stomach lurched as he read the headline:

Searchlight Sweethearts Nicole and Will at home with their cutest case yet.

"I didn't know you had a family," Laura said.

"I don't." Blake turned and headed to the kitchen.

Laura followed and put a hand on his shoulder. "Where are they now?"

"It's no secret. Nicole was a runner on the show. We had an on and off relationship and then she got pregnant. I was over the moon. I almost believed everything was like in that photograph. Beautiful girlfriend, gorgeous baby, nice flat in Manchester and a dream job."

"Sounds perfect."

"Nothing is perfect. And nothing lasts. In 2007, the show was axed. I thought my life was over. It's amazing the hold a little celebrity can have over you. Nicole and I split up. Not long after that our baby girl, Ellie, contracted viral meningitis." Blake felt the familiar burden of grief drag at his very core. Tears were rare these days; just this leaden weight inside him. He sighed. "The poor little mite didn't stand a chance."

Laura squeezed his shoulder. "I'm so sorry. The last thing you need is this psycho raking up the past like this."

"Yeah," Blake said, nodding. "But I get it all the time. People at work, the public. Every time Searchlight is mentioned, it drags everything up again."

"I see," Laura said.

"I was trying to play this down but, it's true;

the killer is fixated."

"On you?"

"I think so. Look at those clippings. He left prints of poems by the poet William Blake and another magazine in the back of Ellen Kevney's car."

Laura raised her eyebrows. "Why would he do that?"

Blake knew what Laura was doing but he allowed her to steer him onto more comfortable territory. Work always chased the demons away, even if it was still close to home. "You tell me; you're the one with a psychology degree."

"Serial killers are often narcissistic personalities. He's involving you on a personal basis but really you need to think about what he's getting out of it."

Blake nodded. That made sense. Although she styled herself as an animal behaviourist, Blake had benefited from her insights into human nature before. "Is it just the thrill of butchering people that he gets off on?"

"Maybe, but why deliberately leave clues lying around. Could be that he thinks he's cleverer than you. He's showing off."

"Who to?" Blake snorted. "A load of cynical coppers? We're the last people who'll be impressed."

"I don't know. The press, maybe? He doesn't have to leave poems for you, does he? He doesn't have to do any of this," Laura said, waving a hand over the cuttings. "If he wanted to be the next Ted Bundy or Peter Sutcliffe, he could have gone out and killed multiple times and just run away."

"God, don't say that. He may well have more surprises in store for us."

"My point is, he's making an effort to draw you into this picture. I think he wants you to be part of his story."

"His story? Why me?"

"You know why, Will. If you were a total narcissist, who would you rather be pursued by: PC Nobody or DCI Will Blake, TV star?"

"I'm not a 'star.' I wasn't back then. I just did a CCTV bulletin near the end of the programme. The director kept asking me not to be so wooden."

"I don't think he sees it that way; maybe to him, you're famous. he wants to beat you, Will. Then the world will know how clever he is."

"Jeez. I'd better phone in and tell someone what's happened," Blake said. "I don't suppose I'm going to get much sleep tonight."

"You need to get your locks changed, too."

"True. But if the killer needs me for his little fame game, then he's not really a threat to me, is he?"

"It's only a theory, Will. But remember, if things don't go his way, he may figure out that he could become infamous as the man who killed the TV policeman. I'd tread carefully."

Suffering is a curious thing. It's meant to make you a better person. But the reality is that suffering just makes you bitter or fearful and distrustful. Survivors are meant to reflect on the horrors they've experienced and learn something from it. Tell that to war veterans suffering from PTSD and living on the streets. And what does it say about those who can bear the suffering no longer and end their own miserable existences? What can we say they've learnt? It's total nonsense but we lap it up because otherwise, the world has no structure; if we can learn from suffering then we can endure.

If the world is just one big gladiatorial stadium of suffering where one man rises only to be cut down by the next, how could we stand it? Or worse still, if we thought for one second that the world had no order to it and it was just a jumbled mess of random cruelty, we'd never get up in the morning. So, we impose a structure, don't we? We tell ourselves that this tragedy will teach us something, that lessons will be learned.

There's a point in every story when our hero faces so great a hardship that it seems unbearable. There's no way he can win through. Somehow, against all the odds, he does. He turns the tide of failure and rises above his enemies. And he learns something about himself. He changes.

Total nonsense, as I said. Lessons are never learned. People rarely change. Ross Armitage was a selfish and venal man; he greased palms and played the old-boy network to get to the top. then he squan-

dered his opportunity. He'd been divorced three times. Left behind him a wake of ruined lives. All his ex-wives and abandoned children learned was to despise him and to take whenever he felt guilty and waved some cash at them. When he tweeted that picture, I could see Blake wasn't happy. I could see my plan going awry, too. Happily, I'm smart enough to see how Armitage could fit into things perfectly. It meant I had a busy night but a worthwhile one.

WEDNESDAY 12TH FEBRUARY

CHAPTER 24

Treading carefully was something done more easily on a good night's sleep. If Blake hadn't been burgled, he would have spent the night stressing about how Martin would react to his sudden appearance on social media next to the gurning Ross Armitage. To put the tin hat on it all, the national news had a feature on Armitage and the Hilbre Grove case. They seemed to know an awful lot. Blake winced as he watched a shot of Aphrodites Club followed by a glamour shot of Ellen Kevney. They even showed Blake pushing his way through the press pack outside Armitage's front gate. He'd only caught glimpses of it between watching the CSI people bag the clippings and jotting down any details that might help. It was a bit pointless; clearly, it was the killer who had done this, and nothing had been taken.

Mallachy O'Hare, Crime Scene manager had given one of his annoying, trademark shrugs. "Looks like he came in through the back. You've got a dodgy sash window there, Will," he said. "I don't think we'll find prints, but we'll have a look."

Blake shook his head. "This is an absolute cat's

arse of a case, Mallachy. We've got two dead bodies, neither we can truly identify. One might be a cleaner from Romania and one might be a chimney sweep or maybe even the mysterious Ralph. We've got a missing woman, and the press crawling all over us and being briefed by a bloody celebrity. Jeez. What else can go wrong?"

"Oh, there's plenty more that can go wrong, Will," Mallachy said, without a hint of sympathy. "I daresay the Superintendent will be chewing the fat with you soon enough. That might shed some light."

"Thanks, Mallachy, you're a real tonic," Blake muttered. "Has anyone ever told you that?"

Mallachy's bushy, white eyebrows shot up in surprise. "No, they haven't, Will."

"I'm not surprised."

*****

Superintendent Martin actually put his head in his hands as Blake reeled off his concerns. "Oh," Blake added, "and I'm pretty certain the killer broke into my house last night and left a load of magazine and newspaper clippings all over my dining room table."

"Good grief," Martin muttered. "Why?"

"I don't know for certain, sir, but I think he may have some kind of fixation on me."

"A fixation?"

"Yes, sir. The clippings were all of me from my...erm... Searchlight days."

"Is that why you were splashed all over the news last night," Martin said. He pointed to a couple of tabloids lying on the desk between them. "And on the front pages of these? You and your pal Ross Armitage."

"Believe me, sir. He's no friend of mine. I went in good faith to ask him if he remembered any strange super fans or people with a grudge. I didn't expect him to turn it into a chimps' tea party."

"You should know what these people are like, Will. What did you expect?"

"He ambushed me, sir."

"This news conference is going to be a complete shitshow. D'you know what they're calling this killer? The Scissor Man. The bloody Scissor Man."

"We need to focus on the positives, sir," Blake said.

"Which are?"

"We've disrupted a major trafficking ring in the city, sir. That we're pursuing a number of lines of investigation? I think we should play down the fixation with Searchlight."

"We need something concrete to give the reporters. A job to do. Anything that'll distract them from pulling us apart."

"We haven't found the chimney sweep's van. We could ask people to look out for that. The killer dumped Ellen Kevney's car in a station carpark, so he might have done the same with the sweep's van."

"Do we have a picture of this Ralph character?"

"We've got footage of him but it's rather pornographic but we can't rule out the possibility that our dead man is Ralph, either..."

"Brilliant." Martin's voice dripped with sarcasm.

"We've taken a still of his face. It's quite clear. So we can share that."

Martin massaged his brow. "Thank God for small mercies, Blake. This better go well. I know we're early on in this case but it's an absolute shambles. I'm worried that your past might turn it into a circus. Don't let it."

Blake felt himself reddening. "I won't, sir."

"Now. I'm sure you've plenty to do before the briefing. I'll let you get on," Martin said and looked down at his paperwork. Blake gave a curt nod and hurried out of the office.

Kinnear waited for him at his desk. "I checked on one of the van registrations from Pleavin's list, sir, and it belongs to a Mark Skelly. He lives out in Widnes. He has convictions for aggravated burglary and sexual assault. Might be worth investigating?"

"You got a mugshot of him?"

Kinnear showed Blake a picture of a stocky bald man, late thirties. "It doesn't really look like our man," Blake muttered. "But we'll need to eliminate him. Check him out."

"Right, sir."

*****

The news conference room was buzzing with voices and a variety of accents. The story had gone international now and the number of reporters had doubled. Blake's palms felt slick as he sat down at the desk next to Superintendent Martin. The cameras and the clamour of journalists dragged him back to a time he'd rather not remember. Ellen's Mother sat on the other side of Martin. She was in her late fifties, her hair was dyed so dark, it made her look ghostly pale. She looked drawn and tired, her mouth a tight letterbox. Martin kicked off with a statement about how they were still searching for Ellen and outlined the resources Merseyside Police were throwing at this case. Then Blake outlined their lines of enquiry.

"We still believe Ellen Kevney to be alive but held against her will. Our resources are focused on finding out where she is and bringing her home safely. As part of the ongoing investigation, we're particularly interested in tracing a white Fiat Qubo Van with the words 'Chimeree' on the side. We are also interested in the whereabouts of this man." Blake held up the picture. "He has used the assumed name of Ralph Vaughan. If any members of the public see this man, they are asked to report the sighting to the police immediately. They should not approach him as he may be dangerous."

Mrs Kevney made a heartfelt plea for whoever was holding her daughter captive to let her go. Her children needed their mother. "If you saw them crying for their mum at bedtime, you'd let her go right away. Please, as a mother missing her daughter, I'm begging you. Let Ellen go. Set her free, now."

There was a moment's respectful silence and then Superintendent Martin cleared his throat. "So, any questions..."

A small, sharp-suited young man held up his hand. "What would you say the Scissor Man hopes to gain from his actions?"

Blake shook his head. "It's hard to fathom what is going on in that mind, to be honest. Maybe power or control. I'm no psychologist..."

"Is it true that the Scissor Man has a personal attachment to you?"

"I can't comment on that."

"But he left prints of William Blake poems at the murder scenes, didn't he?"

"Again, I can't comment on that as it relates too closely to the investigation. All I can say is that we have a number of leads and we'll do our utmost to bring Ellen Kevney home safe." Blake felt Ellen's mother staring at him. "I have to say, it doesn't help us if the media are repeating claims made by people who are not officially involved with the case."

"By that, do you mean Ross Armitage? Is it true he will be assisting you?"

Blake gritted his teeth. "Mr Armitage has no connection with this case."

More questions bounced around the room about the car, the resources but time and again, Ross Armitage and Blake's involvement with Searchlight cropped up. Blake parried each question with a blank indifference that belied his growing anger.

A ruddy-faced, bearded reporter in a brown suit raised his hand. "Is it good to be in front of the cameras again, Detective Blake?"

Blake cast a cold eye across him. "What d'you mean by that?"

"I'm just curious how it makes you feel to have the eye of the public on you again after so long..."

"It means nothing to me other than an opportunity to raise public awareness and bring us a step closer to bringing Ellen home. Does that answer your question?" The reporter shrank under Blake's icy gaze. "Are there any other questions?"

A harassed-looking woman with pointy glasses and her hair in a bun raised her hand. "Julie Irwin, Mirror Newsgroup, can you update us on the incident in Caldy, today, and can you tell us whether or not it's related to the Hilbre Grove case?"

Blake glanced over to Martin who raised his eyebrows. "At this moment in time, we're unaware of any incident..."

"But I've just been notified by our press office. One male dead at the scene. Identified as Ross Armitage. Shouldn't we know what's going on?"

The noise level rose in the room as other reporters competed with each other to get their questions answered. Superintendent Martin stood up and raised his hands. "Please, please, can we have some calm and dignity here? Clearly, this is a dynamic situation and possibly an error. Give us time to get to the bottom of it and we'll brief you just as soon as we know full details."

Blake followed Mrs Kevney and Martin out of the briefing room and wondered what the hell had just happened.

*****

The harder Ellen Kevney listened, the clearer the rumble of traffic became. She knew she was close to a major road. But where? It wasn't constant, so she doubted it was the M53. Every now and then, a train clattered by and she wondered if it was the Wirral line. She tried counting between trains, but they weren't that frequent, and her concentration drifted. It was so hard to think; she was starving, and she ached in every part of her body. She could be anywhere.

Ellen pulled at the chains and handcuffs that chafed the skin on her wrists. If only she could break free. With a sigh, she slumped back down onto the cold metal floor. Some memories of the day she was taken had come back, leaving the club with Ralph and getting into the car. Then a weird series of images and memories; smells and sounds. A door slamming, blinding light, a man's voice. The clang of the metal door. She cursed her stupidity. A rookie error, someone must have spiked her drink. She wondered about Ralph. What had happened to him? Had he been hurt defending her? Or worse? He must be dead; her captor had said as much.

And what would become of her? She tried not to imagine them opening this container and finding her cold lifeless body. And she tried not to think of her children; their faces creased with sorrow.

Panic seized and she tugged at the chains, rattling them through the welded eyelets that held them to the floor, but nothing happened. Her ears rang with the noise and she slumped down again, tears scalding her eyes. She couldn't escape and sooner or later, he'd come back for her.

CHAPTER 25

Kinnear had jumped into his car as soon as Blake had given him the okay to check out Mark Skelly. He was glad to be out of the office. The case felt stuck and the frustration was palpable in that big room. People were snapping at each other and covering their backs. Whoever had Ellen Kevney was running rings around them and making them look stupid. It didn't help that Blake's past in Searchlight was mixed up in it. He knew how some of the others took the piss and he'd seen superior officers have a dig at Blake about it too. But he wondered if it hadn't clouded Blake's judgement.

He inched his way through the city, stopping and starting at traffic lights. He passed the Rocket Pub, with its vintage steam train on the front, then merged onto the M62 and gave a murmur of thanks to the traffic gods as he speeded up.

Mark Skelly lived in a small row of terraces in a run-down part of Widnes. Kinnear had a job parking at first but managed to squeeze the car between two clapped out Vauxhalls. The houses were brick built but painted rust red to protect them from the weather. Some of the paint had begun to peel and a layer of street grime coated the lower half of each house. The front doors opened straight out onto the street and every house had a satellite dish poking out of the wall. He found number sixteen and rapped on the white UPVC front door.

It opened and a young woman, holding a toddler on her hip, looked Kinnear up and down. "What's he done now?"

"Sorry?" Kinnear stammered, taken by surprised.

"Our Mark. What's he been up to? You're a copper, aren't you?"

Kinnear showed his warrant card. "I just want a quick word. Thought he might be able to help me clear up a few things."

She nodded back into the house. "He's not here but if you see him, tell to come home. I need him to help me clear up a few things here, too." She went to shut the door, but Kinnear edged forward.

"I can't tell him, if I don't know where to look for him, can I?" Kinnear raised an eyebrow.

"Oh, he'll be in the One O'clock Gun about now, I wouldn't wonder." The door slammed in Kinnear's face.

The One O'clock Gun was a small street corner pub a few streets away. Kinnear imagined it would be one of those places that would fall silent the moment he set foot in it and he was right. It smelt of disinfectant and booze. A small huddle of red-faced, bullet-headed gorillas sat around a table. There wasn't much room for anything else in there apart from the mahogany bar which pressed itself against one wall.

Kinnear flashed his warrant card. "Hi, I'm looking for Mark Skelly..." He hadn't finished the sentence when one of the identical drinkers broke from the ranks and barged past him, slamming him into the wall and blasting the breath from his lungs.

Gasping, Kinnear staggered forward. "That'll be... him, I... expect..."

"Aye, that's our Mark," one of the lads grinned.

"Thanks," Kinnear said and bolted out of the door.

Mark Skelly was light on his feet and had already made his way to the corner, obviously heading for home. Kinnear yelled after him. "Mark stop! I only want to talk to you!"

The only reply was the pounding of Skelly's feet on the pavement. "Have it your own way, then," Kinnear muttered and speeded up, wishing he'd been better at fending off offers of digestive biscuits all these years. He sprinted after Skelly, the blood pounding around his temples. Skelly nipped down a side alley and Kinnear followed, skidding to a halt when the alley looked empty.

Panting for breath, Kinnear crept along the alleyway. It had turned into a wider passage that ran behind the houses. Each house had a small yard surrounded by a high wall. Gates punctuated the alley wall. Skelly had obviously leapt through one of these and was either hiding or had escaped through a house into the front. "This is ridiculous," Kinnear muttered.

A bin clattered over in front of him and Skelly broke from the cover of a gateway. Cursing and clambering over the fallen bin, Kinnear grabbed at him, fingers grazing Skelly's flannel shirt. He jumped up and sprinted again, this time gaining on Skelly and committing to a bone-crunching rugby tackle.

*****

For the second time in twenty-four hours, Blake found himself on the doorstep of Bramble Cottage. The circumstances couldn't have been more different, though and Blake found himself musing about how so much could change in such a short time. Life could be snuffed out in the blink of an eye; a whole life could change with the arrival of bad news. He knew that himself only too well.

DS Chinn stood beside him, sensing his hesitation at the threshold of the house. "You okay, sir?" she said.

Blake smiled at her. "Yeah," he said. "Thanks, Vikki. I never really liked Ross Armitage, but I'd never wish this on him."

"You don't have to go in, sir," Vikki said.

"Yeah, I do." Blake pulled on the face mask and trudged through the door.

From the inside of the house, it was clear that Ross Armitage's career was stalling. The old, Cheshire sandstone house hadn't changed since Blake had last been here. The only changes were those caused by a decade of neglect. An expanse of dusty, laminate flooring stretched across the hall and into the living room. Faded pictures of Ross's glory days hung on the wall; Armitage shaking hands with Ricky Gervais, on a TV studio sofa with Phillip Schofield, and a magazine shot of him in a red convertible with Jeremy Clarkson and Chris Evans. They clashed with the dark panelling and period furniture which looked tired and old. Thick curtains gave the room a twilight, underwater quality. Crime Scene Investigators busied themselves around the room, taking photographs and dusting for prints.

The man himself sprawled on an enormous, threadbare sofa. If it wasn't for the scissors poking from his left eye, Blake might have thought he was watching the massive TV that filled the old stone hearth. Blood from his gaping throat stained his track suit and the sofa. A single drop had reached the tip of his finger, congealing before it could drop onto the floor. A thousand memories of Ross Armitage flashed through Blake's mind: Ross in his dark suit, holding forth in front of the camera, Ross grinning after some stupid practical joke during rehearsals. He might have been an unpleasant individual, but he didn't deserve this. Blake grimaced. "Jeez," he muttered. "Poor bugger." This is all my fault, Blake thought. If I hadn't come here last night, this would never have happened.

Mallachy O'Hare grunted. "Are you trying to work me into an early grave, Blake?" he said. "I barely slept last night and now this."

"It's our Hilbre Grove man, you reckon?"

Mallachy pointed at the scissors. "Unless there's a sudden craze for doing that, I'd say so. We've got some footprints at the back door. The killer didn't really cover his tracks."

"Did he break in?"

"Looks like he used a bump key on the back-door lock. Surprised Armitage didn't hear it."

Blake looked down at the celebrity's ruined face and then to the phone that lay on the sofa next to Armitage. "Maybe he was too absorbed with himself."

"Perhaps," Mallachy said. He nodded to the wall. "I'm guessing that's for you."

Blake looked at the wall behind him and his heart sank. Painted in huge red capitals, the message filled the blank space. Blake knew the lines off by heart. It was the one poem that was endlessly parroted to him; or at least the first couple of lines. He'd memorised the whole thing as a teenager.

Tyger Tyger burning bright,
In the forests of the night:
What immortal hand or eye,
Dare frame thy fearful symmetry?

"William Blake," Mallachy said. "'Fearful symmetry.' What does that mean?"

Blake shrugged. "I always thought it was something to do with the stripes. You know, they're symmetrical."

"It's the contrast," a quiet voice said. Blake turned round to see Callum, the new CSI. Blake thought of him as new, but he'd been in post a few months now. If he was in need of experience, then these last few weeks would certainly have stood him in good stead. "In the poem, there's mention of the Lamb, which is God, the creator. The tiger is created by God but it's destructive and terrifying."

"So, the poet is asking how God could create such a creature?"

Callum shrugged. "Sort of. I think it's more the symmetry of the world, a kind of duality. Innocence and experience, good and evil, war and peace..."

"God! Let's hope next time he writes that one on the wall; we'll be sure to catch him. It'll take him all night, eh?" Mallachy said. "War and Peace..." Mallachy gave a dry chuckle and squatted down at the corpse's right foot to examine something.

Blake scowled at him and then turned to Callum. "So, the poet is saying there's a symmetry to the world..."

"Yeah, I did it in an Arts enrichment course at Uni,'" he said. "We had to do them in addition to any Science or Technology. I quite liked it. Whoever wrote that thinks he's half of something..."

"And I'm the other half?"

Callum shrugged. "Bit of a leap. Maybe he sees himself as a hunter and his victims the prey, or something." An awkward silence filled the air between them. "Anyway. I better get on."

Blake stared at the writing. "What the hell's he going to do next, Vikki?" he muttered, Looking out of the window. An officer in a hi-vis jacket walked across the rear lawn towards the imposing sandstone wall that encircled the grounds. Blake peered at the man. "Is that a copper, Vikki?"

Vikki Chinn stood beside him. "Yeah. It's a PCSO, sir."

"He looks familiar."

The PCSO paused at the gate, stared straight at them, and gave a brief wave.

"It's the officer from Hilbre Grove, sir," Vikki said.

"Seems like a spare part," Blake muttered. "Why's he wandering across the lawn like that? He looks like he's sight-seeing."

"I dunno, sir."

"I hope I'm imagining things, Vikki," Blake muttered, a horrible realisation dawning on him. "Quickly, let's go and have a word. I've a bad feeling about our PCSO out there."

They hurried through the hall and into a large conservatory that led into the garden. The PCSO stood across the long garden, fiddling with a small gate set into the rear wall. Hearing their footsteps, he turned, his cap pulled down low so that the peak covered his eyes and the collar of his hi-vis jacket turned against the February cold. But Blake could see glittering dark eyes and a thin black beard and recognised him instantly.

"It's him, Vikki! It's Ralph!"

Vikki sprinted across the lawn, but the man was already pulling the garden gate closed behind him. She tugged at the gate as Blake caught up with her, but it wouldn't move. "He's locked it from the outside, sir."

Blake grabbed at the top of the wall, his shoulders and upper arms burning as he pulled himself up. A car door slammed, and he just glimpsed the top of a white van disappearing down the lane. "Call for a car. There must be one nearby. See if they can head him off at the top of that lane." He lowered himself back down and massaged his aching shoulder. Vikki yelled into the radio.

"We've lost him, Vikki. He was bloody watching us. laughing at us from day one. How the hell did he manage to hang around the crime scenes dressed like that?"

"I don't know, sir," Vikki Chinn said and carried on barking orders into the intercom.

"I can't believe I've been so stupid! I bet he's the one Pleavin has been talking to all this time. Tom Dacre. Jeez!" Blake's phone rang.

"Blake," Superintendent Martin's voice was clipped. "I need you back here. Immediately."

"I'm just..."

"Right now."

"Yes sir," Blake said, ending the call. "Shit."

CHAPTER 26

Kath Cryer had always hated hospitals. They were full of sick people for a start and she always worried that she'd pick something up. Now, as an added bonus, they reminded her of her own brush with death only a few months ago and that always brought her up short. Before coming to see Dot Taylor, she had to sit in the car and take several long, slow, deep breaths and let the memories pass. She wondered if she'd ever forget the roar of the shotgun, the pain and the sudden strange detachment from the world as she fell back.

She sat, smoothing the straps of her splint out again and again. It was only when she woke up in hospital that the shock really hit her. There'd been no lasting damage, apart from her wrist. She'd done what any other copper would have done; she saw a mate in danger and reacted. It wasn't as if Kinnear was ungrateful, the opposite, really. Nothing was too much trouble; she was getting a bit tired of it, to be honest. It made her feel vulnerable. She hadn't been tested yet, but Kath worried that next time she was confronted with a knife attack or a gun, she'd freeze. Maybe that was the best thing to do anyway; rash heroics weren't conducive to a long life.

Dot Taylor lay buried in covers on her hospital bed. She stared across the ward at the bed on the other side, but Kath knew that Dot couldn't really see it. Poor old Dot was reliving those last moments when she shuffled out of normal life, where bad things only happened on the news, into a world of madness, blood and insanity.

"Mrs Taylor?" Kath said, gently. "I'm DI Cryer. I wondered if I could have a word. If you feel up to it?"

"Who'd do a thing like that?" Dot whispered. "I'd just come back off my holidays."

"Can you think of anyone?"

Dot looked up at Kath. "Can you?"

Kath raised her eyebrows. She couldn't. She had seen a few killings in her time; usually committed in the height of anger or passion. Others had been cold-blooded executions, criminals punishing other criminals, marking territory, that kind of thing. She'd even seen a few 'ripe' corpses and ones that had been in water for a while. But someone killing with no apparent reason and then leaving the body to be found in that manner. "No," she admitted. "No. I can't. We have some leads. Have you ever heard of a man called Ralph Vaughan?"

Dot shook her head. "We'd just had a lovely holiday. Won a competition and everything. Three weeks in Cape Verde. I thought that, what with everything we've been through, Dave's health scares, and our money-worries, that we deserved this. I wish we'd never gone now. That was our home. The one safe place."

Kath frowned. This wasn't the time to interview Dot and she was pretty certain that the poor old woman didn't know anything that would help them. Dot needed to talk to someone who could help her through this darkness and Kath wasn't that person. "Mrs Taylor. Dot. I'll come back later, okay?"

Dot grabbed Kath's hand. "I don't want to go home. Don't make me go back there..."

"I'll have a word," Kath said. She turned and saw a young man standing by the ward door. He wore a dark hoodie and had lank red hair. A look of shock spread across his freckled face and he turned to run.

"Wait!" Kath yelled and hurried after him.

The young man sprinted down the corridor, pushing people aside and scattering trolleys behind him to block the way. Kath raced behind, apologising and dodging around people. Each floor of the hospital had a bank of lifts and Kath saw the lad disappear into one and the doors shut behind him. "Shit!" Kath cursed, heading for the stairwell. Bounding two, sometimes three, steps at a time, Kath prayed she didn't go A over T and break her ankles. She also wished she'd put a sports bra on this morning.

People yelled and another trolley went clattering to the floor as Kath spilled out of the stairwell into the ground floor just as the young man burst from the lift. Kath grabbed hold of him and wrestled him to the floor. "What's your problem, sonny?" she snapped. "I just want a word."

"Get off me! Help! She's trying to mug me!"

A burly security guard ran up and was about to lay hands on Kath. "DI Cryer, Merseyside Police!" She barked and he skidded to a halt. "Help me to get this suspect somewhere private so I can talk to him."

They manhandled him over to a small consulting room and sat him down in a chair. Kath pulled out her warrant card and waved it around in the direction of the guard and then put it in the young man's face. "DI Kath Cryer," she said again, panting for breath. "Don't do that to me again, son." She looked up quizzically at the guard.

"Lloyd," the guard said, smiling. "Glad to help."

"Thanks, Lloyd. Could you just watch the door while I have a quick chat?"

When Lloyd had stepped outside, Kath turned to the young man. "Okay, let's start with your name."

"You're holding me against my will."

Kath's eyes widened. "Too bloody right I am, sonny. You were seen running away from a murder scene and then you bolted like a startled rabbit just now. So, clear the air and I can let you go. Who are you and what the hell were you doing at Hilbre Grove?"

The lad's eyes swept down to his trainers. "My name is Dylan… Dylan Thomas…"

Kath narrowed her eyes at him. "Like the Welsh poet?"

Dylan rolled his eyes. "I get that all the time."

"I have a boss who might sympathise," Kath said, giving a tight smile. "So what relation are you to the owners of number two Hilbre Grove?"

"Grandson," he said. "I just wanted to see them the other day. They'd be coming back from holiday, after three weeks and grandad likes to see me."

"So why did you run?"

Dylan shrugged. "Dunno, really. Just all them coppers, I suppose. Made me nervous."

"What made you run just now? Do I make you nervous?"

"No," Dylan said, sweeping his long, red hair from his face. "But I knew that once I'd run from the house, you'd be looking for me…"

Kath gave a deep sigh. "Turn your pockets out,

please," she said.

"What?"

"Just humour me," Kath said and rapped on the door. "Lloyd, can you come in and witness this, please?"

Lloyd came in and stood, arms folded. Clearly, he'd decided he was going to be 'tough cop.'

Dylan shook his head. "You're joking, aren't you?"

"Well, I have reason to believe you have a controlled substance on your person," Kath said, throwing her hands up. "And you can either show me here or I can take you down to the station and have you searched..."

"And you wouldn't like that, sonny," Lloyd said, performing an elaborate mime of putting a latex glove on. He even made the snapping sound at the end.

"D'you mind, Lloyd?" Kath said, raising one eyebrow.

Lloyd blushed and put his hand behind his back. "Sorry, Inspector... just trying to help..."

"Yeah, well I'll ask when I need that, okay?" she turned back to Dylan.

"So? What's it to be?"

Dylan huffed and puffed as he emptied his pockets onto the low coffee table between them. A phone clattered on the tabletop, then a lighter, a couple of coins and a debit card. Kath raised her eyebrows and tilted her head. "And?"

"God," Dylan groaned and pulled out a packet of papers and a little block of resin wrapped in clingfilm.

"Is that for personal use?"

Dylan scowled at her. "Of course," he said and then his face softened. "Oh God. You aren't going to arrest me, are you?"

"I reckon your grandparents have got too much to worry about, right now," Kath said. She frowned. "If you'd just walked past their house the other day, nobody would have batted an eye-lid. Even if you'd been stopped, you could have told any officers who you were, and they'd have accepted that. I still don't get why you ran."

Dylan shrugged. "Can I go now?"

"Sure," Kath said, nodding to Lloyd who held the door open and glared at Dylan with laser in-tensity.

Lloyd pointed a finger at Dylan as he sauntered past. "Stay icy," he said. Kath gave him a pained look.

*****

Andrew Kinnear's left arm ached from when he'd brought Mark Skelly crashing to the floor. Now he sat in the man's kitchen sipping a mug of tea while Skelly's wife passed her husband a bag of frozen peas for his eye.

"I just wanted to ask you a few questions..."

"It's about them murders on the Wirral, isn't it?" Skelly said, wincing as he put the peas on his eye. "I didn't do 'em. Honest I didn't."

"But you were in the Grove in the last couple of weeks, right?"

Skelly scowled at Kinnear. "Yeah. I bought a load of cheap cleaning stuff, sponges, brushes, you know. Thought I could sell 'em..."

"D'you make much money?"

"Oh, yeah," Skelly said, giving Kinnear a sarcastic grin. "Made a fuckin' fortune. We're about to sell up and move out to the country, aren't we luv?"

"We've got a shed full of buckets and crap sponges, and no money," his wife said. "Even if you had made a fortune, I reckon Vinnie down at the pub would have it in his till by now, anyway."

"So, what day were you down there?"

Skelly shrugged. "Dunno. Week ago, two maybe?"

"You're going to have to be more precise than that."

"Yeah the Thursday. Anyway. It was nothing to do with me," Skelly muttered. "Whoever was in that house was dead before I called."

Kinnear frowned. "What d'you mean by that, Mark?"

"The stink," Skelly said. "You could smell it outside. I didn't know what it was then, did I? But I do now. I just thought they might be in need of some cleaning equipment given their house smelt so bad but there was no answer."

"Was there anyone with you?"

Skelly looked shifty. "Yeah but I'm not telling their names..."

"Look, Mark, I know you didn't murder anyone. But you've got previous for assault and worse. All I want to do is cross you off my list, right? I'm sure anyone who was with you would want the same. I'm not interested in you selling a few knock-off plastic brushes..."

"They weren't knock-off!"

"Okay. Even better. You've probably committed an infringement of a bye-law or something," Kinnear said, not even knowing if there was a bye-law against door-to-door selling. "It's small potatoes compared to murder, right? Just tell me who you were with and I'll be on my way."

"All right then, if it'll get rid of you."

"You'll never see me again, Mark, I promise."

CHAPTER 27

Having had time to think as he drove across Wirral and back through the tunnel, Blake had thought back through the case; mulled over all the missed opportunities to catch the so-called Scissor Man and he wasn't happy at all. He'd decided what he had to do.

Blake knew there was trouble ahead and, it seemed, so did half of Merseyside Police HQ. He tried to ignore the knowing glances that were exchanged as he made his way up to Superintendent Martin's office.

Martin sat waiting for Blake; another bad sign; normally, he was a master of shuffling papers and ticking off lists while you stood waiting in front of his desk like a naughty schoolboy.

"This is an absolute dog's breakfast," Martin said, even before Blake could close the door. Blake was aware of faces looking up from desks in the office outside.

"I know and I'm not happy about it, either, sir," Blake said. "In fact..."

"Three people dead, Will. One of them a national celebrity. It'll be all over the TV this evening no doubt. This is the case that just keeps on giving, isn't it Blake?"

Blake pursed his lips. "I'm sorry, sir, I was ambushed by Ross Armitage yesterday. I can only assume that when he made our meeting public, it antagonised the killer..."

"And the press knew about it before we did! Journalists crawling all over the crime scene."

"I suspect our killer has been under our noses all along, disguised as a PCSO, sir," Blake said. "He's been feeding the information about the murders to the press. I suspect he's the one who tipped off the press about Armitage so they knew about it before we did. He did it to publicly humiliate us."

Martin looked like Blake had just poured cold custard down his trousers and hadn't quite processed what had happened. "It's a mess. And one of the residents of the Grove ended up in hospital after volunteering for interview. How did that come about?" He said at last. "I've had the bloody Chief Constable and even the Police and Crime Commissioner bending my ear about you. My God, we look like a bunch of clowns. Whoever this Ralph character is, he's running rings around us..."

"Me, sir. He's running rings around me...."

"What?"

"I had him standing right in front of me just

now and he got away. That's why I need to take a step back from this case."

Martin blinked. "What?"

"Whoever this Scissor Man is, he's using Searchlight to compromise me. I need to be out of the equation."

Martin pursed his lips, confused by Blake's change of heart; normally he was like a dog with a bone. "I don't know, Blake. I haven't got the resources just to swap officers around. Matty Cavanagh is back off leave but he's not as experienced as you are. Plus, I'm concerned about what our killer might do if we take his favourite man off the case..."

Blake steeled himself. "Would Ross Armitage still be alive if I hadn't gone to visit him, sir?"

Martin winced. "You can't blame yourself, Will..."

"Can't I, sir?" Martin said, quietly. "It's plain as day to me. Talking to Armitage provoked the killer. Maybe I was getting too close. I don't know. But if I hadn't gone over to Caldy, Armitage would be sitting in some voice-over studio right now."

Martin heaved a sigh and sat back in his chair. "But you didn't kill Armitage. It wasn't your fault. He put himself in harm's way by taking that selfie."

"As far I can see, sir, this psychopath is enjoying rubbing our noses in the fact that we can't catch him. We shouldn't play his game anymore. I don't know who will get hurt next. Take me off the case, put me onto something else or give me a few days off. Let Cavanagh run with this."

Martin thought for a while, twisting his biro around in his fingers. Clearly, he'd intended to tear Blake off a strip and this turnabout had blindsided him. "Very well," Martin said. "It makes sense. I'll be honest, you look terrible. I've been worried about you burning out for some time, Will..."

"I'm not 'burnt out' sir. I just don't want to be responsible for another death. I'll pick up some of Cavanagh's work; the Tuebrook assaults, anything..."

"No," Martin said, narrowing his eyes. "Take a couple of days off. God knows, I was going to have a word with you about not taking your full leave entitlement anyway. Rest. Have a think about it."

"Thanks, sir," Blake said.

"Have a word with Cavanagh and the team. Do the hand over and get some rest," Martin said. "Your mental health is important, Blake. Ours isn't the best of jobs to maintain it." He tried a smile but it looked false. Neither men were great talkers when it came to thoughts and feelings.

An awkward silence fell between them so Martin did his trademark, 'returning to the paperwork' move. Seeing his chance, Blake hurried out of the office before Martin tried to smile again or, even worse, suggest counselling.

*****

If Blake thought stepping back from the case would give him some peace of mind, he was very much mistaken. For a start, he'd underestimated how much Matty Cavanagh would enjoy the turn of events. Cavanagh leaned against Kath Cryer's desk, with that perfect white grin shining through his perfectly trimmed, black beard. But he made sure to keep his brow slightly furrowed so that he could show he was concerned. It also demonstrated to all the staff that although he approved of their efforts, he was slightly disturbed by the direction they had taken.

Handing over the case was the best thing to do but it grated on Blake all the same. He felt a sense of failure; maybe another reason he should hand over. This was a team effort; it wasn't meant to be personal.

Cavanagh didn't inspire confidence; he looked more like a best man at a wedding than a policeman, with his green suit and waistcoat. Blake wondered why he didn't wear a buttonhole too. Also, Blake worried that Cavanagh lacked the imagination to crack this case.

"So, this Ralph was seen with the Kevney girl..." Cavanagh started.

"She's a mother of two, Matty," Blake muttered. "Hardly a girl."

Cavanagh wobbled his head a little and looked perturbed again. DS Bobby Dirkin, Cavanagh's sidekick, whispered in his ear. "Oh, yeah, right, sorry," He gave Blake another frown. "So, this Kevney *woman* left the swingers' club with the mysterious Ralph," he gave Kath Cryer a nod. "Maybe we should go there undercover, Kath. What d'you reckon?"

Cryer reddened and rolled her eyes. "I reckon you should stick to the case, *sir*."

"In the meantime, Ralph kills two people in houses that aren't his. Pretends to be a police community support officer, and leaves fine art lying around at crime scenes." There was a moment's silence. Just enough for the whole case to seem contrived and foolish.

"There's the whole matter of the sex tape made in the house prior to the bodies being discovered. Video footage that links the Whites with Ralph Vaughan and Ellen Kevney," Blake added. "You can't ignore that."

Cavanagh gave a patronising nod. "Yeah, right. So, this Ralph is a bit of a pervert and leaves the house open after their little tryst. Maybe he tells someone in a pub? Or at Aphrodites. It doesn't mean he's our killer, does it?"

"The Taylors and Jean Quinn were sent on holiday, so their houses were empty. It was all premeditated..."

Cavanagh shrugged. "Could still be. I'm not saying your friend Ralph isn't our Scissor Man. I just think we need to widen our focus. It could be that we've got too hung up on the activities of the Whites. Now, any other lines of enquiry?"

Kinnear put his hand up. "There was a van spotted in the Grove belonging to Mark Skelly, he has previous for aggravated burglary and some sexual offences too."

"Great," Cavanagh said, clapping his hands. "Let's reel him in."

Kinnear looked startled. "I checked him out today, sir. He has an alibi. He was in the area with some mates..."

Cavanagh looked at Dirkin and then back at Kinnear. "And you believed him?"

"Well, yes sir. He didn't seem like he was lying. He was in the area selling crap cleaning stuff. The days didn't match up..."

"Let's have another chat with him and his mates, eh?"

"He doesn't look anything like the man we're hunting," Blake added.

"Right," Cavanagh replied, glancing down at his gold watch. "Get him in anyway."

Blake ground his teeth. Cavanagh had as good as said, "Are you still here?"

Kinnear looked uncomfortable. "Yes, sir."

"What about this Albert Green fella?"

"Harmless, sir," Manikas said. "Mad as a box of frogs..."

Cavanagh glanced at Dirkin again, who nodded. "Get him in too. Might be hiding something. Put a bit of pressure on him and see what happens."

"He's an old man, sir," Manikas said.

"Old men do all kinds of weird things, Alex," Cavanagh said. "Being old is not a get out of jail free card. We're investigating three murders and an abduction. Let's be realistic, four murders probably."

"What about Ralph, sir?" DS Chinn said.

Cavanagh glanced over at Blake. "Let's park Ralph for now. See what happens. It's possible he's just an attention-grabbing chancer who's piggybacked this case..."

"He phoned the newspapers and told them he'd killed Ross Armitage," Blake said, almost spitting the words out. "He left that copy of the Radio Times in Kevney's car and spent months disguised as a PCSO, grooming the residents of

Hilbre Grove. You can't just ignore him."

"Okay, where is he, Will? Where can we find him?"

Blake had no answer. And that was the point.

"Bobby," Cavanagh said, turning to his sidekick. "Will you do the honours?"

Bobby Dirkin pulled out his notebook. He looked like a squashed, uglier version of Cavanagh. Short, stocky and balding. "Two of the seventeen vans identified by Mr Pleavin proved to belong to people with known convictions for property theft or violence. One of these lives locally to Hilbre Grove. In the estate around Hilbre Grove, there are five sex offenders, two with previous for burglary, too. HOLMES has thrown up thirty-two recent releases from prison who might be worthy of investigation."

"That's the backdrop to this case, Will. Our psycho might well be calling the shots but there's a shitload of data there that needs crunching, people who need interviewing and that's what'll catch him. Someone in all that lot will have seen something or heard something and we'll be onto him."

Blake frowned. "And in the meantime, we just let him carry on? What about Ellen Kevney?"

"If I could magic her out of nowhere, Will, I would," Cavanagh said, with a sigh. "But you know as well as I do, the odds of finding her alive are next to zero."

A fleeting silence fell across the room and Blake felt the focus drain from him to Cavanagh. The young DCI clapped his hands. "Right people! Let's get moving. Dirkin will hand out assignments. Let's get these people in and start grilling them."

Everyone started moving, except Blake. He watched them and caught DS Chinn's eye. She gave an apologetic smile. Cavanagh strolled over; his hands shoved into his tight trouser pockets. "No hard feelings, Will," Cavanagh said. "Why don't you get home, like the Super suggested? This case is enough to drive anyone up the pole. Just let it go. We'll catch your Scissor Man."

Blake said nothing but gave a brief nod. He strode out of the office, wishing he'd never been allocated the case, never visited Ross Armitage and never appeared on Searchlight.

*****

Blake's mood darkened as he drove home, trying desperately not to think about the case. Cavanagh's idea that Ralph was just an opportunist chancer who had leapt onto the case to make some weird connection with Blake was laughable. But Blake knew that Cavanagh wasn't stupid enough to ignore the facts. He probably had Dirkin and a sub-team of officers sniffing along that trail right now. He just wouldn't admit it to Blake, that's all. It would look better for Cavanagh if he suddenly pulled the killer out of a hat while Blake's old team were poring through lists of van registrations and interview notes.

Anyway, Blake had done enough damage. It was better if he just went home, got some rest and let the others do their jobs. There had been too many deaths on his watch.

The traffic crawled along, increasing Blake's sense of frustration; the whole world seemed to be working against him. A fine drizzle speckled the windscreen, but the wipers squeaked horribly when he put them on. Someone cut in front of him as he approached the tunnel ticket booths and he nearly ran into the back of them. Everywhere looked grey and dismal.

He pulled into the drive, groaning at the sight of Laura's blue Hyundai. What was she doing here at this time? She practically lived here now, and Blake never remembered inviting her. He climbed out of the car and slammed the door.

Laura met him at the door, but he strode past her without a word, throwing his bag down and his coat over the bannister rail.

"Good day at the office, dear?"

He filled the kettle. "No. I'm off the case. How're things with you?"

"Really?"

"Ross Armitage is dead because of me and Ellen Kevney is too, probably." Serafina wound herself around his ankles and he shoved her away. "The killer was watching us all the time. On my watch. I took a step back."

"Oh," Laura said.

"What's that meant to mean?"

Laura looked startled. "Nothing. I was sympathising. So, what are you going to do?"

"Nothing..."

"You've got time off?"

"Yes," Blake snapped. "I'm going to put my feet up and relax while my team hunts for the remains of a woman I couldn't even find."

Laura held her hands up. "Okay. Don't raise your voice like that."

Serafina growled at him.

"What am I meant to do? Laugh it off? Maybe I should do a bit of that ridiculous meditation you seem so fond of..."

"Pfft. Sounds like it might help, right now," she said, picking her jacket off the back of the kitchen door.

"Where are you going?"

"To my place. You aren't very good company."

"Fine," Blake snapped. "While we're at it, you can give me that spare key back."

"Okay," Laura said, pulling it off her keyring and slapping it down on the draining board. "Be seeing you, Will. You know, you're a nice bloke but you need to sort your head out. You aren't responsible for every bad thing that happens in the world."

The front door slammed, and the house fell silent. Serafina stared at Blake, her tail lashing back and forth. "What's up with you?" Blake snapped, but Serafina turned tail and disappeared through the cat flap.

Brand names are important these days. Coca-Cola, Mercedes-Benz, Hilton Hotels; they all carry a weight with the public. If you want to succeed in this world, you need a brand name that people can relate to. One that sticks in their mind.

Apparently, research shows that our response to new brand names is not unlike that of a toddler learning a new word. When a new piece of vocabulary is introduced to a small child, they soak it up without any of the connotations it might hold. connotations might be formed later through experience. So, if a child learns the word fire, they might associate it with warmth and security. If they burn themselves, they might associate that word with pain. As adults, we react to brand names in a similar way; when we first encounter a company, we have no knowledge of it. If their product makes us puke, then their brand name will have bad connotations for us. It's not rocket science, really.

But brand names have a life of their own. Think about logos that appear on clothes or pencil cases or bags. McDonald's don't make pencils or pens, but you'll see the logo on pencil cases. A really powerful brand name has a life beyond the product.

Some companies choose names that already have good or bad connotations built in. So if I wanted to form a company that sells fast cars, it's obvious that I'm going to use words that bring speed and power to mind.

They're calling me The Scissor Man now, which I like. It's a name that will spread, it has all the right connotations. It could be the title of some cheap slasher movie. Just as I intended. It wasn't some random savagery that led me to put the scissors where I did. It was quite deliberate. Scissors don't mean anything, but The Scissor Man does. It's my brand. A modern killer for the consumer age.

THURSDAY 13TH FEBRUARY

CHAPTER 28

There was a familiar, unpleasant stink when Blake came downstairs the next morning. His head throbbed from lack of sleep and he stared mutely at the offensive deposits in the middle of the hall. Clearly, Serafina had embarked on a dirty protest at Blake's churlish behaviour the night before. Not only that, she'd knocked over the picture of Jeff, Blake's little brother. In this regard, she was a serial offender. He could forgive that; Jeff was a pain in the backside.

Having cleared up the mess, Blake took a mug of coffee, sat on the edge of the crumbling promenade outside his house and watched the seagulls skim the grey waters of the Mersey. He didn't mind the cold; it woke him up and cleared the fog that swirled in his head. but nothing could shift the dead weight of guilt deep inside him.

The visit to Armitage had been useless, disastrous even. Blake had provoked the killer by visiting the celebrity. Armitage wouldn't have been targeted otherwise. But it wasn't Blake who had advertised his visit and he had told Armitage not to post that picture. That didn't make Blake feel any better.

He wondered if he should ring Laura and apologise. That might lift some of the burden. But a tiny coal of anger still smouldered inside him. She could see he was upset. Why hadn't she been more sympathetic? She had no concept of what he had to deal with; the things he'd seen in the last few days.

No. He needed to do something practical. Something that would be a step forward. He turned and looked at the house. It stood tall, as if proud of its shabby grandeur. The first thing he should do is see an estate agent and get the house put on the market. It was true that every time Jeff rang, asking about the house, Blake felt less inclined to act. He'd been using work as an excuse for far too long and it wasn't fair on Jeff. Maybe getting out of here would be the change he needed.

Something shifted in the bushes and a pair of orange eyes peered through the foliage at him. Serafina extracted herself from the shadows and padded across to see him. Blake extended his hand to scratch behind her ear and she pressed her head against his fingers. That was one thing he had to thank Laura for; the cat had been psychotic before her intervention. Blake gave a final scratch and withdrew his hand. Serafina spat as he did and sank her teeth into his hand. "Jeez!" Blake yelled. With a long, drawn-out meow, Serafina vanished back into the bushes.

"Maybe I should just phone Laura and tell her to come and take you away!" Blake yelled after her.

He picked up his mug and made his way back into the house. The dining room table lay bare after the Crime Scene Investigators had taken the magazines and papers from it. Blake stared at the grain of the wood, trying to remember the clippings in detail.

They were pristine, not folded at the corners, not faded or yellowed. Someone had cut them out carefully and kept them very safe. That showed a high level of obsession over a long period of time.

It was thirteen years since Searchlight had ended and Blake had fallen out of the public eye almost immediately. If Ralph was in his late twenties, early thirties, he would have probably been a teenager when it was on. There can't have been many young fans of the programme, surely? From what he could remember of the demographics, it was more oldies and married couples who watched it. People who wanted both the thrill of true crime but the reassurance that it would never touch them. Perhaps the team should look at that, younger fans of the programme. Fans who were very keen indeed. Maybe they would. It wasn't Blake's concern anymore. He had an estate agent to call.

*****

The view from Laura Vexley's flat was unremarkable. The flat itself wasn't the most convenient; it was a top floor dwelling in a converted Victorian townhouse. One tiny living room formed the hub giving access to the other rooms: the bedroom, bathroom, and a kitchen. The bedroom was barely big enough to fit a bed in. It wasn't in the most salubrious parts of Wallasey, either. But she'd chosen the flat for that very outlook.

At the back of the flats, dark leylandii hedges hemmed in the overgrown garden where feral rhododendrons battled with brambles and knotweed. A few struggling sycamore trees pushed their way up to the light through the mass. But from the top floor, Laura could see beyond the hedges into the neatly tended garden that backed onto hers.

She could see the neatly clipped shrubs, the wooden-framed greenhouse tucked in one corner and the trimmed lawn that stopped short of the York stone patio. The house was beautiful, too; old but never broken up into flats. The recently painted window frames shone white in the February morning sunlight and Laura glimpsed William Morris curtains peeking from behind them. Mind you, she could already tell by the patio furniture that the couple who lived there were loaded. She'd lived in a house just like that one. The perfect house; the perfect couple.

She gave a hiss of disgust. No such thing. Like the perfect man.

When she'd first met Blake, he had turned up at the cattery she worked at, psyching himself up to give Serafina up to a new home. He had seemed so confused and lost that Laura felt sorry for him. It was more than that.

She looked out across the gardens; the way the neat orderly patch contrasted so starkly with the tangled jungle that belonged to her flats and to nobody. That was the trouble; nobody took responsibility for the land at the back of the building. Every now and then, a contracted gardener would come and hack everything down, cut things back and restore a little order for a few weeks. Maybe it was order she sought. Maybe she thought Will Blake, being a policeman, could bring the stability she needed.

But, outside of the force, Will Blake's life had its own special brand of chaos. Last night, she'd brought a bit of Blake's foul mood home with her. She hadn't slept a wink, going over Blake's unreasonable outburst in her head again and again. She didn't know he resented her having a key. Maybe they should have discussed it a little more; the house was difficult territory. Mind you, everything was difficult territory; some days she felt like she was walking on eggshells.

At the same time, he needed to rest. He was

burning out. The one chance they might have had to spend some real time together and he was too wrapped up in his work to take advantage of it. It wasn't fair.

A sudden thought occurred to her and made her smirk. What she didn't really like was not having the upper hand. Blake was usually quite easy to manipulate; if she wanted something to go her way, she'd just channel him along with a load of closed questions that only required him to say yes. Usually, he wasn't really bothered one way or another about most decisions and so would agree just to placate her. If it was about work, though, he couldn't be budged. She could understand why. And she'd overstepped the mark keeping the front door key and treating the house like her own, when really it was his long-lost mother's.

He'd thrown himself into work after his daughter died. It was all he had left, the last shred of identity. Laura could relate to that. She looked down at the ordered garden and batted away a dark memory that flitted across her mind. From what little Blake had told her, he'd become so obsessed with work that he hardly noticed his mother's decline into dementia until it was severe. Every case now was a chance to redeem himself. This one struck at the very root of who he was and his inability to solve it was a body blow.

Her face hardened and she squinted at the rear of the perfect house; the French windows, the patio and planters. She couldn't help Blake with his eternal guilt trip and she wasn't going to be anyone's doormat. She'd been there and worn the hair shirt. It wasn't happening again.

FRIDAY 14TH FEBRUARY

CHAPTER 29

The one great thing about estate agents, Blake always thought, was that they were more unpopular than police officers. He'd read this fact in a magazine once and it had intrigued him. The young man pacing around his living room right now looked a bit slick in his new suit but he seemed pleasant enough.

"It's a great space," the estate agent said, pivoting round on his heels so he could take in the living room. "When these properties are renovated tastefully, they're really popular with young professionals who want easy access to Liverpool but want the heritage style."

"Great," Blake said, still wondering when rooms became 'spaces' and why they couldn't just be rooms.

"Of course, there's a bit of work required and that could be reflected in the price or you could have it done yourself before you put it on the market."

"What kind of work?"

The man pulled an apologetic face. "Well, hopefully just cosmetic things. You know, wallpaper, a lick of paint. But a survey might reveal other issues. These houses are old and prone to damp, subsidence, the roof can be a weak spot."

"Right." The idea of leaving a load of hairy-arsed builders in here unattended left him cold. "So a price reduction, then. Quick sale."

The estate agent nodded but Blake wondered if the man's face had fallen a little at the possibility of a lower commission. "That's possible," he said. "You could go for an auction if major structural issues are found. That way you can push the price up a bit. Or you could sell it with the potential to split it into a couple of flats."

"Wouldn't planning permission be required?"

"Yeah. Again, you could get that sorted before you sell. It certainly makes the house more desirable." he looked around. "Do you live here?"

"At the moment," Blake said. "I sold my own flat to look after my mother. She had dementia."

"So, are you now the owner?"

Blake felt himself reddening. "Well, it's kind of complicated. My mother walked out of the front door two years ago and we haven't seen her since."

"And you've had her declared deceased?" The young man looked uncomfortable saying it and Blake couldn't blame him.

"It's pretty certain. She was frail, in her late eighties, and went out on a cold November night. I don't think she could have survived long just dressed in her nightgown. The police searched thoroughly but found nothing..."

The man pursed his lips. "I'm sorry to hear that. It must have been distressing for you."

For a second, Blake was back in the front garden on that night, Kath Cryer talking to him, crime scene investigators searching the house. He'd been questioned thoroughly and without any preferential treatment. He'd been made to feel as though he had murdered his own mother and dumped her in the river.

"It was," Blake said. "I know I need to get her declared dead officially, but could we not put it on the market and see what interest there is?"

The estate agent shook his head. "I'm sorry Mr Blake, but until that side of things is sorted out, I don't think we can progress. Put bluntly, as things stand now, the house isn't yours to sell. I can recommend a good solicitor, if you need one."

"No thanks," Blake muttered. "I know plenty of them."

*****

If estate agents weren't popular with the great British public, then solicitors were almost as low on the list that Blake had read. Blake wasn't sure why, but from all the solicitors he'd had the dubious pleasure of meeting, he chose Gareth Cornell. The man was young and inexperienced as far as Blake could tell, but he'd represented a suspect in one of Blake's cases last year and his name had stuck in his head. Anyway, if it was going to be straightforward, why throw a ton of money at some pinstriped, wine connoisseur with a city-centre office?

Blake was even more alarmed when Cornell agreed to see him that same afternoon. Wasn't he that busy? Or did he want to get Blake out of the way as quickly as possible?

Cornell's office was a converted shop in Bromborough village. Blake had a vague memory of it being a travel agent when he was a child. The front reception occupied what would have been the shop floor. A desk filled one half of the space and the other half was occupied by a couple of armchairs and a coffee table laden with lifestyle magazines from last year. A middle-aged woman in a dark suit sat behind the desk and beamed at Blake as he entered.

"Will Blake to see Gareth Cornell," Blake said.

"Ah yes, Detective Blake," she said. "I hope you don't mind but I must say, it's a pleasure to meet you. I loved Searchlight."

"Right," Blake said, trying to keep his voice steady. "Thanks. Is Gareth available now?"

"Yes," she said, unperturbed by Blake's darkening looks. "I was so sorry to hear about Ross Armitage. You must have been so upset."

"I still am," Blake muttered.

"Yes he was such a cheeky chappy, wasn't he? It must have been awful for whoever found him..."

"Is Gareth available? Only I'm on a bit of a tight schedule?"

The woman looked startled. "Oh yes," she said, clearly disappointed in Blake's brusqueness. "If you'd like to come this way."

She waddled in front of him, leading him into a back room. Blake wondered what kind of shop it had been when it first opened. This room was full of filing cabinets and had another desk in one corner. he followed her through another door and up some narrow stairs into another office where Gareth Cornell sat.

Cornell was a slight man but tall. Blake recalled Kath Cryer referring to him as a streak of piss once, which seemed unkind. His pale complexion and long, droopy face didn't really inspire confidence, though. His light brown suit seemed a size too big for him, especially around the shoulders. Even though he'd tried to force his mousey hair into a modern slicked-back style with a gallon of Brylcreem, it still stuck out at the side. Blake wondered if he'd made the right choice.

"Mr Blake," Cornell said, offering a clammy handshake. "Great to meet you again. I was sorry to hear about your colleague from the TV show. Terrible news."

"Thanks," Blake said, sitting down in the padded, leather chair clearly reserved for clients.

"I hear you've taken some time away from the Scissor Man case..."

"Really?" Blake said, bristling at the use of the name. "Where from?"

"It was on local radio this morning. I must say, I was surprised."

"Why's that?" Blake said. He hadn't expected Martin to move so quickly in announcing that he was off the case. It felt like they were trying to provoke the Scissor Man, which didn't seem like a good idea. Blake realised he felt annoyed at the news.

Cornell swallowed. "Well, I mean... I remember you from the last case we both dealt with. You didn't seem the kind to take time off... Not that there's anything wrong with...You just struck me as more dogged, that's all..."

"Dogged? You think I've given up?"

"No! Anyway! There might be a hundred and one reasons why you've stepped away from the case. None of them any of my business. I can imagine the death of Mr Armitage was a blow. He was a friend after all."

Blake leaned back. "The last thing I said to Ross Armitage was 'fuck you.' He was a poor excuse for a human being, but he didn't deserve to die. Now, if you don't mind, I want to discuss my late mother..."

*****

There were several missed calls on the old answerphone in the hall at Rock Lodge. Blake skipped through them. One from Laura. His finger hesitated over the 'play' button but then he erased it; she was probably better off without him. It struck Blake that it was February 14th, St Valentine's Day. He'd never been one for candlelit dinners or grand gestures but it somehow deepened his sense of regret.

Another message was from Kath Cryer, 'just checking in.' This was the woman who called Kinnear a 'soppy get' for sending her flowers after she'd saved his life. She always managed to surprise him. Another one from Laura which he also erased without listening to it.

The visit to Cornell had been fruitful. Blake left with the sense that he was just paying for one of Gareth's secretaries to fill in a form for him, but at least all he had to do was sign on the line and get on with his life. Cornell's frankness at the start of their meeting had made him think. The young solicitor didn't see him as a quitter and yet that's what he'd done. He'd walked away from Ellen Kevney; left her to fend for herself. and, yes, there were plenty of others on the team, just as diligent, and capable of finding her. But Blake couldn't rest until he'd found her dead or alive.

SATURDAY 15TH FEBRUARY

CHAPTER 30

It wasn't every day Laura drove across Wirral to see an incontinent dog. The owner was tired of mopping up after the poor creature and had phoned quite late in the evening. Laura had suggested a vet, but the man was adamant that the animal had a psychological issue. If she was being honest with herself, she agreed to look at the dog to keep busy and not think about Will. She'd phoned a couple of times yesterday, but he didn't pick up. Whether he was sulking or just busy, she didn't know but she didn't like being ignored. When the call came, she decided a new challenge might distract her. The dog was in Frankby, fourteen Corley Road.

"Where the hell is Frankby, anyway?" she muttered to herself. It was an old joke she used to have with her sister who always wanted to live there because of the posh sandstone cottages and country lanes. Laura always joked that you could drive through Frankby and miss it completely. Her journey took her across the Wirral and through fields from the industrial side to the more suburban.

Corley Road struck Laura as being more in Greasby than Frankby, but she wasn't going to split hairs. The bungalow was wedged between two identical twins and more houses flanked them, all the same. Their gables ran right along the road like pointed teeth. A garage fronted each house, partially concealing the living room window and front door. She got out of the car and frowned. The front room curtains of number fourteen were drawn closed. Family saloons and people carriers stood in front of the other houses, but the drive of this house lay empty. She knocked at the door and it swung open slightly.

"Hello?" Laura called. A dog barked in the back of the house and she relaxed a little. It was a playful bark, not a warning or distress. A voice called to it and she realised that the owner and the dog must be in the back garden. She stepped into the house.

"Hello?" she called again. "It's Laura Vexley, the animal behaviour woman." She advertised as the 'Behaviour Saviour' but always felt a little corny saying it out loud. The hallway lay in shadow and the two living room doors were shut tight. Only the kitchen door at the end of the hall was slightly ajar and light from the back shone through. More barking and a voice again, maybe laughter.

Uncertain what to do, Laura crept forward and pushed the kitchen door open. The kitchen was narrow with a sink on one side and a worktop and cupboards on the other. An old-fashioned ghetto blaster sat on the cooker, an old cassette tape turned round and round playing the sound of a dog barking and someone calling to it. The moment she saw it, she knew she was in trouble. She turned to run back down the hall, but a tall, rangy figure blocked her path.

*****

Blake sat on his mother's old bed in front of the cardboard box and held his breath. When he opened the lid, he would fall headlong into the past. A past he'd shut down thirteen years ago. Everything to do with Searchlight, contracts, letters, addresses, lay inside. But he was under no illusion. Each piece of memorabilia would be laden with bad memories. Memories of a time when his life had fallen apart. But a woman's life might depend on it. Last night, he'd decided to see if he could talk on the phone to someone connected with Searchlight.

The idea worried him because of what happened to Armitage but if he could make contact with someone less well -known, he thought they would be safe; the Scissor Man killed Armitage because he was high-profile and advertised his meeting with Blake. A camera man or runner would be completely anonymous to the killer and so unlikely to be harmed. He pulled open the lid and lifted the contents out, placing them on the bed.

There was a pile of leaflets, brown envelopes and other things, a framed photograph of Nicole and him and even some magazine clippings identical to the ones left on his dining room table. But there was a book too; a small, red notebook full of numbers. He doubted that many of them were still operational after all this time but thought he'd try them anyway.

He punched the first number into his phone and was rewarded with a monotonous beep. The second mobile number had been reallocated to a bad-tempered old man. The third, fourth and fifth, delivered similarly depressing results.

Blake flicked through the pages, his eye landing on Nicole's mobile number. Would that be the same? And what would she say if he called after all these years? He shook himself and turned the page.

The name Amy Tyson leapt up from the page. He'd thought of her the other day when he was talking with Armitage. He smiled. She'd been a runner for the programme; a gopher who brought coffees, winkled people out of their dressing rooms and ran various errands for the crew. He'd liked Amy; she didn't take any shit from anyone but kept on good terms with everyone, even Ross Armitage, who thought he was God's gift to everyone, but women especially. As Blake recalled, she lived in Didsbury with her girlfriend and a Great Dane called Henry.

Ross Armitage had mentioned her sexuality and Blake suspected he'd tried it on with her. Blake grinned, imagining the likely outcome of that scenario. He also knew that Amy was a loyal kind of person; a make-do-and-mend type. If anyone would still have the same phone number, it would be her.

Blake punched in the number and waited. The phone rang and then a gruff voice answered. "Yes?"

"Erm, Amy, is that you?"

"Yeah, this is Amy, who am I talking to, please?"

"It's Will Blake... from the Searchlight programme... you probably don't remember me..."

"I remember you, Will, of course I do. In fact, I've been expecting you to call..."

*****

Laura didn't even think; she swung her leg up as hard as she could. The man who blocked her path had stood legs apart to block the way, leaving him open to a good kick in the crown jewels. She followed it with a sharp punch to the side of his head and then leapt over him as he crumpled to the floor. She noticed he was dressed in black jeans and a Puma hoody. He had a ski mask on, but she could see the edge of a beard around the mouth hole. Panting loudly and her knuckles throbbing, Laura slammed out of the house and sprinted towards the car. She stopped, fumbling for the car keys in her bag and pointing the fob at the car. It chirped in recognition. She didn't dare to look back, but she could hear footsteps emerging from the house as she flung open the car door.

Slamming it shut, she pushed the lock button down just as the man threw himself against the passenger window. Laura started the engine and glanced over at him. He grinned at her and slowly peeled his ski mask off. A gaunt, scraggy-haired, bearded young man leered at her, then slowly licked the passenger window. Laura stalled the car, restarted the engine and pulled away, screeching the tyres. She saw him in the rear-view mirror, stumbling into the street and laughing at her. She knew it wasn't just Ellen Kevney who was in danger.

CHAPTER 31

Amy Tyson sat at a corner table in The Lead Station bar. As it was early yet, the place was quiet and mainly serving coffee to the students and the chic inhabitants of the Victorian houses around Chorlton Green. Blake had spent many a riotous hour in the Horse and Jockey pub just down the road when he worked on Searchlight and knew the area quite well.

Amy hadn't changed one bit. Small, dark, hair tied back in a tight bun. Blake was even more surprised to see that she still wore her trademark red check jacket and patched black skirt, a pair of Doc Marten boots poking out from under them. He entered the bar and gave her a wave.

"This used to be a cop shop, did you know that?" she said, without a 'how're you doing' or a 'hi.'

Blake looked around. It was hard to tell apart from a few bits of memorabilia; framed pictures, a truncheon and the like. "I didn't know that, at all, Amy. How are you doing?"

"Better than you by the sound of it," she said, giving him a cheeky grin.

Blake smiled and nodded. "There's truth in

that." He ordered a coffee and then leaned forward, resting his elbows on the table. "You said you were expecting me to call, Amy. What did you mean by that?"

Amy took a sip of her drink. "I dunno. Maybe it was the sudden demise of poor Mr Armitage," she said, without a hint of sorrow. "And, believe it or not, a surprising number of people have been following your career quite closely since Searchlight was scrapped, Will." She picked up her phone, gave it a few swipes with her finger and passed it to Blake.

Welcome to the Campaign to Bring back Searchlight Website, Blake read. *A place for Searchlighters of all ages to exchange their memories and to put pressure on the Independent channels to bring back the valuable and entertaining True Crime TV show.*

"Blimey," Blake muttered. "Some people need to get a life."

He went to hand the phone back, but Amy stopped him. "No," she said, "scroll down. There's more."

"Oh great," Blake muttered. "Don't you just love a 'where are they now?' section." He stabbed the box with his name on it with his finger and then blinked in surprise. "Blimey. There's loads of it..."

"I did a bit of research when I heard about Ross and came across this. Somebody has been watching you for a long time. There are details about the cases you've worked on, appearances in court to give evidence; any mention of you in the papers, however small is catalogued here."

Blake scrolled through the dates and comments, links and pictures. "Whoever did this must be seriously obsessed with the programme..."

"With you, Will. Not just the programme. You. I'm not saying this person is a killer. But they have a similar obsession with you, and they might swim in the same circles. When the link between these murders and Searchlight came up in the news, this website sprang to mind straight away."

"Who runs it?"

Amy shrugged. "The person who replies to any comments just calls themselves 'The Gambler.'"

"But they don't give any more details. Damn."

"It's a pretty amateurish site and there isn't any link up with social media. I guess if you knew somebody who had a certain level of computer know-how, they might be able to get more details about who hosts it maybe."

"That's a thought," Blake said, finding the website on his own phone and saving it. "Thanks, Amy. That's a start, I think."

"You know, there were lots of fans of yours during those years..."

Blake blushed. "I know. The hours I spent signing those terrible photographs of myself. And answering letters. Funny to think but even then, I got letters, not emails..."

"It's a more personal contact, isn't it? And if you don't have an email address, how are you going to get in touch with your idol? I mean nowadays, it's all social media; celebs are almost begging for attention but it was different then."

"True," Blake said, nodding.

"I always liked you, Will. You were a copper first and a celebrity second..."

"Don't think I was ever a celebrity," Blake said. "I got sucked into Searchlight and it's been a pain in the neck ever since."

"That's what I mean. You knew it was all bullshit. Some of those fans were quite persistent."

"How do you mean?"

Amy pursed her lips. "Like I said, most people would send letters or cards, but one or two hardcore fans would wait outside the studio..."

"Really?"

"Old Gary Churchill, the security guard, you remember him?"

"Yeah," Blake said. "Ex-copper as I recall..."

"He was given the run-around by quite a few

boys and girls who wanted to see Ross or Emerald. A few of them wanted to see you, too."

Blake's memory was beginning to awaken. "Didn't one of them make a complaint?"

"There was a young lad who tried to wriggle past Gary, kicked him in the shins when Gary grabbed him. I think Gary literally threw him off the premises."

"That's right. Wasn't there a social worker or something?"

Amy took a sip of her coffee. "Dunno. You'd have to ask Gary. It might be worth speaking to him. He might remember some of the weirder fans; you know, the ones who had him concerned."

"Good idea," Blake said. "Any ideas where he might be?"

"Funny you should say that, Will Blake," Amy said, smiling and picking up her phone from the table.

*****

Laura gunned the engine of her car, grinding the gears as she sped down Frankby Road. Houses and trees flashed by. A car blared its horn, but she didn't care, just as long as she got away from that house. She knew enough from what Blake had told her that this man was dangerous and clever. He'd broken into Blake's house, so he knew where he lived and if he had her phone number, it wasn't a huge leap to imagine that he knew where she lived too.

Turning left, she found herself heading for the M53 and then she was on the motorway, heading South. The exits flashed by and she didn't slow down until she was somewhere near Ellesmere Port. She turned off and found herself sitting in the crowded carpark at Cheshire Oaks shopping outlet. She let her breathing slow and pulled her phone out of her bag with trembling hands. She glanced around as the phone rang. The man could have followed her. He might be here. "Where are you Will?" she cried to the answering service. "It was him. He was at the house I went to... phone me back. Tell me what to do..."

She threw the phone back into her bag and took a deep breath. There were crowds here. There was no way the man had followed her here. She should walk a little, maybe get a coffee and calm down. She picked up the phone again and left another message. "Will. I'm at Cheshire Oaks. There are loads of people here. I'm okay. Just ring me back, please."

She climbed out of the car and strode over to a Starbucks. She should phone the police, but she needed to get her head straight first. It was a long time since she'd had to defend herself like that and she didn't like it. It stirred up too many dark memories.

*****

Gary Churchill arrived at The Lead Station within fifteen minutes. He looked every inch the retired copper. In fact, Blake thought he dressed as if he was still on duty. Grey hair neatly clipped and combed into a side part and held in regimented order by a liberal helping of Brylcreme. He wore a light blue shirt, dark tie and black trousers. Blake stood up when he entered the bar.

"Gary," he said and shook the old man's hand.

"Awright, Will?" he said, grinning. "How's things then?"

"Could be better, Gary," Blake said. They sat down with Amy at the table and Churchill leaned in.

"So, Amy gave me the low down on what's been going on and I've been following the case on the news. Bit of a pig's ear, eh?"

Blake nodded. He didn't mind Gary's assessment of the situation. It came from years of experience and he wasn't making judgements. "It is," Blake admitted. "The killer has clearly linked himself with my past, Gary. He's left clippings about me and Searchlight in the car of the victim, and these William Blake prints with the bodies of his victims."

"We were wondering if our killer could be one

of the super fans," Amy said. "You know the ones who congregated outside the studio after the show."

Gary rolled his eyes. "There were plenty of them. Some of them proper headcases." He frowned. "A lot of them were middle-aged women and men who had the hots for Ross Armitage or Emerald Fisher." He gave Blake a grin and winked. "There were a few there for you, though, Blakey."

"Great. Thanks," Blake said, staring darkly into his coffee. "Have a look through the comments on this website, Gary. Any names jump out?"

Gary perched a pair of reading glasses on the end of his nose and peered at the screen. "Well, Lady Jane, the woman commenting there, she was the landlady of the Golden Fleece just by the studio. She'd pop over after the show. Half cut most of the time. She must be clocking on now."

"I don't think it's her, somehow."

"There's another commenter here called Pauly, he was the gay bloke who used to hang around the studio in the hope of meeting Ross. He was a bit flamboyant but wouldn't harm a flea. Hang on who's this? The Gambler?"

"We don't know," Amy said. "He runs the site, as far as we can tell. Why?"

Gary put the phone down. "Well, you remember that lad who made a complaint against me? Said I threw him into the traffic and nearly killed him?"

"We were just talking about that, yes," Blake said. "Didn't a social worker get involved?"

"Yeah. I nearly lost my job. The kid went bonkers, kicking and biting. I pushed him away to stop him from biting my ear off. He had a social worker who bleated on about him being in care and having a 'troubled life' but the lad was a monster. Anyway. His name was Gambles. Josh Gambles. I'll never forget it as long as I live! He's your Gambler, I'd put money on it."

CHAPTER 32

Matty Cavanagh frowned at Laura as if he was staring at a particularly complex anagram but had grown bored of trying to solve it. "So, you're an," he looked at his notes again, "animal psychologist? And you went to this house in Frankby and a man attacked you."

"That's about the fifth time you've said that, Matty," Blake snapped. "It's not complicated. Our man lured Laura into a trap..."

Cavanagh raised his eyebrows at Blake. "Thing is, Will, I sent some officers round there and they found nothing. The house is secure but nobody home. The neighbours say the couple who live there are on holiday and they didn't hear a thing..."

"Do you think I'm making this up?" Laura said. "Why would I do that?"

Matty Cavanagh glanced at Blake, and it was full of meaning. "I don't know what to think, Ma'am. Your boyfriend, here, is under a lot of pressure..."

"For Christ's sake, Cavanagh," Blake said. "What do you think this is? It's not about my pride. Laura was terrified when she called me. I found her at Cheshire Oaks..."

"You see, that confuses me, too," Matty said. "Why go shopping right after being attacked?"

Laura put her head in her hands. "I didn't know where I was going," she said. "I just ended up there. There were people there. It felt safe."

"Look, Matty, I've been speaking to some of my old friends from the studio..."

Matty heaved a sigh and raised both hands. "Will, we're making some progress on the case at last. We've got that weird loner Green in custody and Mark Skelly isn't exactly as pure as the driven snow. The press has calmed down. Some have already got bored, packed up their toys and gone home."

"And what about Ellen Kevney?"

Cavanagh's cheeks reddened a little. "You know as well as I do, the chances of the Kevney girl being alive still are a hundred to one."

"Just check out a Josh Gambles, please," Blake said. "He was obsessed by the TV programme years ago. He had a history of violence even as a child, apparently..."

"Seems like you're going down that blind alley quite cheerfully yourself, Blake. I'll put it on the actions list in the morning. Now if there's anything else I can help you with?"

Laura looked nonplussed. "That's it?" she said.

"You aren't going to take it any further?"

"I've got your statement, Laura," Cavanagh said. "I sent some officers on a wild goose chase. I don't see what else I can do."

Blake saw Cavanagh to the door and turned to face Laura, who had followed them into the hall. "I can't believe that's it," she said.

"He's full of crap," Blake muttered. "Look, Laura, I'm sorry about last night I..."

The phone rang cutting Blake's apology short. Blake had never had the landline removed from his mother's house and the only time it rang was if Jeffrey or Blake's sister, Rosie called. "That's all I need," he groaned and picked up the phone. "Hello?"

The line hissed,

"Hello?" he said again.

"It's me," a voice said. "I'm aching all over after the mauling your girlfriend gave me. I'd watch that one, if I were you. She's got a history, if I'm not mistaken. You could see it in her eyes when she hit me. Takes a damaged person to know a damaged person." Blake tried to listen beyond the voice and heard what sounded like a distant train rattle by in the background.

"Where's Ellen Kevney?" he said.

"I saw a rather disturbing press conference today, Will. Your Superintendent is telling the world that you're taking sick leave. It would be terrible news for Ellen if you were off the case."

"She's alive, then?"

"For now."

"I'm not off the case," Blake snapped. "I'm very much *on* your case."

"Excellent. You'll have to be smart to catch me, though, Will Blake. I'm not one of your dullards caught on CCTV."

"I'm coming for you, Josh," Blake said and ended the call. He looked at Laura. "That was our man."

She frowned. "Why did you call him Josh?"

"Because I'm convinced that's his name. It'll rattle him, too. Put him on the back foot. First thing tomorrow, we're going to start looking for Joshua Gambles."

*****

Josh Gambles looked at his phone and blinked. Blake had used his name. A thrill of excitement shivered down his back, turning suddenly to cold dread. How had he known? Who had he been talking to? Josh Gambles jumped up from the plastic chair he was sitting on. How much more did he know?

"Maybe I should move," he said aloud. No. This was all part of the plan, surely. He looked around at the portacabin where he now lived. A table in one corner held all his files and notes. He'd pared his belongings down to a sleeping bag, a pillow, and a camping stove. That stood on the sink in the corner. It made him agile and able to change location quickly if needs be. Switching the light off, he hurried into the yard, wincing at the ache that still nagged his groin. That Laura could certainly kick.

Anyone who came into this place would see a high fence surrounding a space filled with shipping containers. The main road ran alongside it, hissing with the constant flow of traffic. Every now and then, a train rattled along the line on the other side of a tree-lined embankment that formed its other border.

Josh made for one particular container and prised open the door. When he'd taken the job of caretaker, he'd made sure he hired one of them straight away. The one at the far end where nobody went. Not that many people came here anyway. It was a storage yard; a place where people kept things that they didn't want but couldn't part with. He wondered sometimes what guilty secrets might be hidden in some of the other containers. He pulled the bolt down on the door and heaved it open, wincing at the squeal of metal on metal.

Ellen Kevney crouched in the corner, her hands still handcuffed and the chain running through the cuffs and a hoop on the floor. Josh wondered if he should let her exercise but had decided against it. She was in pretty good condition, considering she'd been cooped up all this time and he kept her fed and watered. She'd given up pleading with him, now which was a blessed relief. He found it hard to be nice to her when she was whining.

"He knows my name!" Josh said, clapping his hands. "He *is* a worthy rival, then. I thought for a moment that he was going to mess things up. I worried I'd made it too hard for him. But the story is unfolding, Ellen. This is his darkest hour. All stories have a darkest hour, don't they? You know, the false defeat, everything is going against our hero and you think, 'things can't get any worse, can they?' But they can, Ellen. They most surely can..."

Dogged. Have you ever considered that word? It probably doesn't have full resonance unless you've lived with a dog. One foster home I stayed in had a dog. It would sit and watch while you ate. Watch and watch with those big brown eyes. Waiting for one scrap, one morsel. And if you took a chunk of meat or a sliver of bacon and hid it, the dog would push and scratch and dig until it had found it. Dogged. Relentless. Never giving up. That's Blake.

He's clever but a lot of detectives are. The thing about Blake is, he doesn't stop. If I fled the country, I suspect he'd come looking for me.

This may well be my last journal entry. They are closing in and I need to move Ellen Kevney before they finally figure out where I am.

The events of the next couple of days could possibly end in my death. I don't want that, obviously. I'm not suicidal. I want to live to enjoy my notoriety. But I'm not sure Will Blake will let me live.

In all my planning, I didn't once entertain the idea that he might actually kill me. But to hear his voice the other day; the hatred in it; he wants my blood. And if I tell him everything I know, everything I've done, he'll end my life for sure. I think I underestimated him. The last domino is about to fall.

SUNDAY 16TH FEBRUARY

CHAPTER 33

When the phone rang so early in the morning, Blake half expected it to be Josh Gambles or Ralph or whoever he was. It was DS Chinn. "Hi, sir," she said. "Just checking up on you. Seeing if there's anything I can help you with?"

"Vikki, are you sure you're meant to be contacting me?"

"Dunno, nobody has said we can't, sir, but Cavanagh has put me on recording evidence for the rest of the week. I can do that in my sleep. And Kinnear is sifting through all the registration numbers again. It's Sunday, and Matty Cavanagh has swung us all overtime. We thought you might want a bit of assistance with your gardening leave."

Blake grinned. He could kiss Vikki but that would be a bit weird down the phone. "Well, as it happens, I have an old friend who I want to get in touch with. His name is Joshua Gambles. He went through Social Services in Manchester back in 2007. He also had a criminal record. Reckon you could track him down. I think we have some old magazines that belong to him."

"I could give it a go. D'you think he's our man,

sir?"

"I'm hoping so."

Laura snaked her arms around Blake's waist as he ended the call. "So, what do we do next?" she asked him.

"I'm going to look for Joshua Gambles."

"Then I'm coming with you."

"Laura, you can't..."

"He broke into this house like he had his own key. I'm too spooked to sit alone here all day while you swan around."

"But it's work..."

"I'd say that was a bit fuzzy, wouldn't you? Didn't your boss tell you to take some time off, if you wanted?"

"Yeah but..."

"No, Will. I'd freak out if you left me here alone."

"All right," Blake said, wiggling his eyebrows. "How do you fancy visiting a swingers' club?"

*****

It was nearly midday by the time Laura and Blake reached Aphrodites. Laura didn't look impressed.

"All we're going to do is ask the manager to check an address. Just to satisfy my curiosity.

I'm not going to ask if we can use his dungeon."

"It isn't that," She said, staring up at the sign. "Why is there no apostrophe?"

Blake nodded, his face grim. "I wondered that too. Maybe we should ask him." He rapped on the door. "Remember, we aren't strictly on official Police business or you wouldn't be here. Don't you say anything. Just look stern."

"Stern. Like 'facing down a Doberman' kind of stern?"

"Exactly that."

Bob Courtney opened the big red door and physically winced when he saw Blake. "Bloody Hell, Blake. Haven't I had enough grief? I've had reporters camping outside for three nights, half my punters have disappeared, and I doubt they'll come back. What do you want now? Free membership? Anyway, didn't I hear that they'd taken you off the case?"

"No, Bob, that doesn't happen. I'm working back of office at the moment. Sifting through fiddling details, checking any minor infringements of the law as we go along. It occurred to me, have we reviewed your licence recently?"

Bob Courtney looked like he was going to cry. "Please, Blake. It's not funny. I've had to cancel a holiday to Florida 'cos' of you..."

"I'm having to fingertip search the North

West for a missing mother of two because of you," Blake countered, raising an eyebrow. Laura scowled and folded her arms in apparent disgust at the club owner but said nothing.

Bob pursed his lips. "It wasn't my fault. I thought Ralph's ID was okay. Anyway, what do you want?"

"I want you to have a quick scan through your guest list and tell me if there is anyone who goes to this club from Cowley Rd Frankby?"

"I don't have to look; I know the answer to that one: Roz and Derek Fulton. They're regulars."

"Friends of Ralph, are they?"

Bob laughed. "They're everybody's friend," he grew serious. "But, yeah, they spent a lot of time with him. They're okay, aren't they?"

"They're fine. That's all I need to know, thanks," Blake said.

"How come you didn't check the list I gave you already?" Bob called after him.

"Just wanted to hear it from the horse's mouth," Blake called back as he climbed into his Opel Manta.

Laura grinned. "That was exciting. So, what do we know now?"

"The house you went to was only a stone's throw from Hilbre Grove and we know how Josh

Gamble got access to it, now."

"You did believe me, didn't you?" Laura muttered, her face falling.

"Of course I did, and now we have a concrete link between our man and the owners of the house. We can throw that in Cavanagh's face, too."

Blake's phone rang. "Kinnear," he said. "How's the paperwork going?"

"Driving me insane, sir," he said in a low voice. "Listen. Vikki came up trumps with your Mr Gambles. He was in care in and around Manchester for some time. Back and forth to foster homes but they always seemed to break down. Anyway, I've got the name and address of a social worker who used to try to help Josh. She's retired now but she's happy to talk to you. Cavanagh is watching everyone. I don't think he wants us to pass anything on to you."

"No worries, Kinnear. I won't tell if you don't. Where is she?"

Kinnear gave him the address and he entered it into the phone. "Fancy a drive out to Warrington, Laura?"

"Wow, Will Blake," Laura said. "You know how to show a girl a great time."

They drove in silence for a while along the Mersey side of the Wirral until the houses gave way to green fields and trees and then they turned onto the motorway. After a while, Laura gave a shiver. "Is it always this exciting?"

Blake frowned at her. "Really? I thought you were afraid. You were nearly killed yesterday."

"I know," Laura said, her green eyes flashing. "But I wonder if he just wanted to frighten me."

"I'm not sure. Whoever this man is, he's not stable and I wouldn't describe any of this as exciting."

Laura looked out of the window. "Well it has its moments, doesn't it?"

"Most police work is a dull grind, Laura. When I come home late, it's not because I've been involved in car chases or shootouts with desperate gangsters. It's usually because I've been filing reports and refreshing databases and filling in time sheets. And being attacked by a psychopathic killer is in no way 'exciting.'"

The chemical plants of Runcorn flashed by as they crossed the River Weaver. Laura looked at her nails. "You don't have to tell me," she said.

"Gambles could have incapacitated you the moment you stepped into the hall, but he made that elaborate pantomime of drawing you in and standing behind you..."

Laura shuddered this time and nodded. "Yeah, it wasn't that exciting, I suppose," she muttered.

"I was frightened witless..."

Blake frowned. He'd only known Laura a few months; he knew very little about her past, but she'd become an integral part of his life. There were moments like this one when she veered from one emotion to another: excitement to a sudden quietness. Blake wondered what had happened in her past to make her so volatile. *'Takes a damaged person to know a damaged person.'* That's what Josh Gambles said. Was he just winding him up or had that psychopath seen something in Laura's eyes and recognised it?

"So who are we going to see?" Laura said, interrupting his thoughts.

"Josh Gambles' old social worker. If we have some background on him, we might be able to run him to ground. We tend to think of ourselves as free spirits going where we please, but most people run along in the same ruts most of the time. Hopefully, Mr Gambles is a creature of habit like the rest of us and we can use that against him."

Blake turned the Manta off the M56 and followed the A road into a pleasant market town. He'd never visited Stockton Heath, but he quite liked its bustle and activity, even on a Sunday; some towns seemed stagnant, shops closing down, people hanging around. This place felt busy. The satnav on his phone took him to

Glamis Street. The houses were all well-kept red brick Edwardian villas with planters and pots in their small front gardens.

A plump, round-faced old lady in a red cardigan stood in her front garden as they pulled up. "Are you Inspector Blake?" she said.

Blake nodded. "This is my assistant Ms Vexley. Are you Mrs Whiteford?"

"Yes. Come on in and I'll make you a coffee."

Jenny Whiteford's house was small but beautifully decorated. The hall tiles had been polished and sealed so that the colours shone out and the wallpaper matched them perfectly. "You keep a nice house, Jenny," Laura said. Blake flashed her a look; the deal was she kept quiet. He didn't want her to derail any conversations.

Jenny smiled, clearly flattered. "Thank you. I try my best, but it isn't easy when you get to my age. I like a bit of wallpapering and painting, though."

They settled in the cosy front room and Jenny soon came back with coffee and biscuits. "The officer who called said that you were interested in a boy called Josh Gambles," Jenny said, and her face clouded as she said the name.

"If possible, Mrs Whiteford. I believe you were his social worker."

Jenny Whiteford sighed. "I was for all the good

it did him. I tried my best for that boy, you know but sometimes, the odds are stacked against you. I wouldn't call Josh Gambles one of my success stories and it breaks my heart to say that. People often paint social workers as interfering do-gooders and I'm fine with that as long as we do good. I'm not sure I can say we did Josh any good at all."

"Can you tell us anything about him; his past or where he might be now?" Blake said.

Jenny frowned. "I'm not sure. It would be breaking a confidence..."

"Jenny," Laura said, leaning forward and putting her mug down. "We wouldn't normally ask but we're afraid that Josh might be in terrible trouble and other people might be in danger."

Blake held his breath and bit his tongue.

"It's no surprise," Jenny said at last. "Josh was hamstrung from the start. His father was physically abusive, and his mother left the house when he was nine."

"When was this?" Blake asked.

"Around 2004 or 5. I became involved with Josh when he was ten or eleven. I worked for Wirral Social Services then. Josh was taken into care and fostered but he could never settle. Fiercely bright boy. Did very well at whatever school he landed in, but he could never settle. He was obsessed with crime and violence. A bit of a fantasist, too."

"A fantasist?"

"He told the kids at school stories about his parents; he'd tell them they were film stars. I remember one occasion when we were called to an emergency meeting because he'd dressed up as a policeman and tried to direct the traffic. He was a very mixed up kid."

"He must have got a hard time from the other kids in school," Blake said.

Jenny nodded. "Ooh, terrible. Bullied mercilessly. He didn't help himself, though. He'd target other vulnerable kids. There were some serious incidents..."

"What kind of incidents?" Laura asked.

"He was accused of sexually assaulting a younger girl in his school. Some foster carers refused to have him again because he'd been cruel to their family pets. He was difficult to place. The incidents increased and we moved him out of area in the end. To Manchester. I was still involved. We moved him around a lot to spread the load on foster carers."

Blake shifted in his seat. He felt sorry for the boy Jenny described but, at the same time, he'd seen the carnage caused by the man. "Did he continue to be obsessed with crime and violence?"

Jenny nodded. "Yes. That's why it's funny... funny peculiar, I mean... that you've turned up, Inspector Blake. You see, Josh was an avid fan of Searchlight and you..."

Blake nodded and held up a hand. "Yes. It was a long time ago..."

"But it is relevant," Laura cut in. "When you say an 'avid fan' what do you mean?"

"He never missed an episode. He would record each programme and watch them incessantly. One foster family ditched him just for that. When the show ended, he was about twelve, but he carried on watching them. He'd recorded them on an old VCR."

"These foster families," Blake said. "As he got older, would they have tended to be in or around Manchester?"

Jenny nodded. "Yes, and in care homes in Cheshire, too but he still returned to the Wirral from time-to-time. There were a couple of families who could work with him."

"You wouldn't remember who they were, by any chance, Jenny?"

"Only one sticks in my mind because they were such an eccentric family and they fostered so many children. Literally hundreds of them. I wrote their name and address down so many times, it stuck in my head. Albert and Maggie

Green, 1, Hilbre Grove, Upton.

CHAPTER 34

Andrew Kinnear sat at his desk and looked at the list of phone numbers and van registrations. What a waste of time. Ever since Cavanagh had taken over, Kinnear had been pinned to the desk by paperwork. There must be something better he could do.

"You're deep in thought, there, mate. Found something?"

DCI Matty Cavanagh stood right at Kinnear's shoulder, leaning over him. He had his hands in his pockets and his Hugo Boss aftershave almost choked Kinnear.

"No, sir, just wondering, really..."

"Wondering what exactly?" There was something about Cavanagh's tone. It was too friendly. Kinnear had been here long enough not to trust Cavanagh; he was pally and one of the lads one minute and then he'd be at your throat for some minor cock-up the next. At least with Blake, you knew where you stood. Blake would bollock you for shrugging, but he acknowledged good police-work when he saw it.

Kinnear felt his collar tighten. "Well, most of these van numbers, they're all legit and DS Dirkin has already gone through them. It seems like a waste of time..."

Cavanagh frowned thoughtfully as though he was considering a deep philosophical question. "Do you know, you're dead right, Andrew," he said at last. "You come with me and we'll pop over to the custody suite in St Anne Street..."

"Sir?"

"We pulled Mark Skelly last night. He's kicking his heels at the moment. Got him on selling knock off goods but I thought we could go and ruffle his feathers a bit. See what he comes up with."

Kinnear felt the blood drain from his face. The last person he wanted to face now was Mark Skelly, especially after he'd promised him that no more would be said. He stood up and caught Vikki's eye as he left the room. She gave him a sympathetic smile and went back to her cataloguing evidence.

They took Cavanagh's car, even though it was only a short walk and, by the time they'd negotiated the Liverpool traffic, it would take the same time if not longer. He looked left and right as they pulled out of the carpark and onto Liver Street.

"So d'you think Skelly is capable of murder, Andrew?" Cavanagh said, keeping his eye on the traffic.

"I'm not sure, sir. He's shacked up with a girl-friend and they've got a little kid..."

"Harold Shipman had a wife and four kids, mate. Didn't stop him."

"No, sir."

"A few years back, Skelly was burgling a house when he was disturbed by the owner; a frail old man in his late seventies. He beat him almost to death. In another break-in, he raped a teenage girl in her bedroom. He's no pussycat."

"No, sir," Kinnear muttered, blushing. He'd not really dwelt on Skelly's previous crimes in too much detail because he wanted to eliminate him from the enquiry. "But he's an opportunist. The murders at Hilbre Grove were planned."

"If you were going to plan a series of murders. Why would you commit them right next-door to each other? Seems like bad planning to me."

"Well, I suppose that depends on the reason for the killing, sir," Kinnear said.

"How is Blake, by the way?" Cavanagh said, out of the blue.

"Fine, sir," Kinnear blurted out before he could stop himself.

"So, you've spoken to him?"

"Just briefly, sir."

"Just checking he was okay. That sort of thing?"

"Yes, sir."

Cavanagh took his eyes of the road and looked hard at Kinnear. "I wish I could command that kind of loyalty, Andrew. I really do."

Kinnear said nothing as they pulled into the carpark of St Anne Street Station.

*****

As soon as Kinnear and Cavanagh left, Vikki Chinn switched screens on her computer and reviewed the information that had come in since Blake had left the case. There was a lot of noise but very few concrete leads. The victim at Jean Quinn's house had been positively identified, though. She picked up the phone, glancing around as Blake answered.

"Hi, sir," she said, lowering her voice. "Yeah, I thought you might like to know that the body you found at number three was, surprise, surprise, a chimney sweep by the name of Charlie Hulme, forty-five. His wife reported him missing ten days ago but he had a history of going off on drinking binges. So, there wasn't a massive search party as you can imagine."

"Is he local?" Blake asked.

"Prenton on the Wirral, sir."

"Did his wife have a list of appointments?"

"Apparently, he kept the appointment book in his car because he got so many calls as he was working."

"Is it worth talking to her?"

"I'd steer clear if I were you, sir," Chinn said. "There's Family Liaison Officer round there who'll tear you a new one if you go asking questions without permission, if you pardon the expression."

Blake laughed. "Point taken."

"Anyway, I suspect he was just chosen randomly. The killer needed a chimney sweep to fit with the picture and he was the first available."

"What about Albert Green? Have they interviewed him?"

"Cavanagh and Alex Manikas brought him in. Grilled him for ages," Chinn almost whispered into the phone. "Alex wasn't happy at all. The poor old man didn't know what day it was. At least Cavanagh has crossed him off the list of suspects."

"Hmm, yes. Or maybe he just didn't ask the right questions," Blake said. Vikki could hear the doubt in his voice.

"D'you think Green was involved?"

"I've just been talking to Gamble's social worker of old. Guess who was a foster parent for little Josh?"

"Albert Green?"

"Exactly. Listen, what's Hilbre Grove like now? Many reporters?"

"It's pretty quiet, sir," Vikki said. "Cavanagh has managed to make it really dull for them by having a huge list of suspects, leads and requests for information…"

"Plus, our little friend, Josh, isn't stirring them up, right now. I dread to think what he's busy with. Okay, thanks Vikki, I appreciate this."

"No worries, sir, take care, yeah?" Vikki put the phone down and looked up, straight into the eyes of DI Kath Cryer.

"Anyone we know?" Kath said, grinning.

"Just the boss, Ma'am," Vikki said.

"Yeah but which one?"

"The one who knows what he's doing, Ma'am," Vikki said, with a smirk as she returned to her keyboard.

"Nice one," Kath murmured and returned the smile.

*****

Blake slipped his phone back into his pocket and pulled the Opel Manta out into the road again. Laura watched his face carefully but couldn't work out what he was thinking. "So, are we calling in on Albert Green?" she said at last.

"I think it might be useful," Blake said.

Laura felt her stomach lurch, but she said it anyway. "Maybe you should wait in the car and I'll talk to him."

Blake flashed her a concerned look. "I don't think that's wise, Laura. I thought you didn't want to be left alone."

"I know but Albert Green's an old man. He hardly poses a threat and if you go thundering around the Grove, then Cavanagh will get wind of it and the Superintendent will have your head on a pole. He's just told the world that you're off the case. Anyway, if Cavanagh has given Green a grilling, he's hardly going to want to talk to another policeman is he?"

Laura could see the emotion in Blake's face now and felt quite gratified; he was actually conflicted.

"Alright," he said at last. "But I'll be right outside. You just need to ask him a few questions about Josh."

Laura patted Blake's knee. "You keep your eyes and ears open."

They drove on and Blake outlined what he wanted to find out. It was growing dark when Blake parked the car around the corner from Hilbre Grove and Laura followed him as he crept to Green's house. The end of the Grove still had barriers across it and a marked car sat in the middle of the cul-de-sac presumably to reassure the other residents. Albert Green's drive was shielded from the police car by the dark bulk of the house. Laura felt Blake's hand on her shoulder, and he nodded, his face in shadow.

She sneaked up the drive to the front door and knocked gently. At first there was no answer and she turned to Blake who hid behind the bushes at the bottom of the drive. He made a knock-again gesture and Laura was about to do so when the door swung open. Albert Green peered out. He looked haggard and licked his lips. "What do you want? I've told the police all I can..."

"I'm not the police, Mr Green. My name is Laura Vexley. I'm an animal psychologist..."

"Are you?" Albert Green blinked at her.

"Yes. Mr Blake sent me. He thought your pets might have been upset by the intrusion yesterday. All those nasty policemen upsetting your cats."

Green frowned. "William Blake sent you?"

"Yes, that's right."

"All right then," Green muttered and pulled the door open. Laura tried not to wrinkle her nose at the pungent smell that filled the house. "Can I make you a cup of tea?"

"No thank you, Mr Green," Laura said and cleared a space on the edge of an armchair. "How have your cats been since the ordeal?"

Albert Green picked up a fat white cat with a pink nose and sat it in his lap. "I think they've all been upset but Minky, here has been off her food."

"Minky looks lovely, Mr Green. How old is she?"

Albert thought for a moment. "One hundred and forty-three."

"A good age, then," Laura said, not missing a beat. "I would recommend plenty of warm milk and wrap her in a blanket when she sleeps. Is she used to visitors?"

Green shook his head. "No. Then, suddenly, we have all these policemen trampling all over the house."

"And nobody else?"

"No," Green said.

"Not even your children?"

Albert Green frowned at her. "My children?"

"I met an old friend of yours Jenny Whiteford, the social worker. Do you remember her? She said you looked after hundreds of children in your time."

"Literally hundreds," Albert said. "Yes. Some of them visit every now and then..."

"And Josh," Laura said. "Does he visit?"

Albert Green's eyes narrowed and he settled back into his chair. "Sometimes," he said, his voice hardening. "Why do you want to know?"

Outside, Blake kept to the shadows of the bushes that fringed the side of number one. He scanned the area for any police activity but it was quiet. On the other side of the road, a lone dog walker stooped to pick up the mess his pet had just deposited and then walked on. Blake held his breath. The walker had gone but Blake found himself staring at a van. A white van with 'Chimeree' written on the side. If it had been there the other day, officers would have noticed it. And it would have been spotted by the mass of journalists crowded at the entrance to Hilbre Grove. That van had arrived very recently and there was only one person who could have driven it.

CHAPTER 35

Laura stared at Albert Green as he crushed the growling cat against his chest. "Mr Green, you're hurting the cat..."

"Who are you to come here, questioning me?" he hissed, his face a mask of hatred. "Bitch! Prying and nosing around." Saliva dribbled from the corner of his wet mouth. "Josh told me you'd come. He warned me you'd be all nice as pie but a snake underneath. Why is everyone interested in old Joshy all of a sudden?" The cat gave a final growl and wriggled from his grasp. "You wanna know how often Joshy Boy visits? Why don't you ask him yourself?"

Laura's heart thumped against her chest as Green twisted in his seat and looked over his shoulder. "Oh, Joshy Boy," Green called in a reedy voice. "There's a nice lady to see you..."

The door to the hall creaked open and a dark shape emerged from the shadows behind. Laura recognised the man from the house in Frankby straight away. He was still dressed in black and still grinning horribly. His dark hair hung to his shoulders and a well-kept beard finished the look. Laura would have said he was quite handsome under other circumstances but, with his face twisted into this evil smile, he looked like a demon. “Hello again, Laura. Come to visit my old friend Albert?”

Laura leapt to her feet, but Green threw his arms around her legs as she passed him and they both fell onto the floor in a tangled heap. Gambles saw his chance and hurled himself forward, straddling her and bringing his face close.

“What was it so damaged you, Laura? I’d love to know,” Gambles hissed. “I know there’s something there. Was it an abusive boyfriend? It was my old dad who did it for me. Beat the living daylights out of me. And my mum left me behind with him.”

“Bitch!” Green snapped, making Laura struggle but Gambles had pinned her with the weight of his body.

“Yes, Albert,” Gambles said. “You’re right.” He turned his attention back to Laura. “You see, Laura, I can tell you’ve got a secret. Something dark.”

Laura bucked and kicked, trying to unseat him. “You don’t know a thing about me.”

“Touchy,” Gambles said.

“Touché!” Albert shouted, lying on his back and waving his hands in the air.

“Both!” Gambles said, slapping his thighs. “You’ve got a skeleton in the closet, haven’t you?"

"No," Laura snapped. Gambles hands snaked around her throat as she kicked and flailed her arms, desperate to land a damaging blow.

The front door exploded inwards and Blake came staggering up the hall, his eyes wide in horror. Using the distraction, Laura heaved Gambles away from her, sending him rolling backwards. She staggered to her feet as Gambles leapt towards the kitchen and the back door.

"It's Gambles!" Laura yelled. "Get him!"

Blake made to move forward but suddenly, Green stood between them and the door to the hall. He was snarling and whirling a poker around in the air. "Leave him alone. He's suffered enough!"

"Mr Green, he's killed at least three people..." Laura pleaded.

"Don't waste your time, Laura," Blake said, raising his hands. "Okay, Mr Green, we're leaving." They backed out of the room to the front door, Green snarling at them like a wild animal all the way. Blake pulled the front door shut and dragged Laura up the drive just in time to see the Chimeree van speed off.

"Come on!" Blake said, running towards the Manta.

The engine was rumbling and the car rolling

forward as Laura threw herself into the passenger seat. Then Blake floored the accelerator and she almost slid down into the footwell as they took off. The tyres screeched on the tarmac and it took Laura a few moments to get herself straight in the seat. She tugged at the seatbelt, cursing as it snagged repeatedly.

"He's just up ahead," Blake said. "Careful with the belt, this is a classic car you know."

"Green was harbouring him," Laura said.

"It explains how Gambles knew so much about Hilbre Grove." The streetlights flashed by and then suddenly, blue lights appeared behind them. "Damn," Blake said. "Looks like our friends on guard duty finally caught up with what's going on."

"Are we going to pull over?"

"No." Blake said and put his foot down, overtaking the taxi in front of him and getting behind Gambles in the Chimeree van. The police car had its siren on now and was repeatedly flashing Blake to stop.

Gambles suddenly turned right onto the main road, narrowly missing an oncoming minibus which slammed its brakes on, Blake used the chance to follow but the police car had to stop as the minibus started moving again. It stalled and the police car accelerated out of the side road.

"What are we going to do?" Laura yelled above the throaty roar of the Opel Manta's engine.

"I don't know," Blake said. "Keep on his tail and hope the boys behind us realise that they're chasing a copper's car and look at who I'm chasing!"

Laura's heart pounded and she gripped the door handle, her knuckles white as the Chimeree van swerved around two cars and Blake followed, narrowly missing an oncoming bus. Horns blared and lights flashed, dazzling Laura and Blake but he kept to the van's tail. They careered through red lights, cars swerving to right and left. It was a miracle nothing hit them. Blake realised they were on Upton Road. "He's heading for Moreton," he said. "The roundabout in the town centre might slow him down."

The Chimeree van almost went up onto two wheels as it hurtled around the roundabout. Blake tried navigating it in the wrong direction and for a moment, he was alongside the van. Gamble looked pale but he gave Blake a manic grin as he swerved into the Manta. Laura shrieked, leaning into Blake as the impact shuddered through the car. Blake winced as he heard the metal buckle. Finding himself on the wrong side of the road with a motorcycle screaming towards him, he fell back in line behind the van. "Damn, that'll cost me to fix," he muttered.

Two police cars followed them now and Laura thought she could hear the thrum of a helicopter above their heads. A supermarket flashed by and more red lights. They had turned into a narrower road. A row of shops flew by on one side, a school on the other and then they were replaced with rows of semi-detached houses and trees.

"What time is it?" Blake asked Laura.

"What?"

"The time. What is it?" Blake barked.

Laura glanced at her Fitbit watch. "Nearly twenty-five to," she said. "Why?"

"We're in luck."

Laura looked up ahead to see the raised arms of a level crossing barrier. "Leasowe Station," Blake said to her. "And there's a train due." The arms wobbled and slowly came down.

"He isn't going to stop!" Laura screamed.

The Chimeree van accelerated towards the sinking gates that slowly guillotined the road. The bottom of the gates rattled noisily against the roof, a few pieces snapping off against the roof rack and then the van had squeezed under and the gates were shut. Blake slammed the brakes on and for a moment, Laura thought they were going to crash into the side of the train that now thundered along the rails in front of them. She slumped forward, slapping the dashboard with the flat of her hands. They sat staring at the rumbling wall of Merseyrail blue in front of them.

"I thought your work wasn't all car chases..."

"Shit," Blake hissed as the two police cars, lights still flashing, pulled up behind the Manta and two officers jumped out.

Holding his warrant card aloft, Blake climbed out of his car. "DCI Blake," he called. "I was pursuing a suspect..." His phone rang and Laura watched as he listened intently. Then he said something to the officers and hurried back to the car.

"That was Matty Cavanagh giving me an earful," he spat, banging his palms on the steering wheel. "Apparently they've found Ellen Kevney's bloodstained clothes hanging on a gate down by Birkenhead Docks.

MONDAY 17TH FEBRUARY

CHAPTER 36

When DCI Matty Cavanagh had asked DS Vikki Chinn and DC Andrew Kinnear to interview one of the many van drivers who had been unlucky enough to deliver a package to Hilbre Grove, they jumped at the chance.

"We can pop into Wellington Road on the way back," Vikki had said.

Kinnear had frowned. "What's in Wellington Road?"

"A friend of Josh Gambles," Vikki said, with a grin. "Just keep it from Cavanagh until we have to tell him we've been there.

The houses along Wellington Road had obviously once been grand townhouses, owned by wealthy managers and bankers who worked in Liverpool. They'd have had servants and dinner parties and taken the air on Sundays in the nearby Vale Park. Many of the houses had been dismembered; split into bedsits and flats. Georgie Grant lived in the ground floor bedsit at number twelve.

DS Chinn and DC Kinnear paused at the door and scanned the doorbells at the side. Years of being painted over, pressed, rained on and frozen had left them looking dead and useless. "D'you think they work?" Kinnear said.

DS Chinn shrugged and pressed the bell. To their surprise, a buzz sounded inside the house. After waiting for a minute, Chinn pressed again. Eventually, the door swung open and a pale, spindly man, dressed in a blue dressing gown stared at them with half-closed eyes. Blond stubble covered his pointed chin and he raked his long fingers through a tangle of straw-gold hair. "What d'you want?" he yawned.

"Mr Grant? I'm DS Chinn and this is DC Kinnear. We'd like to talk to you about Josh Gambles if we can."

Grant's face crumpled into a look of discomfort. "I'd rather not talk about him, if it's all the same to you." He went to close the door, but Kinnear's foot was already wedged in it.

"It could be a matter of life and death, Mr Grant," he said.

With a sigh of resignation, Grant opened the door and gestured to the first floor flat. "Do come in. You'll forgive the mess only I couldn't be arsed to tidy up even if I'd known you were coming."

Grant's flat was a pigsty. Chinn had grown up in a small flat above a restaurant and the place got cluttered, but she'd never seen a mess like this. A bed sat in one corner of the room and next to it stood a coffee table laden with a teetering pile of magazines and CDs. There was a TV on the other side of the room but to get to it, you'd have had to step over fourteen similar piles of magazines. Rows and rows of vinyl records leaned against the other walls. There was a small space where Grant stood to access the tiny sink, draining board and kettle. Otherwise, not an inch of floor could be seen. Various clothes and takeaway foil dishes lay scattered on top or between these piles.

"Take a seat," Georgie said, waving a hand at some chairs that were buried in records, CDs, and DVDs.

"You're a collector of music, then, Georgie?" Kinnear said, picking up a vinyl from the top of a nearby pile.

"I buy and sell on eBay. Get them from charity shops, mostly. Keeps me in pocket money. So, what do you want? Has Joshy been up to mischief again?"

Chinn folded her arms. "You know him well?"

"Well enough to insist you use the past tense, for a start. KNEW him. I KNEW him. I wouldn't go near that psycho again if you paid me."

"You had a bad experience with him then?" Chinn asked

Grant pulled his dressing gown aside to reveal

a white semi-circular scar on his shoulder. "See that? Joshy Gambles, that is. Bit a chunk right out of me like I was KFC."

Kinnear winced, sympathetically. "You must've upset him..."

"I turned the telly over from his favourite programme. That Searchlight thing. He was well into that in a big way. He just went berserk. It took two of the screws to pull him away from me."

"Screws? You were in prison?"

"Secure unit, mate," Georgie said. "Thing was, I kept getting lumped with Joshy boy. We'd get dumped in the same foster places, same homes. Social workers said it helped us socialise. Just left me with bad dreams."

"You shared foster homes?" Kinnear said. "Any interesting tales to tell?"

"Too many," He said and chuckled. He seemed a little too friendly to Kinnear; it was a brittle, shallow friendliness that could suddenly turn to anger and vitriol. Whether that was years of drug abuse, mental illness, or a combination, who knew? But Kinnear could see that Grant was fragile. The young man sat down on the bed, his dressing gown flapping open to reveal a little too much thigh and boxer short. "There was one place. Yeah, I was thinking about it just the other day 'cos' it was in the papers."

"Really?" Chinn said.

"Yeah, really. I'm not making this up, you know," Grant snapped. "I invited you in. You could be fuckin' vampires for all I know..."

"We're not vampires, Georgie," Kinnear said. "DS Chinn said that because she's interested in what you have to say."

"She is?"

"Yeah. Go on. The foster placement in Hilbre Grove..."

"The woman was lovely. Like an old grandma, all smiley and plump, like, you know. But the fella. He was a perv."

"In what way was he a perv, Georgie?"

Grant was looking at his fingers now as he knotted and tangled them into each other. "He had a dungeon. With metal walls. He'd give you a hot chocolate and then you'd pass out and wake up in the dungeon, chained up. Then he'd torture you or do stuff. Touch you and get you to touch him."

Chinn's face softened. "Did you tell anyone?"

"Course I did but they said I was making it all up. That it was impossible..."

"This dungeon," Kinnear said. "Any idea where it was?"

Grant shook his head. "Nah. Like I said I was

zonked out me head. But it was like one of them container things. You know like they put on the back of lorries?"

"A shipping container?"

"Yeah, that's what I said, didn't I? All metal and cold." Grant shivered and pulled his dressing gown tight around his shoulders.

"What about Josh Gambles?" Vikki said. "Did the fella from Hilbre Grove hurt him too?"

Georgie Grant looked up. "That's the thing," he said through gritted teeth. "He didn't touch Josh. Josh helped him. He watched and laughed and joined in sometimes too. He bloody helped him!"

*****

Blake stood in front of Superintendent Martin's desk while Matty Cavanagh slumped on a chair at the side of the office. Martin's voice was icy cold and barely above a whisper which chilled Blake more than if he'd been bellowing in his face.

"Chasing another car at breakneck speed in your own vehicle. One that barely passes its MOT every year let alone stands up to the standards expected of official police vehicles. What were you thinking of Blake?"

"sir, I was pursuing the Chimeree van that belonged to Charlie Hulme, the victim at number three..."

"And how the hell do you know that, Blake?" Cavanagh muttered, folding his arms.

Blake shrugged. "I've kept in touch. Our killer is a man called Josh Gambles, a local lad, went through loads of foster homes here and over in Manchester. He was fostered by Albert Green."

"Oh, come on, Blake. We already interviewed Albert Green. He didn't mention any Josh Gambles," Cavanagh said, stretching out his legs and looking at the tip of his pointed brogues.

"Gambles was thrown out of the Granada Studio as a boy back in 2006, he assaulted a security guard. Nearly bit his ear off just trying to get in to see the Searchlight team. I spoke to his social worker who told me he was obsessed with the programme. There's a website he runs. Everything."

"And you didn't think to share this with the team?" Martin said, quietly.

"I'm not sure DCI Cavanagh would've been particularly receptive to my information."

"If he hadn't withheld that information, sir," Cavanagh said. "I'd have collared this Gambles joker days ago."

Blake closed his eyes. "I did suggest that you follow up the Searchlight link. Gambles was at Albert Green's house last night. Laura recognised him as the man who attacked her at the Frankby house..."

Martin frowned and looked over to Cavanagh. "Laura? The Frankby house?"

"Blake's missus said she'd been called out to this house in Frankby. It was more like Greasby to be honest. She said she'd been attacked. We sent some uniforms round, but the house was secure. No sign of a break-in..."

"Are you comfortable there, Cavanagh?" Martin said, his voice really quiet now. Realising the danger, Cavanagh leapt to his feet.

Blake took some small satisfaction in Cavanagh's discomfort but kept a straight face. "The reason there was no sign of a break-in is because Josh Gambles is pally with the owners of the house who are on holiday. They also happen to be patrons of Aphrodites. Does any of this sound familiar?"

Cavanagh opened and closed his mouth but couldn't think of anything to say.

Martin gave a grunt of dissatisfaction. "It's not good enough. This case has been a mess from start to finish. Blake, I'd hoped you'd take the hint and have a break; not go off on your own personal mission to solve the case. Cavanagh, you're too cocksure of yourself. I'm not looking to pin this on just anyone. I want this killer found. We've got three dead bodies and now the

Kevney girl's..."

"She's not dead," Blake said.

CHAPTER 37

"Oh, behave!" Cavanagh snapped. "If you'd seen the amount of blood on that dress. You'd say she was dead, Blake..."

"It'll prove to be fake or pig's blood. Where's the body? What's this guy's MO? He leaves the body for all to see. That's what he wants. That's how he operates."

"And why does he do that?" Martin said, massaging his temples.

Blake felt himself colouring. "I believe he wants me to solve this case." Blake saw Martin open his mouth, but he carried on before the Superintendent could stop him. "sir, I know you don't like my history with the Searchlight programme. I've said before, I wish I'd never stood in front of a TV camera, but I did, and we are where we are. Now Gambles doesn't know the Wirral that well. He grew up here but was moved around a lot. His knowledge seems restricted to the Upton/ Greasby area, maybe a little bit of Birkenhead. It's a small enough area. If we put the word out that we're still actively looking for Ellen and flood the place with officers, I reckon we'll find her safe and sound."

Martin drummed his fingers on the table as he looked out of his window, deep in thought. "Okay. Do it," he said.

"Thank you, sir," Blake said, taking a deep breath. "We need to search for anywhere that might be easy to hide someone..."

"It'd have to be somewhere away from other people," Cavanagh said. "If the Kevney girl kicked up a fuss, then people would hear. So, storage facilities, sheds, garages."

Martin nodded. "Cavanagh, you coordinate the search for likely premises. Blake..."

Blake raised his hand. "If I can be in the background, sir. Returning me to the case will only stir up the press and that, in turn, might make him react. I'd hate to see another fatality."

"Right, let's get to it," Martin said, standing up at his desk as if he was about to run off and join the search.

Cavanagh turned to Blake once they were outside the Superintendent's office. "Think you're smart, don't you Blake? Well, I won't forget this. You stole a case off me..."

"Don't panic, Matty, you'll get all the credit when it's over. I'll make sure of that. I've had a bellyful of publicity," Blake said, turning and walking away.

*****

Josh Gambles panted for breath as he peeled back the corrugated iron sheet that covered the bottom of the old chapel window. Outside, the odd car rumbled by but in this boarded-up old building, he could have been a million miles away from anywhere. There were plenty of houses around here, but they were well set back from the road and the nearest building was a shop that never seemed to open or sell anything and that was across the busy road.

He'd managed to get rid of the van last night but then getting back to the church had been a nightmare. He'd walked for what seemed like hours, using an old A to Z. He'd thrown his phone away long ago. As he scrambled over the piled-up pews and fallen beams in the old church, he realised that this was all coming to an end. The fruition of all his plans. So he had to make it good.

Ellen sat in the corner, dressed in the old boiler suit he'd found at the storage yard. He had chained her to a thick, lead pipe that ran up the brickwork. She looked heavy-eyed after the Midazolam he'd given her but she was coming round enough to recognise his face.

"What're you looking at me like that for?" he panted.

"Ralph? I thought you were dead... I thought..."

He gave a short laugh. Did she think he had

come to rescue her? The look on her face was priceless; she was hoping against hope that he wasn't a hallucination. Then the truth dawned on her.

"Well, you didn't think hard enough, did you, Ellen? I'm not really called Ralph, by the way. My name is Josh Gambles. Pleased to meet you." He held out his hand, as if to shake hers and then gave a pained look at her chains. "Oh, sorry. I forgot you can't shake my hand."

"You drugged me at the club," she said.

"Not quite. That idiot Bob Courtney would have kicked me out if he thought I had GHB on me. I put it in your water as we came out."

"Bastard!" Ellen spat, lunging at him. The chains clanked and pulled her back.

He squatted down, close to Ellen and stroked her head. She winced and shrank away from him. "So much life and energy, even after all these weeks. Impressive. But it doesn't really matter if you die begging for your life or cursing me to the rooftops. Nobody remembers the victims, do they? Or the arresting officer; who knows who arrested Fred West or Ted Bundy? It's the killer who gets all the credit!"

CHAPTER 38

Matty Cavanagh preened himself as the cameras pointed at him and journalists crouched on chairs scribbling down his every word. Blake had to admit, Cavanagh looked quite the policeman when the spotlight was on him. But then, someone had said that to Blake when he was young and ambitious. "This'll be great for the force, good P.R. A young fella like you, easy on the eye, appealing to the nation's housewives for help and information..." Blake remembered it all and winced. He'd lapped it up at the time.

Now he leaned against a wall, happy to be at the back of the conference room watching with folded arms as Cavanagh told the assembled press about a new tack they were taking.

"We're looking for Joshua Gambles," Cavanagh said, suppressing his scouse accent as much as he could. They had used the still from the Whites' sex tape and cropped it into a headshot. "But we also have intelligence that Ellen Kevney may well still be alive. We're imploring the public..." Blake frowned 'imploring.' Was that one of Cavanagh's ad-libs? Where did he come up with a word like that? "...to report anything unusual; old garages that are suddenly being used; disused building that may have been broken into. We'll be flooding the area around Hilbre Grove with police in order to find Ellen."

A reporter raised her hand. "What about DCI Blake? Is he still off the case?"

"After the death of his good friend, Ross Armitage, Will Blake is on compassionate leave. He is not actively involved in this investigation at this moment in time."

He could have just said, 'no,' Blake thought as he strode out of the room before anyone saw him.

DS Chinn and DC Kinnear stood frowning at a huge OS map that had been stuck to the wall. They'd had it blown up and it covered the northern half of the Wirral. The operations room was crammed with officers, both uniformed and plain-clothed.

"Good to see you back, sir," Chinn said, flashing him a smile.

"Yeah, sir, welcome back," Kinnear said.

"Thanks," Blake said, clearing his throat. "I owe you." He turned to the crowded room. "Okay, while DCI Cavanagh is batting his eyelashes at the cameras, we'll crack on and find Ellen Kevney. Some of you may know that we found her bloodstained clothes yesterday, but we believe her to be still alive. I want everyone to focus on the area around Hilbre Grove and then gradually spread out from there. We're looking for any likely hiding places nearby. Vikki and Andrew have some new intelligence."

"Thanks, sir," Andrew Kinnear said. "We interviewed an acquaintance of Gambles this morning and he said that he'd been held in some kind of dungeon by Albert Green and Gambles when he was younger. He thought it was a shipping container. We haven't been able to verify this story, but it may be useful to know."

"So bear that in mind. Somewhere you could keep someone captive for this long without being detected. Garages, lockups, sheds, anywhere you think is suspicious. Be particularly suspicious if you come across any shipping containers being used for storage. Kath has allocated teams and areas in the vicinity. So let's get out there." The crowd began to murmur and disperse. "Oh, one more thing. If you encounter any journalists, DCI Cavanagh is heading this case, understand? We want Josh Gambles to think I'm off the case. Thank you!"

DS Chinn turned to Blake. "What are you going to do, sir?"

"Bring Albert Green in for a chat. I want to get to the bottom of this container story if we can."

Vikki hurried off and Blake stood in front of the map, willing a likely bolt hole to leap out at him.

Just to the north of Hilbre Grove and the surrounding roads was the town of Moreton. Blake shuddered as he remembered the chase in the car the night before. Gambles had seemed to know where he was going; leading Blake straight to the level crossing but, what if that was just blind good luck? Where was Gambles heading? Blake traced his finger along the railway line. He'd heard a train in the background when Gambles had phoned him. His finger came to rest next to the Tarran Way Industrial Estate in Moreton. A quick Google search gave Blake a satellite view of the estate. There were storage yards, a caravan storage area, warehouses, and row upon row of shipping containers "Kinnear," Blake said. "Fancy a trip out?"

Kinnear grinned. "Too right, sir."

*****

There were two storage yards on the industrial estate. One, was a large affair offering containers to store household contents and also a space to store caravans securely. It seemed well-run and staffed by several people. Judging by the cars parked around it, the place kept busy day and night. Kinnear shook his head. He couldn't see Gambles heaving a body over his shoulder and hiding it in there. Way too many people.

A man in a hi-vis jacket knocked on the car window. "Can I help you?"

Kinnear showed his warrant card. "I'm wondering if there are any quieter yards around here. Places not used as much maybe?"

The big man rubbed his stubbly chin. "There's Sanford's Yard down by the railway line. That's been more or less closed for years."

"More or less?" Kinnear said.

The man nodded. "Yeah. Old man Sandford used to run it but he's not so well now. Some young fella was helping out down there last time I heard."

"Could you show me where it is?"

"Sure."

Sandford's Yard was a dismal place; a huddle of containers pocked with rust formed a square around a patch of muddy, rutted ground. A rickety portacabin crouched in one corner. The large iron gate that should have barred Kinnear's entry hung open, the padlock dangling from its chain. Kinnear drove the car into the yard and climbed out, trying the door of the portacabin. It opened, revealing an empty office table and a couple of chairs. It smelt damp and musty. "Nobody home," Kinnear muttered to himself.

He checked each container, finding them locked or rusted shut. One at the corner of the yard stood, its door yawning to reveal the darkness inside. Kinnear pushed the door further open with his elbow and saw a toilet, dirty plates, and tins of beans. There was also a pile of rope and some chains. "Well, well," Kinnear said. "Looks like we've just missed them. We're one step behind all the time."

He phoned Blake with the news. "He must have needed a vehicle to move Ellen Kevney, even if she was alive. The Chimeree Van is pretty distinctive, sir. Maybe there's some CCTV from last night?"

"It's worth a punt," Blake said. "You check that out and I'll go and see what Albert Green has to say for himself."

*****

Chinn had brought Green to the Birkenhead Custody Suite as there was a voluntary Interview room available there. It also meant that Blake didn't have to go to Hilbre Grove where things would be getting busy once again as the press got wind of the increased police activity in the area. Green looked frail and bewildered in the sleek offices of the custody suite. He wore a beret and a long purple overcoat. Blake reminded himself of the snarling old man who had confronted him the other night when Laura had encountered Gambles. Although he had grabbed Laura that night, the case against him was scant and he claimed not to have any memory of it. Now he sat in the interview room, meek and smiling like an innocent child.

Vikki Chinn brought a cup of tea in and Green grimaced after sipping it. “Sorry,” he said. “I’m used to full cream milk.”

“Thank you for coming in to see us, Mr Green,” Blake said, as he entered the room. Green looked up in surprise.

“Blake!” He said. His face went through a thousand contortions as he tried to regain his composure.

“You remember me, then?”

“How could I forget you with such a name?”

“You seemed surprised to see me, Mr Green.”

Albert Green stared at Blake. “It was just that someone told me you’d been taken off the case, that’s all.”

“And who might that be?” Blake asked, leaning forward in his chair.

“I don’t recall. Memory’s a slippery devil in these winter days of my long and blessed life. ‘Old John, with white hair, does laugh away care,’ as Blake wrote...”

“You’d remember me kicking your door in, last night, surely.”

Green gave an apologetic smile and waved his hands in the air. “I thought that was a bad dream. It gets hard to tell the difference some days.”

"Did you know that Josh Gambles had murdered a woman and a man in the houses next to you, Mr Green?"

Green pursed his wrinkled mouth. "I don't believe for one moment that Josh would do such a thing."

"He's quite capable, Mr Green and you know it. The sad fact is, he has done it. The only question is: did he do it alone?"

"I'm sorry, Blake, you've lost me. Forgive my befuddled and bemuddled old brain. I was never good at murder mysteries..."

Blake leaned over the table that sat between them. "Okay, you can drop the confused old eccentric act, now," he hissed. "I saw you the other night. I saw who you really are. I know you, Albert Green."

A malevolent light sparked in the old man's eye. "Then you'll know, Inspector, that I'd never come here voluntarily with the intention of giving you enough rope to hang me, now would I?"

Blake frowned. "Your garden runs alongside the Taylors', doesn't it?"

"Why, yes but alas, I'm not a gardener. My roses are all sick ones, Inspector Blake."

"You see, I was wondering how Josh managed to gain access to the houses without being spotted at the front by Don Pleavin."

"Delightful, Mr Pleavin," Albert said, smiling benignly once more. "A veritable Argus Panoptes..."

"Josh could easily have climbed over the fence at the back and then he could access Jean Quinn's from the Taylors'."

"It doesn't take a genius to work that out Inspector but it's straws you are grasping at," Albert Green said amiably. "I was probably having a cup of tea with my beautiful cats."

"Have you heard of Georgie Grant, Mr Green?" DS Chinn said, suddenly.

Albert Green's face twisted horribly. "That ragamuffin. Good for nothing son of a harlot. Making false accusations..."

"They were true though, weren't they?"

"No!" Green spat and jumped up, knocking his tea over. "Joshy is a good boy. I'll not have him dragged into the dirt by scum like Georgie Grant!"

Blake frowned. "Did I mention Josh, in this context, Mr Green?"

Green gave a horrible grin. "I remember what Grant said. His accusations were total fantasy. I live in a modern bungalow. How could I possibly have a dungeon? It's ridiculous."

"How about a lock-up at Sanford's Yard? An old shipping container? Are you going to deny that?

All we have to do is look through Sanford's accounts. Your name will be there."

"It seems that someone has been held captive there for some time, quite recently," Vikki added. "Would you care to comment?"

Albert Green's face fell. "I kept my artwork and paints in it, but I later burnt them. I haven't been down there for years. I don't know anything more about it."

"But why rent a shipping container for all this time and not use it, Albert?"

Green licked his lips. "I do many things for no reason, Blake. It's my age and dotage," he said. "Now, unless you're going to arrest me for something, I want to go home."

CHAPTER 39

Ellen Kevney slumped against the rotten old pews and groaned. Every part of her body ached. The cuffs chafed her wrists, her arms ached from being held at awkward angles by the chains and the ground felt hard and cold. She just wanted to go home. High above her some pigeons cooed in the shadows between the streams of weak light that shone down through the holes in the roof. This was an old chapel or church. The shape of the windows and the style of the decaying furniture around her told her that much.

She hadn't seen Ralph or whatever his real name was for some time. How much time, she wasn't sure. A small spark of hope kindled inside her. Perhaps he wasn't coming back. Perhaps the police had caught him, and they were searching for her. A wave of cold dread extinguished her hope. What if they had and he refused to tell them where she was?

She'd seen that on the news once; a killer who wouldn't tell where he'd left his victims. Didn't Ian Brady and Myra Hindley do that? She let out a moan of horror. Imagine dying here. Starving to death and nobody finding you. What would they tell her children? They'd grow up never knowing what had become of their mother. And then, one day, someone would find her desiccated remains chained to this drainpipe.

"No," Ellen Kevney said aloud. "No." She began pulling at the chain, ignoring the burning pain in her arms and wrists; ignoring the slippery red blood that trickled down her arms. Her shoulders burnt with the effort and the days of poor sleep and poor nutrition were telling on her. Her muscles felt like rubber and, exhausted, she fell, gasping to the floor. But, looking up, she noticed that the pipe had moved ever so slightly.

*****

DS Vikki Chinn had definitely drawn the short straw, when she was asked to drive Albert Green home. She'd given Blake a pained look, but he'd not noticed it. Now she drove through the Birkenhead traffic with the old man in the back of the car. He was looking down at his mobile phone and chuckling to himself. So much so, that Vikki kept glancing at him in the rear-view mirror. She couldn't understand him; one minute he played the dotty old codger and the next, he was staring into a state-of-the-art iPhone. Blake was right when he said it was all an act. Vikki generally had a positive view of humanity, but this man was evil; he knew about Joshua Gambles and may even have encouraged him.

Glancing forward, she slammed the brakes on just in time. A taxi in front of her had swerved into the side of the road to let a passenger alight. Vikki had only just seen it in time. Another split second of looking at Albert Green and she would have ploughed into the back of it.

Green gave a grunt as the seatbelt stopped his forward momentum, but the phone took flight from his palm. It hit the passenger seat headrest, bounced off the dashboard and settled in the footwell to Vikki's left. She stared down at the phone and then picked it up. "What's this?" she said.

Green had been watching an online live feed from somewhere.

"Give it back," Green snapped. "That's my private property. You've no right to have that."

A woman lay on a bed, gagged and tied. The taxi had moved on and cars were blaring their horns as they negotiated their way round Vikki, but she was oblivious. Picking up the phone she stared closely at the woman on the bed. It was Tina White and she looked close to death.

*****

Ellen Kevney gathered her wits and dragged herself to her feet. The realisation that she could be trapped in this crumbling church until she died had spurred her on. Now a new terror seized her.

What if he came back?

The pipe had bent a little and one of the bolts holding it to the wall had lifted; a small trail of stone dust formed around the bolt and some had drifted down on to the floor. The wall was damp and old. It was weary like her. She just had to have more fight.

Bracing her feet against the wall, Ellen leaned back, so that all her weight gave the chain that snaked around the pipe a whipcord tension. She was slight and never physically strong. The last week or so had taken its toll. She gritted her teeth and threw herself backward. The chain jagged her wrists, making her cry out.

The pipe shifted.

She was almost horizontal now; her feet planted firmly on the crumbling stonework, suspended by the chain and the leverage of her legs. A crazy notion came to her that she could walk up the wall, like Batman in those stupid 1960s programmes she'd watched with her dad as a girl. Grinning she jagged her arms upwards, suddenly slackening the chain and flicking it up. The chain climbed up the pipe, clinking loudly in the echoing church.

Now Ellen was a couple of feet off the ground, but the height had given her more pull. The pipe creaked. Ellen whimpered as more blood streamed from her grated wrists. She threw herself back again and again, and the pipe grumbled at her more. It hissed as chunks of stone and dust trickled out of the bolt holes. One bracket that held the pipe to the wall had twisted. She pulled back again, her yell bouncing off the rotting pews and the metal grilles on the windows.

A scraping noise sounded behind, and she froze. The blood pulsed around her temples. Something had moved in the shadows at the corner of her eye. All she could hear now though was the beating of her heart and her ragged breathing.

Was he back?

Something metallic clanged to the floor and for a moment, Ellen imagined him, Ralph striding towards her with a huge iron bar in his hand. Then a blur of rusty red burst from behind the pews and Ellen gave a short, strangled laugh. She'd never seen a fox this close-to before. It gave her a brief, contemptuous look and bounded across the church and leapt up onto the window where the boarding had broken away. For the first time in weeks, Ellen smiled.

That was her way out of this building.

Turning back to her work, she gathered up the chain, pulling herself closer to the wall and the ever-yielding pipe. Her scream came from the very pit of her stomach as she hurled herself backwards. There was an indignant grating of metal, a ping of several bolts landing on the stone flags and then she was flying. It seemed like she was weightless and for a fleeting moment, Ellen thought this sense of freedom would last forever. Then gravity took over and she landed hard on the cold floor, gasping as the impact beat the breath from her lungs. She lay there for a second, trying to breathe and then with a gasp, she sat up.

Scrambling to her feet, she gathered up the chain and followed the fox. But she couldn't leap up onto the window ledge. She didn't have the energy. Leaning against the wall, she sobbed. It couldn't end like this. She was so close. Scanning around, she saw some old, wood-wormed chairs and dragged a couple over. The first one she trusted with her weight let her down badly, crumbling to dust beneath her feet and sending her careering off across the church. The second felt more secure. She clambered up and pulled at the broken planking that covered the window, making the escape hole big enough for her to slide through.

Wriggling through, Ellen found herself facing a two- or three-foot drop. It wasn't much but dangling face-first from that height made it feel much further. Extending her aching arms, she squeezed out of the window and fell face first into brambles and old bin bags that had been dumped there. She didn't care, she was free! She could hear the rumble of traffic on the road just a few feet away. Her arms and face were bleeding and she staggered like a drunkard, falling back down into the brambles a couple of times as she dragged herself towards the low perimeter wall and the road.

And then she saw him, Ralph, striding down the pavement towards her. She didn't even look what was on the road as she ran out to get across and away from him. A horn blared and she heard a screech of tyres. She stood with her hands flat on the bonnet of a box van that had just managed to stop in time. The driver jumped out, a burly man in a checked shirt. Another car pulled over.

"Are you alright, love?" The burly man asked, looking at the chain and the blood on her arms.

"She's fine," Ralph called hurrying over. "She's my sister, just a bit, you know," Ralph pointed at his head and twirled his finger. The man frowned. A small crowd had gathered at the side of the road. Somebody pulled a phone out.

She backed away from him. "I'm not his sister. My name is Ellen Kevney. He's been holding me against my will..."

Ralph jumped forward, trying to grab her but the man in the checked shirt pushed him back. "She doesn't want to go with you, pal."

A woman came over and put her coat around Ellen's trembling shoulders. "An ambulance is on its way love," the woman said. She glanced up at Gambles. "The police too."

Ellen blinked as her captor ducked under the arm of an onlooker and ran. And then he was gone, sprinting down the street away from the crowd and away from her. She was free. Ellen Kevney slid down onto the road and sobbed with relief. It was over. She would hold her children again. She would hear their laughter. She would live.

*****

"Give me my phone back, you bitch!" Albert Green hissed, tugging at the door handle but Vikki Chinn had locked the car.

"I've reason to believe that Tina White's life is in danger and I'm holding onto it until we get to Hilbre Grove," Vikki said, fairly sure she was on thin ice but what else could she do? If she gave the phone back to Green, he'd probably end the call and clear his browser. Possibly even destroy his phone, which would be evidence. But evidence of what? Was Tina White dead?

Kath Cryer had described how the Whites had a studio in their back room, kitted out as a bedroom. Vikki was certain that Tina was still at her house. But in that case, where was Paul White? Vikki put her lights on and headed for Hilbre Grove.

CHAPTER 40

Josh Gambles paused for breath. He didn't think anyone had followed him. Once the big man had squared up to him, Josh had realised the game was up. He couldn't have got Ellen Kevney back if he'd wanted to. He pressed his forehead against a high brick wall and kicked hard. "Bloody people!" He shouted. Who would have thought it? He'd *wanted* Blake to find Kevney, but it seemed like Blake *had* been taken off the case after all. That strutting show-off Matty Cavanagh wasn't the man to catch him. It had to be Blake.

On the other hand, a moment like that would go down in folk history. What drama! The victim running into the road, the brave townsfolk of Rock Ferry ganging up on the killer and saving the damsel in distress. That's a story that would be told in pubs up and down the Wirral for years to come. The kind of story that would add to his notoriety.

He paused, noticing his surroundings for the first time. He had been on the New Chester Road in Rock Ferry when he'd seen Ellen and he'd run down towards the river, but his path was blocked by old, rusty railings and a thick thorn hedge dotted with saplings. Beyond them was the by-pass. The gods were smiling on him still, but he needed to hurry. This place would be crawling with police.

Smiling, Josh set off at a jog up the road that ran alongside the by-pass; sooner or later there would be a bridge across. Blake's house wasn't far away and once he got wind of Ellen's escape, the detective would guess where Josh was going next. "And if Muhammad won't come to the mountain... or was it the other way round?" Josh forgot but he knew just how he could bring Blake right into the middle of the story again.

*****

Laura Vexley sat in Blake's house, stroking Serafina and sipping a cup of herbal tea. She had hoped that it might calm her down, but it did little to drive away the memories of the previous couple of days. She'd been attacked and nearly killed in a car chase. There were moments when she felt excited at having shared something of Blake's life. But there were darker moments when the adrenaline rush dragged her back to a time she had buried deep. Until now.

Blake had told her all about his own past but that had been because circumstances demanded it. If she hadn't been with him when they discovered the magazine clippings on the table, then she wouldn't have known. But she could never tell him about her past. As gently as she could, she lifted Serafina off her lap and stood up, placing the cat back on the armchair. *At least one of us is settled,* Laura thought. It was a bad idea to stay here; the locks on the doors and windows were old. Gambles had shown he could break in easily.

A floorboard upstairs creaked. Laura crept out into the hall and looked up the stairs. Shadows danced on the walls, but she could see no movement. Outside the wind blew up from the river, making the leaves on the trees around the house hiss. Another creak upstairs convinced Laura that she wasn't going mad. There was someone in the house.

Snatching the car keys from the coffee table in the living room, Laura made for the front door. She didn't look back until she was safely locked in her car. A shadow moved in the living room window. Laura searched around for her bag and phone but, with a sinking feeling, realised they were still in the house. The only thing she could do was to find Blake. She started the engine and reversed out of the drive, nervously accelerating a little too much the engine as she did. Her foot dabbed the brake but nothing happened. She pressed harder as the car rolled backwards out of the drive and across the narrow lane. With a yell, she slammed her foot on the pedal, but the car had picked up speed and rolled towards the river. Laura tore at the handle and began to open the door. The car bumped up and over the low wall that fringed the old promenade and upended, sending her tumbling back inside. Her stomach lurched and the grey clouds filled the windscreen, as the car plunged backwards down the promenade wall.

Kinnear slammed the phone down. "They've got Ellen Kevney, sir," he said. "She's alive and well, considering what she's been through."

"Great," Blake said. "Where?"

Kinnear tapped the map they were looking at, his finger landing on the Rock Ferry area. "She staggered out of an old, abandoned chapel on the side of the A41… nearly run over apparently. Gambles was there too but the public chased him off."

Blake frowned and looked closely at the map. "Gambles was there?"

"Are you alright, sir?"

"No," Blake replied. "That's too close for comfort…" His phone rang before he could say anything else and he saw Laura's name flash up. "Laura. Thank God listen…"

"I love your house, Will Blake," Gambles said. "It's so old-fashioned. Like it was stuck in a time warp. Wasn't it your mother's?"

"Where's Laura?"

"That's for me to know and you to find out. I was just saying to your cat. Serafina, isn't it? I was just saying. This is turning out even better than I thought it would."

"Give yourself up, Gambles. Stop playing games."

"I stopped playing games a couple of years ago, Will Blake. You just weren't paying attention. I think you better get over here quickly. It's looking a bit ropey for poor old Laura. And the cat's growling at me now. That's bad manners. I don't like bad manners. Or cats."

Blake slammed the phone down. "Kinnear get some officers down to my house. I'm going on ahead. Gambles is there and it sounds like he's got Laura." Emotions tumbling over themselves, Blake hurried out of Police HQ and into the carpark. The Opel Manta was still standing outside Blake's house, sad and crumpled after the chase but Blake had taken a marked car and started the lights before he left the carpark.

"I swear, Gambles, if anything has happened to Laura..." He muttered. And what about Serafina? He hated that cat at times; she was a legacy of his mother's disappearance; a reluctant inheritance but she was part of the family.

Even though he was concentrating on the road, weaving in and out of the traffic, something nagged at him. How did Gambles know the cat's name? It troubled him. The idea that he'd somehow been eavesdropping left Blake cold. It was possible, he supposed. Blake powered through the tunnel, lights ablaze, siren shrieking. He changed lanes, overtook vehicles and the barriers at the tunnel exit went up automatically for him.

Racing past Cammell-Lairds, he took the roundabout into Rock Ferry and turned left down the road Gambles must have run down earlier. He glimpsed police cars outside the ruined church but didn't stop. The roads narrowed, slowing him down. He hissed with frustration as slow cars tried to pull in and allow him past. "Come on, come on..."

Finally, he brought the car screeching to a halt outside his house and stared in horror. Laura's blue Hyundai lay, upended in the thick mud of the River Mersey. The door hung open and the engine still roared. Blake half scrambled, half fell down the promenade wall to get to the car. He looked in, turning the engine off and frowned.

"She's not in there, Will," a voice said above him. "I brought her inside. Come and see me!"

CHAPTER 41

Knots were never Vikki Chinn's forte and now she struggled to get Tina White free. The woman's arms had swollen, making the job harder. Her breathing was shallow, her lips cracked from days without water.

Along with two officers assigned to watch over the crime scenes in Hilbre Grove, Vikki had broken into the White's house when there was no answer. Paul White lay in the kitchen, a pair of scissors poking from his eye. Vikki was no expert but, from the state of the body, he'd been dead a while.

She'd hurried through the house and found Tina unconscious on the bed. The poor woman was close to death having been bound and gagged for days.

The ropes came free and Tina let out a small groan. "Come on Tina, ambulance is on its way. You're going to be alright," Vikki said. Tina's eyelids fluttered but she didn't respond. The camera winked at her and Vikki felt confronted by Albert Green's evil. Had Joshua Gambles done this just to entertain the old man? Green was watching all the time. Watching this girl's slow and miserable death. He took pleasure in it.

Stepping outside, she returned to her car where Albert Green sat smiling at her. She opened the driver's door. "Can I get out and go home now, Detective Sergeant?" Albert asked from the rear seat.

"Not likely, sunshine," Vikki Chinn said. "Albert Green, I'm arresting you for conspiracy to murder. You do not have to say anything, but it may harm your defence if you do not mention, when questioned, something which you later rely on in court. Anything you do say may be given in evidence."

Green's face twisted into that mask of hatred again but Vikki just slammed the door shut before he could start ranting. The ambulance would be here soon enough and then she could take him back to the custody suite. An uncomfortable night would be the least of Albert Green's worries over the next few days.

*****

By the time Blake had scrambled back up the promenade wall and got into the house, Gambles sat in a chair next to the sofa. Laura lay unconscious on it, a livid bruise on her forehead and a trickle of blood at the corner of her mouth.

Gambles held his hands up and Blake saw that one held a kitchen knife. "I didn't do anything, Will, honest! I was just upstairs and she upped and ran out of the house. Reversed herself into the river. Not part of the plan."

"Oh, stop it. There is no plan," Blake snapped. "Give it up, Gambles. This has gone too far."

Gambles' face hardened. "It went too far years ago for me. You know, I hero-worshipped you? You were the one stable thing in my life. You and Searchlight. If the world seemed to be going to shit, I could pop you on the TV and everything would be fine."

"I wish I could say the same," Blake scoffed. "For me, it was a white-knuckle ride every episode and then a sudden bump back down to earth when it was over. That programme ruined my life and you keep dredging it back up."

"You'd have grown into the role if they'd let it run. You'd be a celebrity by now and none of this would have been necessary."

"Is that what this is all about? Revenge because they axed Searchlight?"

Gambles traced the knife point lightly across Laura's exposed neck. "It wasn't about that, Blake. It ISN'T about that. It's about *you. I did all this for you!*

Blake stared in disbelief. "For me? You think I'd approve of the suffering you've caused? of all the deaths?"

"No, no. Of course not; You're not a psychopath. That's my job! You're the genius detective.

You solve all kinds of crimes but do you get any recognition? No. Well, *now* you'll be famous again. More famous than you'd ever be."

"You're insane, Gambles, this is all about you."

Gambles smirked. "Well, yes. Can you imagine the hours of news that'll be dedicated to this case? The Scissor Man. You're wrong, you know. I *did* plan what I could of this. I chose the venues and made it as difficult as I could for you. I even injected a bit of sex to spice it up. The whole story has been like catnip for the journalists..."

"This isn't really about me. You did this for yourself, Gambles."

"At first, it was all about you, Will. You were my hero. My plan was simply to thrust you back into the public eye. But you disappointed me. You really don't want to be famous, do you?"

"I just want to be left alone to live my life. Isn't that enough?"

"Not really," Gambles said, flatly. His eyes lit up again. "Peter Sutcliffe, the Yorkshire Ripper, he gets fan mail. They sent him money! Did you see the woman he was going to marry? Imagine becoming a folk hero like that."

"You're sick."

"People will write about me. They'll pore over the killings and recount them in every gory detail. They'll want to interview me. I'll refuse at first. Give it a few years. Scarcity bumps up the price, doesn't it?"

Blake took a step forward. "I swear, I'll..."

Gambles wagged a finger and hovered the blade over Laura's throat. "One more step and I'll stick this right in her gullet."

Blake froze. "So, what do you want?"

"You're going to arrest me."

"Okay," Blake said slowly pulling a pair of handcuffs out of his jacket pocket. "Joshua Gambles, I'm arresting you for the murder of..."

"No! No! No!" Gambles hissed, scowling at Blake like a petulant child. "Not here. This isn't nearly dramatic enough. We need some height. And an audience! Turn around and put your hands behind your back. Now, can you cuff yourself? Do it!" He lowered the blade towards Laura's throat. She moaned a little, twisting on the sofa. Blake turned around and put the cuffs on his own wrists behind his back. He felt Gamble tighten them. "And the keys?" Gamble said.

"Jacket pocket. Your left."

Again, he felt Gamble reach into his pocket. "Do anything silly and I'll stick your girlfriend." He pulled the keys out and Blake heard him back off and return to his seat next to Laura.

"Now what?" Blake said.

"We're going on a little drive. Call off any men who are out there. I'll be walking out of this house behind you with this huge kitchen knife just ready to whip out your kidneys if anyone tries to intervene, Okay?"

Blake turned round and held his hands in the air. "Okay. But I want paramedics for Laura as soon as we're clear."

"She can have the Easter Bunny and Father Christmas for all I care. You know, I've been paying special attention to you for several years. I've been watching you, and making background checks on any new friends or associates in case they messed up my plans. I could tell you things about her but maybe later. Now move slowly."

They shuffled out, Gambles with his hand firmly on Blake's shoulder like they were engaged in some strange dance. Two police cars had arrived and the officers stepped forward. "He's got a knife in my back, don't come any closer. There a woman in the house in need of medical attention. Get an ambulance up here as quickly as possible."

"Yes, sir," one of the officers shouted and ran back to the car. The others stayed where they were, shuffling back to give Gambles and Blake space to pass.

"I want them gone," Gambles said. "Right down the promenade so they can't rush me. "Move back!"

"You heard him," Blake said to the officers. "Fall back to the far end of the prom. Go."

Reluctantly, the three remaining men slid back, looking for some chance to free Blake but not seeing any. Gambles pushed Blake over to one of the cars. "Ah, the keys are in it. Excellent. Get in the back."

Blake slid onto the back seat and Gambles climbed into the front. He started the engine and began to drive. "Where are we going?" Blake said. He considered overpowering Gambles or even just stunning him with a headbutt. The chances of it being successful seemed very slim and it would result in the car crashing and possibly hurt innocent bystanders. For now, he just had to go with the flow. One of the cars from the house was following them but Gambles didn't seem to be in any hurry.

"There are some flats near here, aren't there? In Birkenhead. I think we'll go there. We can get nice and high-up for the cameras. It's important to have a stage, you know." Gambles fiddled with the car dashboard and finally worked out how to put the blue lights on and work the siren. "Do you know, I've always wanted to do this!" He shouted and put his foot down. He glanced back at Blake. "I was going to be a copper, just like you but I never had the chances. My monster of a father, lazy teachers and as for that cow of a social worker! Nobody cared, you see. But in my head, I'd convinced myself that *you* did."

"That doesn't excuse what you've done. You've taken lives. There are plenty of people like you who have had a bad start and yet they rise above it."

Gambles ignored him. "My favourite part of Searchlight was the update from last programme. I loved it when you told people how you'd followed a lead that a caller had given and caught a suspect. I thought one day you'd burst through my front door and stop my dad from hurting me. It never happened, though."

"Is that when you gave up trying?" Blake said, trying to goad the young man. Another police car had joined them and Blake was pretty certain there'd be a helicopter above them.

"I never stopped trying," Gambles snapped, glancing at Blake in the rear-view mirror. "If anything, I intensified my efforts."

"Really? How? By helping Albert Green abuse your friends?"

"When I was thirteen, I saw your face in the local paper. I was living on the Wirral then. I tried to contact you. My letters never reached you and I couldn't get through on the phone or by email. Nothing worked. So I started to commit crimes to get your attention."

"You've only yourself to blame for this predicament, Gambles. I don't remember anyone trying to contact me."

"I saw what the trouble was, the crimes I had committed were too petty; shoplifting and dealing a few drugs wasn't going to get you on my trail. Sadly, I ended up in detention. But it was there I realised that I needed to do something much more serious."

"Well, it worked. You got my attention. Now why not just drive to the station and hand yourself in. I'll even caution you if that gives you a thrill."

"No," Gambles snapped. "I've crafted this story and it won't end with an anti-climax like that, believe me." He turned off Price Street and Blake saw the block of flats looming above them. Gambles parked the car at the door of the flats and climbed out. Blake considered kicking at Gambles from the back seat when he opened the door but again, the possibility of any kind of follow up seemed impractical. He slid out and stood before Gambles who quickly huddled behind him, knife poking into Blake's back. Four marked cars screeched into the carpark, lights flashing. The officers got out, barking commands but Blake called out to them.

"Stay back, he's got a knife. We're okay as long as we do what he says."

"We're going up in the world, Will Blake," Gambles said dragging Blake back towards the door of the flats. He pressed all the doorbells and looked to Blake. One intercom clicked on.

"DCI Will Blake, Merseyside Police, could you open the door please?" Blake said using his most officious tone. The door buzzed and Gambles grinned pulling Blake in.

They took the lift to the top floor and they stumbled around for a few moments looking for a door that led up to the roof. "It'll be locked, Gambles," Blake said. "You haven't thought this through. Just give up. Let's go downstairs again..."

"No," Gambles said, as they approached the door. "There's something I want to tell you and I want us to be up there when I do."

CHAPTER 42

The door gave in surprisingly easily; years of rust on the hinges and weather beating against the fibreboard had left it brittle and hanging from its frame. Gambles almost fell over, dragging Blake with him. The brisk wind slapped Blake in the face and blew his hair back as they staggered out. The roof was lined with water tanks for the flats below and a knee-high wall edged the space. Blake felt dizzy as he looked across Birkenhead to the river and the city of Liverpool beyond.

"Go on then," Blake said, leaning against one of the water tanks. "What have you got to tell me?"

Gambles strode to the edge and for a moment, Blake thought he was going to jump. Instead, he paced back and forth. "I came out of prison three years ago and you were still here on the Wirral. You hadn't moved or done anything with your life."

"I had a career," Blake said. "I was caring for my parents. Those were pretty important to me."

Gambles snorted. "Parents," he said. "Over-rated. You were in *Take a Break* magazine with a beautiful wife and a little girl when I was a kid. You had the perfect life..."

"I never had the perfect life and what's so amazing about being in bloody *Take A break*?"

"To be known," Gambles said, crouching and looking over the edge. "To be seen and noticed. Those are things everyone wants. Look around you Blake. Who lives in these flats? Do you know? It's a huge pile of rooms containing a bunch of nobodies. Anyone of them could die and you wouldn't know or care. But to have been known. That's something."

"Sounds a bit needy to me," Blake said.

Gambles strode towards him, still brandishing the knife and Blake backed away, expecting an attack. Instead, the young man rummaged in his pocket and pulled out the handcuff keys. "Turn round," he said. Blake frowned and did as he was told. "Now. When I was just out of prison, I searched high and low for you." The cuffs clicked and Blake felt them slip off his wrists. He turned, ready to headbutt Gambles and drag him downstairs but something in the man's eye stopped him.

Gambles walked away from him. "And I found you. It took a bit of detective work, believe me. But I'm a clever man. I was quite pleased with myself when I found you trapped in your parents' house. Your father had just passed away and you were coming home to an increasingly chaotic household as your mother slipped away into dementia."

"Why are you telling me this?"

"Because I was there. That night when you came home to the open door. I was there. I saw her wander out."

"Bastard!" Blake launched himself forward, grabbing a fistful of Gambles hoodie and lifting him up off the ground. "You're lying!"

"That's it! See? You feel alive now, don't you?" Gambles yelled. Blake looked down and realised he had Gambles half dangling over the edge. "Go on," Gambles hissed. "Do it. Cast me to the four winds and watch me fly."

Blake panted through gritted teeth. "You're lying."

"I'd never lie to you Detective Blake," Gambles said, raising his hands. "She was wearing her dressing gown. The pink one with the blue piping up the collar."

"You could have read that in any one of a dozen press releases," Blake growled, shaking him. "Why are you telling me this?"

"Because it's true. You know it. I saw her walk out. I even spoke to her. She told me to look after Serafina and I realised she thought I was you! Imagine the honour. I saw she wouldn't last the night. She didn't want to..."

Kinnear burst up the stairs and onto the rooftop with three uniformed officers. “Sir? You’ve got him. Now bring him over here to us.”

“And.. what? You… just let her die? Or did you kill her?” Blake snarled, pushing Gambles further over the edge. Gambles gave a high-pitched shriek and started giggling.

“I did you a favour, Will!” He spat. “I set you free!”

“I was a ghost! A bloody ghost trapped in my mother’s house! Not knowing what had happened to her…”

“Sir,” Kinnear said. “Let him go. It’s not worth it.”

“Where is she, Gambles? Tell me what you did or, so help me, I’ll drop you off this building.”

“Sir, NO!” Kinnear shouted.

“But I’m not scared, Will Blake,” Gambles said, softly. “Kill me and you’ll never know. Let me live and I might tell you, one day. Kill me and I’ll become a legend, the stuff of nightmares to frighten the kids of Wirral at bedtime. Let me live and we’ll become celebrities together. There’s a kind of symmetry to that, don’t you think?”

Blake straightened up, staring deep into Gambles’ eye. “So, either way, I lose?” Blake said, lifting him higher.

LATER

CHAPTER 43

Kath Cryer stood in the hospital, tugging at her sleeve. Donald Pleavin lay in the bed, looking washed out. His eyes were squeezed shut as if he was trapped in a bad dream. Wires and drips snaked from his arms. Helen Pleavin sat at his bedside. She smiled at Kath when she arrived.

"How is he?" Kath said.

"He'll pull through," Helen said, with a gentle smile. "But he's got to take things easy."

"I came to apologise," Kath said. "I never meant for this to happen."

Helen Pleavin gave her a sympathetic smile. "You've nothing to apologise for. Donald painted himself into a corner with his terrible behaviour. He would have had this heart attack at some other point without your help. It serves him right."

"And how about you?"

"I'm fine. Never felt better. I'll see he gets better, then he's on his own."

Kath raised her eyebrows.

"Your DC Kinnear is a man of wisdom," Helen said. "It's a leap of faith but I know Donald will never change and I need to be able to breathe. Jean Quinn has offered to share a flat with me. She doesn't want to go back to her house after all that happened there."

"Well, good for you."

"How is Tina White?"

"She's sitting up but still in shock. I think she'll pull through. She was badly dehydrated but she'll recover."

"Physically, yes," Helen Pleavin said. "I don't know how she'll recover from her ordeal. Imagine her being trapped like that, knowing that her husband was dead in another room..."

Kath shuddered. "Sometimes, it's just best not to imagine anything, Helen."

*****

Laura Vexley sat next to Blake on the crumbling prom outside Blake's house. She'd been discharged from hospital with a couple of stitches and a letter saying to come back if she started throwing up or feeling dizzy. Now they sipped coffee in the freezing February morning and watched the steel waters lap against the slick, grey mud of the Mersey. "I don't ever want to be involved in one of your cases again, Will Blake."

Blake gave her a sidelong glance. "You don't want to sign up as a PCSO, then?"

"Think I'll stick to psychotic cats," she said,

stroking Serafina, who stalked up to her almost on cue.

"Well, if you change you mind, just let me know," Blake said. "I'd write you a glowing reference."

"So, how are you doing?" she said.

"Me?" Blake said. "I'm fine. I nearly threw a murderer from a great height, but... you know, decided not to. It would have been a poor career move..." He thought back to that moment. It was touch and go. Part of him wanted to see Gambles' remains splattered in a bloody starfish at the foot of the block of flats. But he'd pulled back, thinking of a better revenge.

Dragging Gambles back from the edge, he slapped the knife from the man's grip and dumped him on his backside.

"Kinnear. Is there a PCSO downstairs?"

"I dunno, sir."

"Find out and get them sent up."

Gambles frowned and then his eyes widened as the realisation hit him. "Blake, no! You can't do this!" He scrambled to get away, clawing for the edge to throw himself over but Blake gripped him tight.

A few minutes later, a breathless PCSO appeared at Blake's side.

"PCSO Hilary Stone," she said. "What can I do, sir?"

"Kinnear, give Hilary your cuffs. She's going to make a citizen's arrest."

Blake could hear Gambles' petulant scream as he stumbled down the stairs to the bottom of the flat, "No! No! Come back and arrest me! It's got to be you!" He sounded like a toddler having a tantrum. It would be gratifying if only so many people hadn't had to suffer.

"So now what?" Laura said, snapping Blake to the present.

"I don't know," Blake admitted. "I need to get out of this house. So that's a priority. But Gambles said he knew something about my mother's disappearance..."

"Will, he's messing with your head. Don't listen to him."

"Maybe but before my mum disappeared, she kept going into the garden and telling me there was someone out there. I thought she was imagining it but what if it was Gambles?"

"You'll never know, Will, but if you give Gambles this hold over you, then you'll be shackled to him forever. You'll never get any peace."

Blake shrugged. "Yeah, you're right. That's what Gambles wants; fearful symmetry: he and I as two players in some depressing double act.

But I don't have to play his game. He craves attention and I don't have to give in to that." He smiled. "Tyger, Tyger," he muttered, scratching Serafina behind her ear. "There's only room for one predator in this house."

The End

ACKNOWLEDGEMENTS

As ever, there are so many people I'd like to thank.
You, for reading the book!

Once again, none of this would have been possible without the patience and support of Barry Hutchison aka JD Kirk. Thanks, you're a true gent!

Lin, my wife and business partner, for reading the various iterations of this story and for the cups of tea, sympathy and tough love!

Rod Yates for giving me the lowdown on local policing. The usual disclaimer applies: if there are any inaccuracies, it's my fault!

Kate bendelow, author of The Real CSI, who has been benerous to a fault with her time and advice, once more!

A shout out to the Wirral posse: Clare Hulme, Jan Jones, Amy Rebecca Thomas, Laura Colwell, Suzanne Thomas and Frauke Hoffman! Thanks you lot!

The ever-patient Meg Cowley for her killer covers.

Everyone in the Collective - you know who you are! Cheers!

ABOUT THE AUTHOR

J. E. Mayhew

Jon Mayhew lives on the Wirral with his family and has done all his life. A teacher for many years, he enjoys traditional music and plays regularly in ceilidh bands and sessions. Jon is also an award-winning author. His dark children's books are published by Bloomsbury.

Find out more at
www.jemayhew.blogspot.com

Find JE Mayhew on Facebook and twitter.

BOOKS IN THIS SERIES

DCI Will Blake

Read all the exciting DCI Will Blake novels set on the Wirral.

A Poison Tree

Would you forgive your child anything?

The murder of a young girl found barefoot in a country park and the re-emergence of shoes from the victims of a serial killer from over forty years ago. A coincidence or a connection? Will Blake is determined to find out, but as he unearths the past, questions are raised about the original investigations and it becomes clear that The Wirral has a killer on the loose once again. Victor Hunt, the father of the last dead girl from the original case, lies in a hospice with weeks to live. The truth lies hidden in Hunt's tangled family tree, and the actions of his wayward daughter. Time is against Blake and his fractious team. If they don't get to the root of past crimes, then innocent blood will flow again.

A Poison Tree is the first thrilling mystery in the

Will Blake crime series. A great read for fans of Luca Veste and JD Kirk's Jack Logan series.

Discover A Poison Tree and get involved in this exciting investigative series today.

Printed in Great Britain
by Amazon

80895796R00226